Praise for Christina Freebu

"A snappy, clever mystery that hooked me on page one and didn't let go until the perfectly crafted and very satisfying end. Faith Hunter is a delightful amateur sleuth and the quirky characters that inhabit the town of Eden are the perfect complement to her overly inquisitive ways. A terrific read!"

– Jenn McKinlay,
New York Times Bestselling Author of *Copy Cap Murder*

"An enjoyable read with a comfortable tone, plenty of non-stop action and pacing that was on par with how well this story was told...A delightfully entertaining debut and I can't wait for more tales with Merry and her friends."

– *Dru's Book Musings*

"Christina's characters shine, her knowledge of scrapbooking is spot on, and she weaves a mystery that simply cries out to be read in one delicious sitting!"

– Pam Hanson,
Author of *Faith, Fireworks, and Fir*

"A fast-paced crafting cozy that will keep you turning pages as you try to figure out which one of the attendees is an identity thief and which one is a murderer."

— Lois Winston,
Author of the Anastasia Pollack Crafting Mystery Series

"A little town, a little romance, a little intrigue and a little murder. Join heroine Faith and find out exactly who is doing the embellishing—the kind that doesn't involve scrapbooking."

– Leann Sweeney,
Author of the Bestselling Cats in Trouble Mysteries

"Battling scrapbook divas, secrets, jealousy, murder, and lots of glitter make *Designed to Death* a charming and heartfelt mystery."

–Ellen Byerrum,
Author of the Crime of Fashion Mysteries

"Freeburn's second installment in her scrapbooking mystery series is full of small-town intrigue, twists and turns, and plenty of heart."

– Mollie Cox Bryan,
Agatha Award Finalist, *Scrapbook of Secrets*

"Witty, entertaining and fun with a side of murder...When murder hits Eden, WV, Faith Hunter will stop at nothing to clear the name of her employee who has been accused of murder. Will she find the killer before it is too late? Read this sensational read to find out!"

– *Shelley's Book Case*

"Has mystery and intrigue aplenty, with poor Faith being stuck in the middle of it all...When we finally come to the end of the book (too soon), it knits together seamlessly and comes as quite a surprise, which is always a good thing. A true pleasure to read."

– *Open Book Society*

"A cozy mystery that exceeds expectations...Freeburn has crafted a mystery that does not feel clichéd...it's her sense of humor that shows up in the book, helping the story flow, making the characters real and keeping the reader interested."

— *Scrapbooking is Heart Work*

DASH AWAY ALL

Mysteries by Christina Freeburn

The Merry & Bright Handcrafted Mystery Series

NOT A CREATURE WAS STIRRING (#1)
BETTER WATCH OUT (#2)
DASH AWAY ALL (#3)

The Faith Hunter Scrap This Series

CROPPED TO DEATH (#1)
DESIGNED TO DEATH (#2)
EMBELLISHED TO DEATH (#3)
FRAMED TO DEATH (#4)
MASKED TO DEATH (#5)
ALTERED TO DEATH (#6)

DASH AWAY ALL

Christina FREEBURN

HENERY PRESS

Copyright

DASH AWAY ALL
A Merry & Bright Handcrafted Mystery
Part of the Henery Press Mystery Collection

First Edition | July 2020

Henery Press
www.henerypress.com

Author photograph by Kristi Downey

Trade Paperback ISBN-13: 978-1-63511-599-4
Digital epub ISBN-13: 978-1-63511-600-7
Kindle ISBN-13: 978-1-63511-601-4
Hardcover ISBN-13: 978-1-63511-602-1

Printed in the United States of America

To my husband Brian, who helped make everything possible.
I love you.

ACKNOWLEDGMENTS

A huge thank you to my editor Maria for encouraging me to ignore my self-imposed rules and allow the book to be what it needed to be, even though it meant I'd write a new ending after the first revision. I appreciate all your hard work and dedication to this book. You're the best!

ONE

The last ounce of sunlight was fading into the night as I pulled into the housing quarters for the cast and crew of *Dash Away All*, a new television Christmas movie being filmed in a small town in Indiana. One wouldn't know Christmas was coming to town from this particular area. It was plain, ordinary, run-of-the-mill RV park appearance. Gravel ground with small patches of grass throughout and rows upon rows of small trailers. It even had a large picnic and concession area.

Then again, it was July and it wasn't like the film needed the off-camera areas Christmas ready. My RV would stick out amongst the rest of the homes away from homes. I received a lot of odd looks but also some honks and thumbs up as I drove down the interstate in my Christmas-themed RV. The main image was Santa Claus flying over a town, but our business logo for Merry & Bright Handcrafted Christmas was still visible.

I parked in my assigned space and turned off the engine, checking on Ebenezer who was still snoozing away in his pet carrier strapped into the passenger seat. Nerves and excitement had kept my adrenaline high the whole seven-turned-into-nine-hour drive from my hometown in Season's Greetings, West Virginia to Carol Lake, Indiana.

I had been hired to work on a television Christmas mystery movie. Marie McCormick, the cousin of my friend Paul McCormick, had decided to take up a second career after leaving the police force and found a job being the assistant to Luna Carmichael, the grande dame of Christmas movies. The movie featured a handcrafter solving a mystery and Marie had dropped my name as the perfect person to create some of the pieces needed for "authenticity" on the film set for the up-and-coming television movie star Anne Lindsey's character who specializes in home décor crafts. Paul heard from his cousin about difficulties in finding the perfect crafter, especially since the others hadn't worked out, and she had a week left. He told his cousin that I was a great fit. I loved Christmas, crafted, and had a moving craft studio. Marie had emailed me a script with notes, letting me know what the key pieces were needed for the scenes and which were for the background.

The movie featured some new actors and I was thrilled at getting a chance to know them before they made it big in the Christmas movie market. It would be great to say I was there when they launched into Christmas stardom. What I loved most about this movie was that the director had chosen "older" actors for the key roles. The heroine and hero of the movie were both in their mid-forties, my age. It was a nice change of pace.

I slipped out of the RV. There was enough light left for me to attach the electrical power cord of my RV into the remaining receptacle without fumbling around in the dark. I had planned on arriving late in the afternoon but a rainstorm revving itself into a monsoon had me pulling into a rest stop for a few hours. While I was growing more confident driving my RV, I wasn't so confident to assume it could double as a boat. It was better waiting out the storm than driving through the downpour, especially on roads I wasn't familiar with. A large portion of the drive was on the interstate, but it still wasn't wise to travel through a storm.

The casting director had sent instructions for me to park on the outskirts of the space marked off for the trailers where the cast and crew lived. The majority of the dwellings around me were white trailers with green, tin-like roofs, storage for props and other offices. From what I was told, the only person who had an actual office, dressing room, and a room in a house was Luna Carmichael and Marie.

Voices rose in the distance. Two women. I plugged in the

power cord and dusted off my hands, making my way toward the argument. I couldn't help it. The peacekeeper in me demanded I help out. Slight arguments could easily turn into something much worse, as two recent experiences in my life had proven.

Two figures moved in the near dark, heading toward a pavilion area a few yards away. One woman stalked behind the other. Both postures were rigid. Straight back. Tightened fists. The lead woman had short dark hair and took long purposeful strides toward the coffee urns. The other woman's blonde hair swung around her shoulders in limp tendrils as she hurried to catch up.

The blonde snagged the other woman's arm and spun her around. "You have no right."

"Trust me, it's better this way." There was a firmness in the brunette's voice, and she yanked her arm away.

"You think it's better to hide the truth."

"Just because you believe it doesn't make it true," the brunette said.

"What makes you so sure you're right and I'm wrong?"

"Research."

A twig snapped. I glanced down and lifted up my foot. I hadn't stepped on one, so someone else was watching the exchange in quiet or was leaving. Most people would rather not get involved in an argument than force their way into it, like me.

"Hope the coffee urns are filled," I said, making myself known.

The women drew closer to each other, their angry words turning into harsh whispers as I ventured toward the food area. The two women were near the coffee carafes, the only things still out in the open and accessible. The rest of the drink area and food service, set up like a huge buffet, was covered with metal lids and locked.

One of the women had an arm draped over the top of the smallest carafe, the phone in her hand held her interest. "Decaffeinated is in this small carafe, full charged in all the others."

The blonde shot one more glare at the woman then stormed off.

"Everything all right?" I asked.

"Yep." The woman kept her gaze on the phone and drew out an exasperated sigh. Her hair still hiding her face. "Some people can't turn off their fan girl moments. Just because you're working on the set, doesn't mean you get a private get-together with Ms. Carmichael. The woman deserves privacy like everyone else."

My face heated. Luna Carmichael. The reigning queen of Christmas movies, or rather, former as Luna had appeared in less movies over the last few years. She was the person I was most excited about meeting. I was sure to bump into her sometime during the next two weeks or hoped Marie might introduce us. No one could fault me for saying a quick hello and maybe a small gushing session.

For a decade, Luna had appeared in every, or it seemed every, Christmas romance television movie. I owned all the movies she starred in. She had this mix of strength and innocence, perfect for a Christmas heroine who was learning to stand on her own but also willing to fight for the love she knew she deserved. The starting over trope was my favorite of all the romance storylines. I think it was because I felt like I was perpetually in that stage of life.

A shrill sound came from her phone. She pulled out her cell and swiped a finger across. Shaking her head, she tucked her phone into the back pocket of her jeans and fixed her gaze on me. There was something familiar about her features. Her tense smile morphed into a more welcoming one, like she recognized me. "There's no rest for the wicked. Let Paul know you've arrived safely. I know he'll worry about you. We'll chat tomorrow."

Paul's cousin. She had the same wide set eyes and high cheekbones. I really should've made time to stop at Paul's before heading for Indiana but the last week had me camped out in front of my die cutting machine making as many Christmas projects as possible for the movie. At least I could've requested a picture of his cousin or stopped for a visit and looked at a family album. Instead, I was engaged in what was becoming a new hobby for me—avoidance. Paul had once again hinted about moving our friendship toward a romance. I still couldn't get past our thirteen-year-age difference, though Paul had no qualms about it.

Before I could say a word, Marie strode off into the dark. I watched her, trying to decipher her tone. It had turned firm. Almost like an order. Maybe it was just from all her years being a police officer and leftover anger from her conversation with the other woman.

Or maybe a scolding for eavesdropping was in my future.

Tiny claws scratched at my arm and a pitiful sound echoed in my ear. Ebenezer. Something was wrong. I jerked awake, gathering my furry companion into my arms as I sat up in bed. My mind was fuzzy, trying to remember where I was. This wasn't my bedroom. The RV. I was in my RV. In Indiana. Ebenezer whistled, twisting and turning to escape my arms. At the set of a Christmas movie and my guinea pig was having a major meltdown.

"What's the matter?" Panic welled up in me. Was he hurt? Sick? A thousand horrible scenarios ran through my mind, all of them ending with a trip to the vet. How close was a veterinarian? There was a cat in the Christmas movie, so the casting director must have a name of a vet to call.

"I'll be right back." I dropped a kiss on Ebenezer's head and placed him under the covers.

I slipped off the bed and changed from my pajamas to more appropriate attire for a mad dash outside. Ebenezer shot off the bed and ran for the bedroom door, clawing at it. There were voices near the RV. He wasn't sick. Ebenezer had sensed people outside and was alerting me. He wasn't much of a people person.

I peered out the small window in the bedroom. It was still night. I tapped my phone that was on the bedside table. Four in the morning. I held in a groan. I sure hope this wasn't the time the cast and crew started readying for a day of shooting. I was not a morning person. Being woken up at this time for the next two weeks by a curmudgeonly guinea pig wasn't an experience I wanted.

The voices were growing louder. Frantic. Was this first day of shooting jitters or was something else going on? I scooped up Ebenezer and deposited him into the playpen I set up in the living space. "Sorry, buddy, but I can't have you running outside in the dark."

He whistled and shrieked his outrage at the containment. Ebenezer enjoyed the great outdoors. Too much. The moment a door was opened, he made a break for it.

"Either this or your pet carrier."

After slipping on my canvas sneakers, I stepped outside. There was a smoke smell in the air. In the dark, I noticed a group of golf carts zipping by and other people running, following the carts out of the cast area and toward a small road.

"We can't let the fire spread to the main house."

A whitish plume rose into the sky and I made out the faint flickering of a yellow and reddish glow coming from a distance away.

"Where's the fire trucks?" someone yelled.

"It's a small town. Volunteers have to leave their house and head to the station first. It'll take time."

A golf cart jammed to a stop near me and before I knew what was going on, I was hustled into it by a young man wearing a "Dash Away All Crew" shirt. Our butts had barely touched the seat before the driver of the cart pressed the accelerator and we shot forward. I held on for all I was worth as the cart sped through the night down a dirt path. Branches smacked and scraped against the cart and I drew back and winced at each scratch and thump.

I spotted flames dancing through the trees. There was a large vacant area, a mix of dirt and grass behind a huge house on a slight hill. As we drove closer, I noticed a tiny shed a few yards away from the house. Some people were hosing the burning structure while others fixed hoses on the vegetation on either side.

Cars were parked near the building, the brights turned on to illuminate the shed, which was more of a tiny house, and the people desperately trying to put it out. Tendrils of smoke escaped from the windows and the bottom of the door. The light from the flames flickered over the faces of the people closest to it.

The driver stopped the golf cart a few yards away from the burning shed and motioned for me and the other passenger to get out. "Check in with Ike with what jobs are needed. I'm heading back for more help. There's a lot of our props in that shed."

"Who's Ike?" I asked.

The crew member looked at me oddly and pointed at an attractive man with long brown hair tied into a ponytail who was directing people putting out the fire. "Him. How can you work here and not know Ike? He's the casting director and hired all the crew."

"I'm the crafter. Luna's assistant was the one who contacted me." The guy seemed suspicious about me and I figured dropping Luna's name was better than Marie's.

"That explains it." He hurried toward Ike.

There was something in his tone that generated multiple questions. Right now wasn't the time to ask. I ran toward the group. Marie was standing off toward the side, frantically tapping away on her cell phone.

"Everyone should back up and wait for the fire department. No one here is trained to put out a fire and could get hurt," Marie said, gaze still trained on her phone. "I doubt having all the cast and crew over here to put out a small fire will be appreciated. There's just more people in their way."

"If we wait until they arrive, the fire could reach the house. I'm sure that's not something your employer wants happening." Ike said. "Continue hosing it down and bring the water jugs, filled, we'll use those also."

I was assigned one of the roles of filling empty buckets and water jugs with a garden hose. I waited, with one hand on the spigot, for an item to fill with water. The flames weren't growing or being put out, the fire burned at a consistent rate. I sensed a movement behind me and turned. Near the windows of the main house was a group of people watching the makeshift fire brigade.

"Someone find the director and let him know what's going on."

Ike held a clipboard in one and waved it around. "I also need the status of the police chief or sheriff's arrival."

A group of people ran toward me. I turned on the water and filled up the buckets and the water jugs shoved toward me. The flames burned steadily. At this rate, we'd run out of energy before the fire.

"Edward is on his way," a young woman pointed at a man charging toward us. "He was looking for the sheriff. Said the man was here not too long ago. Something about a trespasser on the premise."

A bald man who was just shy over six-foot-tall, and all lean muscle, pushed his way through the crowd. My guesstimate on his age was somewhere in his sixties. There was an air of authority about him. People instinctively moved out of his way without a word or look from him. It was like watching the Red Sea parting for Moses. "Where's Luna?"

"Garrison relocated Ms. Carmichael to one of the trailers," Ike said.

"Wise decision," Edward said. "This situation could become unsafe and it's best Luna is away from it."

"I was instructed to remain behind and apprise her of the developing situation." Marie held her phone out toward the director. "Luna wanted me to tell you she is not happy being forced to vacate. As anyone could see, the fire is contained and of no threat to her. She would like to return home as soon as possible."

Ike sighed. "It was a recommendation not an order. If Ms. Carmichael preferred staying and risk her safety, I certainly wouldn't have dragged her out of the house. Garrison was the one who insisted."

"Yet, instead of helping put out the fire, you're texting her." The director settled a look on the Marie that was hard to decipher. "That would get her back into her house quicker."

"Do I look qualified or dressed to put out a fire?" Marie waved her hand from near her head down to her mid-thigh. Marie wore tailored slacks, a silk short-sleeved blouse and low-heeled boots. A round, gold locket glittered at her throat. "Besides, my loyalty is to Luna and Luna alone. I was instructed to observe and report, which is what I shall do."

Matter of fact, Marie looked well-dressed considering it was four a.m., and she was rushed out here, presumably, to give Ms. Carmichael updates about the fire.

"Someone has to take her safety seriously since she isn't concerned about it," Edward said.

"I did convince her going with Garrison was the best option, and I moved her car from the garage to the crew parking lot and put on the high beams." She gestured with a tilt of her head to one of the vehicles lined up and facing the burning building.

Edward glanced around, a frown deepening. "Has anyone seen where the sheriff went? I'd think the man would have made his way over here by now."

Marie took her eyes off her phone long enough to shoot a glance over at him. "Are you sure he was here? It's not like the sheriff department is nearby."

"I'm positive I saw him earlier."

"Maybe he's otherwise engaged at the moment," a man wearing a polo with the words "security guard" embroidered on it quipped. He took a bucket of water from me.

"What are you insinuating about Ms. Carmichael?" Edward put a hand on the man's chest, stopping him from walking away.

The man held up his hands in surrender. "I heard there was a commotion between Ms. Carmichael and someone in the house. Maybe the sheriff is removing the person."

"Why aren't you or one of the other guards handling it?"

"Our shifts don't start until five in the morning. Only reason we're out here now is because of the fire. Then there's the conflict of interest."

"I knew it was a bad idea hiring him for the security staff," Edward said.

"But what Ms. Carmichael wants..." The guard trailed off and headed for the fire with a bucket of water he was handed.

Marie twisted her wrist, flashing the screen of her phone at the director. "Luna says the shed can stay or go whichever is quicker. She's not happy being shoved in a trailer."

"If she doesn't care about this she shed, let it burn. I don't want anyone getting hurt," Edward said.

"The props. It'll be a huge loss," Ike said.

"Not as big of a loss as someone getting hurt or killed," Edward said.

The director was right. The flames were no longer shooting toward the ceiling and were barely seen through the windows. All of the craft items I had created for the movie were still in my RV or in the underneath storage compartment. I had planned on moving everything this morning after the promised golf cart for transportation was dropped off.

Ike walked closer to the trailer, straining his neck to see inside. "I don't think anything will be salvageable. Shooting will be delayed. There will be nothing to decorate the main house. Ms. Carmichael will not be happy. She wanted this production wrapped up in two weeks." Ike shuttered. He didn't like the idea of displeasing her.

I was getting a little nervous about meeting her. From the reactions so far, it didn't seem she was a filled-with-Christmas-spirit type of person.

"Everything I made is still in my RV," I said. "I hadn't brought them over."

"Great. We should be able to manage with those items. Whatever you can't make to replace those items, you can buy in town," Edward said.

Buy? When did I turn into the personal shopper? There was no way I had time for shopping for crafts if the director wanted more crafted. Right now, I was a one-woman operation. My partner and best friend, Bright, had declined tagging along on the trip; she was deeply enmeshed in a genealogy project for her family. I had hoped being hired to work on a Christmas movie was the opportunity for an in-person meeting. Our ten-year friendship and business partnership were built on texts, Facebook messages, and one phone call. But alas, business, even a once-in-a-lifetime moment came after family.

"Not going to find anything in Carol Lake," Marie said. "They have a grocery, toy, mechanic, and general store, along with a diner and the police department. I doubt you'll find any Christmas decorations. Whatever they have, they're using for the storefronts. Luna promised a few scenes would be filmed in town."

"What the—" Ike stepped closer to the window. He drew in a sharp breath and stumbled backwards. "There's a body in there. Someone was in there."

People ran toward the building. Sirens flowed in the air. Near the trailer, a small object twinkled. Lights from the cars bounced off of it. I hurried over to it. My breath caught in my throat. A magnesium firestarter. This was no accident. It was arson. Murder.

I snuck a glance over at Marie. Why wasn't she jumping in to help preserve the scene? She stood silently, only fixing a hard gaze on me and shook her head, placing a finger on her lip for one moment. *Don't tell.*

TWO

White smoke drifted into the black sky, highlighted by the red and blue lights from the police and sheriff cars. Two police cruisers were parked at the end of the line of cars the cast and crew drove over to light up the area for the firefighters. A sheriff department's SUV was parked so close to the open driver's door of one of the police cars, someone banging a hip into the SUV's bumper would jolt it forward and close the door of the cruiser. Either the sheriff had a problem at night with depth perception or there was some animosity between the departments. The parking job seemed very much like a power play.

The cast and crew who had created the fire brigade now stood on the outskirts, waiting for their turn to answer the police's questions. The sky had a hint of color and it was likely we'd be here until the sun was burning down on us.

A deputy walked over to where I was standing guard near the evidence. I was afraid we'd lose it in the dark or someone would step on it. Marie sat in Luna's car, sipping her coffee, attention on her phone. For all I knew, she was playing Candy Crush or texting Luna every small detail of what was going on, without doing anything to actually help. She had been a police officer. Why was she so unconcerned about a murder? My fingers were itching to text Paul and ask what was up with his cousin.

The sheriff's deputy knelt on the ground near the firestarter, carefully picking it up and depositing it in an evidence bag. His weathered face was stoic. "Did you see someone drop this?"

"No." My gaze flickered toward the trailer where through the window I saw firefighters and police officers examining the body. I shuddered. What a horrible way to die, not that anyway was a good one, especially when it wasn't from natural causes.

The deputy stood, gaze taking everyone in, or more accurately Marie who was typing madly away on her cell. A scowl deepened the lines on his weathered face. "There's something about this that's not sitting right with me."

Edward broke into our conversation. "Like how your boss was here before the fire and disappeared after it started."

"Are you insinuating something?" The deputy straightened his spine, maximizing every inch of his five-foot-six frame. Even with the bulk of his bullet-resistant vest, his presence still wasn't as intimidating as Edward.

Marie finally left her car and walked over to the trailer and peered through the window, watching the lone officer and a sheriff deputy shift through the rubble in the house to get to the body. Luna must've wanted a first-hand account from her assistant on who was in the trailer.

"The arsonist was likely in a rush to get away before someone spotted him. Or her," I said, hoping to break up, or at least stall, the brewing fight between the deputy and the director.

"At four in the morning? Most people aren't up at that time." The deputy squinted his eyes, focusing on Edward's face and leaned forward. "Is that soot?"

"We had to put it out. The emergency services around here are a little lacking." Edward swiped his wrist across his jaw. "This is a movie set. Our working hours aren't standard."

The deputy shifted the bag in his hands, the starter tumbled around. "How did you see it? There isn't much light."

Fighting back a yawn, I pointed at the cars lined up and facing the trailer. "All those cars had their brights on. It was glittering."

"It could have been dropped here months ago. This field was used by teenagers and groups for parties," the deputy said.

"The prop shed was almost burned down." Why was the deputy unconcerned about what happened? There was a fire. There was a body. If he was so disinterested, why did he come? The police could've managed without his not-so-helpful help.

"It seems to be holding up pretty good." He frowned. "Don't look like there's much damage. The roof and floor are stable otherwise the fire department wouldn't have cleared the building for the police to go inside."

I copied his expression. He was right. The outside was dirty but not damaged by the fire.

"What do you think is going on, Deputy?" Edward asked. "Someone staged the fire—"

"To cover up a murder," the words flew from my mouth.

Slowly, the deputy turned his head to focus solely on me. He leaned forward and down, trying to stare directly into my eyes. "A murder. Why would you jump to that conclusion?"

"Because there's a body in a building that was burning." It was pretty obvious to me.

A body flew out the door of the shed followed by a wig. The adult-sized body-shaped object flopped onto the ground with limbs twisted in all different directions. The officer stormed out of the building and kicked the body. It flopped over. It was a dummy.

Another disgruntled officer and fire fighters stepped out of the trailer.

"The chief was right. This is a waste of time." The officer who just stepped out of the trailer lifted his chin toward a squad car. He kicked "the body" closer to the deputy. "Sheriff Rhodes can have jurisdiction on this."

"This a local matter." The deputy held out the evidence bag with the firestarter. "You might get some prints from this. We were only here to assist. Rhodes made that clear when Chief Quinn insisted the sheriff's department send backup."

Marie shoved her phone in her pocket. "Ms. Carmichael would rather the police handle these incidents."

The officer practically vibrated with anger. "I don't really care what Carmichael wants. Contrary to her belief, she doesn't own everyone in town. This is a stupid hoax. We don't have time or resources to waste on this. Our volunteer fire crew jumped out of bed at four a.m. because of a fire. Multiple structures were in danger. The dummy was your body, and the fire was set in an outdoor firepit placed in the middle of the room and one on a table on the other side. Expect a bill from the town."

Edward gaped at the officer. "What?"

"If someone would've went inside and checked," the ranting officer continued, "you'd have known it was a joke and not wasted our time. This is the third stupid incident since Ms. Carmichael returned."

"You seriously wanted the director to send untrained individuals into a burning building?" I asked. "Smoke was pouring from underneath the door. We saw the flames in the windows."

"Probably because it was burning for a while and the smoke built up in the shed." The officer clenched his fists. "I should run every single one of you in. The next time something happens around here, call the sheriff's department. We're out of it."

"The police department is required to protect and serve those in their jurisdiction." Marie pulled out her phone and typed away on it.

"The people who need our help. We won't sacrifice our officers' well-being and time for some elaborate hoaxes so this production gets attention. Everyone knows Ms. Carmichael's career has gone stale."

"You might want to do your job and figure out why it caught on fire," Marie said. "Her almost ex-husband was spotted last night. He could've placed the firepits inside with the intent to ruin the movie or her reputation."

"Of course, he's here," the officer yelled. "Didn't the dang woman hire him as a security guard? Tell her he's not a trespasser if he works here."

The deputy crossed his arms. "The officer has a point. If he works here—"

"He doesn't need to be in the house or around it. Does he?" Marie's eyebrow quirked up. "And did you just insinuate Luna burned down her own she shed?"

The officer raised his arms in the air then slapped them against his side, clearly frustrated in the logic of hiring someone Ms. Carmichael didn't want near her house where some of the filming was taking place. I had to agree with the poor officer.

"Actually," a volunteer fireperson broke into the conversation, "what ruined everything was the water sprayed over everything and the smoke. The fire didn't actually destroy anything."

Then what was the purpose of the fire? The thought swirled around in my head, demanding an answer. I gazed around the area, searching for a reason for what turned out to be a cruel and elaborate hoax. Had the culprit hoped someone would rush into the burning shed to save the "victim"? Or had they just wanted everyone in one location.

"How many people were helping with the fire?" I asked.

Ike glanced down at the clipboard in his hand. "Pretty much everyone. I sent word that all cast and crew members were needed here."

I turned around and stared toward the area where the crew trailers were located. "So practically every other area is vacated. Is there anything on the set someone might want to steal?"

Marie drew in a sharp breath and ran for the back door of the house.

"I need to check my office. You—" Edward pointed at an officer, "come with me."

"Is something wrong?" I asked.

Ike had a tight smile fixed on his face. "Nothing to concern you."

I frowned. I was here. That made it my concern. "I'd like to—"

"The front door was opened." Marie yelled out.

Edward paused and held out his arm, stopping the officer from moving forward. The director slowly turned and stared at Marie.

She stood in the doorway, one hand on her hip, the other holding a coffee tumbler. "The cat is gone."

Ike groaned and smacked a hand against his forehead.

"The cat?"

"Luna's co-star. And Sheriff Rhodes' pet," Marie said.

"At least we know why Vernon was lurking around," Ike said. "What better way to get back at the man you think your wife is sleeping with than losing his cat."

THREE

Great, I left my drama at home and stepped right into someone else's. On the positive side, I could ignore it and go about my business of crafting and reveling in being on the set of a Christmas movie. At least this drama I was able to walk away from permanently in two weeks. Unlike my own, which I had to return to and deal with. And this form of revenge was on the less violent side. Or was for right now, it all depended on how Sheriff Rhodes viewed his cat—pet or fur baby.

"Someone get the leadman over here," Edward said. "We need an inventory of what was destroyed. Ask him to drop me and our crafter, Merry, a list of what needs to be replaced. I'll be in my work trailer. There's a chance we'll have to rearrange the shooting schedule, depending on what's gone. Some of the pieces were key to solving the murder mystery."

I stared after the man. No request? No asking if I had time, ability, or the supplies needed to recreate the lost items. The sun was starting to rise. After all the excitement, there was no way I'd get back to sleep, and I had a lot of crafting and caffeinating to do.

"The director forgets not everyone is his to direct." Marie pocketed her phone. Steam rose from the lip of a Yeti mug with a decal in a bold font stating Drama, It's What I Do. "I guess now's the time for a more formal introduction than last night. I'm Marie. I recognized you from your picture." She looked me up and down, a slightly troubled look on her face.

I pressed my lips together, stopping the defensive words taking root in my mind, unsure of why she was looking at me like that. What had Paul told her about our friendship? That he was interested in more than being friends. That I was thirteen years older than him. That at the moment I was still navigating in my head how I felt about our age difference and wasn't sure testing the waters was a good idea. One just didn't jump in the deep end of the pool if they didn't know how to swim.

"Thanks for recommending me for the job," I said. "This is a dream come true for me."

"Everyone deserves a dream or two coming true. Have any others?" She smiled.

There was something hidden in the gesture like she was prying for information. Maybe wondering if I dreamed about having a man in my life. "World peace. Happiness for all. Meeting Luna. And yours?"

Her eyes sparkled. "One of those can be arranged. Luna would like to meet you."

My heart thudded. She wanted to meet me. That right there was a dream come true. Luna must've really loved the craft items I sent for her perusal. "Just let me know when's the best time. I've been anxious to meet her."

"Have you?" Her mouth dipped in a frown for a moment and her eyes narrowed on me. Did she think I was a crazy stalker?

"Every Christmas aficionado I know has meeting Luna Carmichael, the Queen of Christmas, on their bucket list. She isn't one known for doing meet and greets so having a chance to meet her is a once in a lifetime opportunity. I promise I won't take up too much of her time. I know she's busy and I do have some extra craft projects to complete."

She tilted her head and studied me.

"Is something wrong?" Was I too excited about meeting my Christmas idol? Was I blowing it? "I'm harmless. Ask Paul. He'll tell you. Overly excited about Christmas, but harmless. I promise."

"Sorry. I can't help being a little nervous. Especially after the fire. Everyone thinks it's a prank, but I think there's a little more to it."

"Because the cat was let loose?"

"No. It could've just as easily been Garrison or Luna who left the door open when they left. They were a little preoccupied. Letting the cat escape isn't Vernon's style. Well, at least not starting a fire to do it. He'd just point blank open the front door while the sheriff was present. No sense doing something to aggravate who he considers a rival if that person doesn't know he did it."

"Vernon, I'm assuming that's Luna's husband, isn't fond of the Sheriff."

"He thinks they're having an affair. Luna told him they're not and she isn't a woman who explains herself to anyone. He kept pressing her and now he's her soon-to-be ex-husband. You either believe her or you don't and if you don't...you leave. Luna changes for no man."

"Vernon left?"

"My opinion is he wanted Luna to chase after him. But Luna doesn't chase after a man."

"It sounds like Vernon is working here and Luna is okay with it. Why? I know I wouldn't want my ex-husband around." Okay, my first ex-husband and father of my children I didn't mean too much. The second one I wanted nowhere near me when I ended the marriage.

Marie glanced around then heaved out a sigh. "Paul trusts you so I will too. The director had received some threatening letters about Luna, and she feels it's better Vernon is nearby."

My eyes widened. "Did someone threaten him?"

One of Marie's eyebrows rose.

If that wasn't it there was one other option bouncing around in my head. "She thinks he might have written them. Why not tell the police instead of keeping him around to watch?"

"He's not responsible for the letters but factors into it. The notes are about revealing secrets about Luna and she's afraid people will believe them. The public likes a good scandal about a celebrity, especially a woman who's only marks against her are her multiple marriages. Vernon knew her back when the incident took place and can help clear up the matter. Her only real problem with him is that he thinks he can win her back."

I understood that. I had that issue with one of my ex-husbands also. "The police should still be told. They can look into it."

"She's afraid it'll get leaked before she can find the source of the information and what evidence they plan on using against her."

"What is this secret?"

"It's one Luna is willing to share, but on her conditions and timeline. Have you read the entire script or just the highlighted notes?"

I hadn't thought I was expected to read the whole thing. "I skimmed it but mainly only paid attention to what I had to create. Sorry. I was short on time. I was only—"

Marie patted my arm. "I didn't think you had time. We only contacted you a couple weeks ago and you had a long list for crafting."

"The items are still at my RV. You can come take a look at them."

"I would but Luna has errands for me this morning. She has a manuscript with changes she wants mailed to her agent. Make sure nothing in there can get her in trouble."

"I'm surprised she doesn't email it. It's quicker."

"Luna doesn't trust technology. She's afraid someone else will get ahold of it. She prefers typing, handwriting corrections, and good old snail mail."

"What if it gets lost?" My business was mainly done through the mail and even with tracking packages were lost. I hated thinking about something as valuable and one of kind as a typewritten manuscript getting lost. "I hope she at least has a copy."

"One of us isn't that leery of technology. I have her back."

"What's it like working for Ms. Carmichael?"

"Call her Luna, she hates when women call her by her last name, makes her feel old. Men, on the other hand, she insists call her by her last name. Unless she was or is in a relationship with them."

The scent of coffee, bacon, and other breakfast goodies filled the air. My stomach rumbled. Might as well grab my first cup of coffee for the day and maybe a few slices of bacon. I wasn't a big breakfast eater, but it was hard passing up bacon.

"I hope the coffee around here is good."

Marie shook her stainless-steel Yeti cup. "Got myself some decaf a little bit ago before the mad rush. But I'm not a coffee snob. Luna hates the type that's provided here. I have to go into town and get her some."

I wanted to ask her what made her change careers from law enforcement to basically being an errand person, but we just met. It was a real nosy, and potentially insulting, question.

"Maybe I'll walk into town and get some too." The director was providing coffee and meals to the cast and crew, though it was also important to support the local businesses, especially since the officer hinted there was some bad blood between the town and the movie crew. What better way to build a bridge than spend some money in town?

Her phone pinged. Marie removed it from her pocket and frowned at the number flashing on the screen. "You'll be out of luck. The bakery in Carol Lake doesn't serve good coffee. I drive into Harmony, a larger town about twenty-five minutes away. Great coffee, lovely restaurants, antique shops, and has the closest post office."

"That's a long drive for coffee."

"Not for Luna. Thankfully, I have Yetis." Her phone screen lit up and Marie began tapping her finger on the phone again as she walked to a silver BMW.

"Ms. Winters..." a frazzled looking young man ran up to me and shoved a piece of paper toward me. "Those are items we've cataloged so far with fire and water damage."

The list contained thirty items. I groaned. Where would I find two-foot-tall handmade, plush elves, mesh wreaths, and hand drawn Christmas prints by tomorrow?

"I don't actually possess Christmas magic," I said. "I can't conjure these out of air. Where am I to find all these items? I don't sew. It's not one of my crafting talents."

"I'm just the messenger." The young man ran off.

"Edward isn't one to think about the practicalities of what he wants. He thinks it and expects it to happen," Marie called out to me.

"He's going to be disappointed."

Marie's lips dipped into a tight frown for a moment. "I have list of local crafters in my car. Luna had me vetting them for the job, but once Paul mentioned you and I passed it on to Luna, she knew you were perfect. Some of them might be willing to give a hand."

I jogged over to her, hoping they had time in their schedule to help me out and weren't bitter about not receiving the job.

She slipped into the driver's seat, adjusted the seat, then leaned over and flipped through a stack of papers on the passenger seat.

A handsome man walked up and grabbed the frame of the driver's side door. "A word with you, please."

"Not now, Garrison." She shut the door and slowly pulled out of the area, maneuvering around the people who were either too tired or too careless not to walk in front of the car.

I fought the instinct to gape at the man. There was a rugged mystique about him, a mix of boy next-door and mountain man. His dark beard, peppered with gray, was trimmed close to his face. This was Garrison Tyler. The former behind-the-scenes man, and son of the director, who Luna was dragging in front of the camera. *Dash Away All* was the brainchild of Luna Carmichael and she insisted the lead characters were in their mid-forties and there was no romance. While I liked a good Christmas romance, I loved even more that the movie had a woman and man best-friend team.

With an eyebrow quirked up, Garrison met my gaze. "Have we worked together before?"

I blushed. "Sorry, I'm Merry Winters."

He grinned. "This day has been a little overwhelming already. Luna mentioned you. You're the crafter. Good thing she had the foresight to have you on set."

Right. Crafting. The fire. The items lost. The list. Ugh. I was distracted and Marie left before I reminded her about the list of crafters. Now, I was on my own. First item on my to-do list: coffee.

People were moving toward the food concession area. I followed along with the crowd. At the edge of the pavilion a coffee station was set up. There were four commercial grade coffee urns. I bypassed the one marked decaf and headed for the shortest line of the urns filled with the caffeinated coffee. I planned on grabbing a cup of coffee first then get into the food line. I wasn't sure if being a crafter qualified me to partake in the meals supplied to the cast and crew by the producers and director, but I doubted anyone would frown upon me having a couple of pieces of bacon and a muffin. Or two.

Someone cursed. Then another person. I was bumped into and edged backwards. Everyone was stepping back. Something splattered to the ground. A touch of heat hit my leg and I instinctively jumped back.

"This isn't funny," a voice yelled.

Coffee poured from the urns. A man was trying to close the spigots on two of them, while a woman struggled to stop the coffee from the other two urns.

"What did you do?" yelled an irritated voice.

"I opened it to get a cup and now it won't stop." The man flicked the lever back and forth. The coffee continued draining out.

"Who's doing this?" A disgruntled voice asked.

The river of coffee was slowing. A couple of crew members searched for mops while two offered to go into town and pick up some coffee for everyone.

Edward walked into the pavilion area and stared at the mess. The director heaved out a sigh. "I hope nothing else goes wrong."

"It'll stop once you find out whoever is committing these pranks," Ike said.

"I'll be willing to let it all go as long as it stops now." Edward turned in a slow circle, doing his best to take everyone in with his hard stare. "Anymore antics and there will be some dire consequences. Our reputation is being harmed by all these pranks. Rumors will reach town and we don't want them changing their minds about allowing us to film some scenes there."

I turned and headed back for my trailer. At least this prank was less destructive than the fire that took out some of the props and made us think someone had been killed. The coffee prank was harmless, but the earlier one caused a lot of damage and to fake a death was incredibly evil. What if we had spotted the "body" in the trailer? Someone might've rushed inside to save the person.

A mama bear protectiveness rushed through me. It was an attitude developed over the twenty-four years I'd been a parent and then fine-tuned over the last nine months with the murders that plagued my small town. These pranks, especially the first one, wasn't something to let go.

After I checked on what supplies I needed for my additional work, I'd walk into town and speak with an officer. This wasn't something for the director to deal with, no matter how the town and the police department felt about the crew. Someone could've been seriously injured or killed with the dummy being placed in the prop room.

I opened the door to my RV and stepped inside, freezing when I saw two women in the living room, pawing through my crafting supplies. A flash of fur aimed for the door. I blocked the path with my body, scooping up Ebenezer before shutting the door.

Anne Lindsey was in my craft studio. Her long, dark hair fell in soft waves around her face and back, flawless makeup highlighted all her features and made her seem younger than the forty-six years I knew her to be. She was dressed in blue jeans, boots, and a sweater. They must've been on the way to film a scene and the fire interrupted the shooting.

I held Ebenezer in a football hold. "I wished I would've known I was having visitors. I'd have returned sooner."

A woman with long, lanky blonde hair fought back tears. Was this the same woman who was in the disagreement with Marie?

"Is everything okay?" I asked.

Anne held out a piece of paper to me, smiling at me in a pleasant manner. "I'm Anne. Luna requested I join her waiting in your trailer while all the ruckus was happening. Hope you don't mind. She hadn't wanted to be alone and Garrison was required on set earlier than me."

"Not at all," I said. "I stopped for coffee, but the carafes are malfunctioning. Except for the decaf. It worked for a little while."

"I'm surprised they make a whole carafe of it in the morning, Marie is the only one who drinks it." She rested a hand on the blonde woman's shoulder. "This is Katrina, my assistant. She's having a stressful morning like the rest of us, and it looks like it's only getting to be more hectic for everyone. Oh, the prop department dropped a script and a list off for you. They thought you might like a copy."

"I was just given one." Hopefully, it was a copy of the list I was given earlier and not one with more items. I took the paper and my hopes were immediately dashed. It was a longer list of items needing to be replaced and when the director wanted them. Panic raced through me. Fifty ornaments by this evening. How in the world would I complete them along with signs and a whole slew of other items over the next two days? Along with the stuffed elves, there was now a Santa and Mrs. Claus on the list.

"I don't think the prop department knows long it takes to handcraft an item," I said.

"I could help," Katrina said. "I love to craft and am great at following directions."

Anne beamed. "That's a great idea."

"Are you sure? Don't you need your assistant?" *Please say you don't need her.* While Katrina was working in my studio on decals, I could drive over to Harmony and pick up some items from the other crafters.

"Heavens no." Anne blushed and smiled apologetically at her

assistant. "I don't need an assistant. Luna insisted I have one as I was now a starring actress not background. If there's one thing I've learned, it's best not to argue. In the end, Luna always gets her way."

Looked like my plans for the day were changing. First thing, a trip into Harmony for some needed supplies. "Do you either of you have a car I can borrow?"

The road to Harmony was a long, flat stretch surrounded by corn fields, or what looked like abandoned corn fields, along the way. The large expanse of land was a straightaway as far as the eye could see. The field was filled with corn stalks, brittle and dry, reaching up toward the sky with browning grass mixed in. The farmland seemed not to have been taken care of for a long time.

I yawned, shaking my head, and turned the air conditioner to full blast, hoping the cold kept me wide awake. The long road was dulling my mind and taking away my attention. I needed to focus. I should've caught a quick nap before I ventured to Harmony to pick up the craft items, but I wanted to return to the set and work on the items I still had to complete for today's filming.

I passed a dilapidated farmhouse, the roof caving in and the windows broken. Half of the roof of the wraparound porch collapsed onto the porch, the columns barely holding up the remainder of it. My heart twinged with sadness, imagining the family that had once called the farmhouse home. I bet it was a magnificent house, now forgotten along with the land that had supplied a livelihood and food for hundreds of people.

In the distance, I spotted a section of flattened cornstalks. As I neared, I saw a BMW near a rusted, faded green baler machine. Was it Marie? Was she having car troubles? I pulled off onto the side of the road. The car went over a deep rut and the steering wheel almost jerked away from my grasp. My breath tightened in my throat and I willed myself to remain calm. Panicking wouldn't help the situation. I tightened my hold, eased off the accelerator, and directed the car onto a flatter part of the makeshift shoulder.

Tucking my phone into my back pocket, I walked toward the car. The driver's door was open, glancing down I checked the tires. Not flat. Why had Marie pulled off the road? And where was she?

Shielding my eyes, I glanced around the open area and walked closer to the car. Marie's cracked cell phone was on the ground. The bumper and the side of the car were dented. I leaned over and picked up the phone, my gaze drifting into the car. I froze, a coldness swept through me. There was blood, a lot of it, on the steering wheel. I fumbled for my cell. The front of the BMW was smashed into a corn baler. I called 911 and frantically scanned the area, hoping to see Marie.

The dispatcher immediately answered.

"There was a car accident. The driver left the car. Her cell phone is on the ground broken." I explained my whereabouts as best I could and the state the car was in. "I know the person who was driving. She left Carol Lake about two hours ago."

I squinted into the distance. There wasn't a barn or house nearby. Maybe one of her errands was nearby at a place I hadn't passed yet.

"Emergency services are on their way," the calm voice said. "Please remain near the car."

"But she's wandering around by herself hurt. It's hot." Glancing into the car window, I spotted paper scattered on the floor of the passenger side. One of those sheets might be her itinerary for the day.

"Ma'am, it's better if you stay with the car. Especially since you don't know the area."

I knew the dispatcher was right, but I couldn't just stand and wait. Every moment out in the heat was harmful to Marie in her injured condition. I had to look for her. Pressing the phone tightly to my cheek, I opened the passenger side door. The call ended.

A moment of regret twinged through me at my accidentally-on-purpose hanging up on the dispatcher. She was doing her job by trying to sway me toward the more practical—and safe—choice.

There wasn't another option for me. I had to look for Marie.

Carefully, I opened the door, making sure nothing fell out. There was a list of five names. My name was on the list along with a Katrina Emerson. Was that the same Katrina who was helping me out? She had said she crafted. Had she been up for the job also and was assigned to help Anne instead?

I folded it and placed it in my back pocket and resumed my search. Hopefully, Marie didn't get upset I was rummaging around in her car and took something. The rest of the sheets looked like the script for the movie with notes. Was this the manuscript she was mailing? The pages must've slipped from the seat and were now in a jumbled-up order.

The glove compartment was partway open. Inside was the manual for the car, a first aid kit, and a permanent marker. The kit seemed like a good item to take, yet she left it. This wasn't making any sense. There wasn't a cup in the holder. I knew Marie had her drink and Luna's cup when she left. Why would she have taken the cups with her and not the first aid kit? It was obvious she was hurt, though small bandages and a couple rolls of gauze and tape might not have been helpful. How much good would hot coffee do on a sweltering day? Then again, some kind of beverage was probably better than nothing when stranded out in the heat.

Sweat trickled into my eye. I slipped out of the car and swiped it away. Was it better to stay put and wait for the police or start searching for Marie? She was hurt and the heat wouldn't help. Where could she have gone? I squatted down and inspected the ground. With the area being dry, there wasn't any footprints. A few yards away, there was a patch of flattened grass. That was a promising sign.

On the back of one of the pages of the script, I scribbled down the facts that I knew: car accident, blood on steering wheel, driver wasn't with the car, saw flattened grass, heading in that direction. I debated between leaving it on the seat and slipping it under the windshield wipers. Since the car was littered with papers, and I had just called 911 so they knew someone had seen the accident, I placed the paper under the wiper. It was easier for the rescue crew to see it.

I headed for the squashed grass, being careful of where I stepped in case there was a clue. Something slithered away. I held in my scream, fearing startling the creature might have it turn and bite me. I knew there were venomous snakes in Indiana and I'd rather not find out what kind had just moved out of my way. I shuffled my feet, hoping the movement and sound of the grass crunching sent any other snakes in the area far away from me.

"Marie!" I called out, more worried. If the heat or her injuries didn't get to her, a snake might. With her likely head injury, she probably wasn't considering all the dangers out here. I sure didn't. There was no response. I continued forward. Every few yards, I'd look behind me and check out the trail I was leaving behind. The last thing I wanted was to get lost out here too.

I stopped to catch my breath and checked the time on my phone. A half-hour had passed since I called 911. The sun beat down on me and I licked my dry lips. Dried corn stalks were all around me. My heart thudded. I was regretting my hasty decision. I had no water and a bad sense of direction. Being five-foot-tall didn't allow me to see over the cornstalks.

I'd head back. The police and paramedics should've arrived by now, and I'd let them know the area I searched. A faint crunching sound came from the left. I stared through the corn stalks and saw some movement in the distance. It was either Marie or the search party.

"Marie?" I called out. More sweat dripped from my forehead. The sun was brutal today. How would Marie hold up against the heat and a head injury? I was assuming she hit her head on the steering and that was what the blood was from. Head wounds bled a lot.

The fluttering of the cornstalks stopped for a moment and then the parting of them moved closer and closer to me, like a scene in a horror movie. Large hands moved the stalks out of the way. The tip of a brown sheriff's hat peeked out from the top of the stalks.

A tall man in his mid-sixties emerged from the stalks and spoke into the radio attached to his vest. "I found the woman who left the note. Any luck on the victim?"

"Negative," a crackly voice responded.

The man reminded me a little of Edward Yale, confident, strong, not to be messed with it. Though, it was a look most law enforcement had in their uniforms. His crew cut hair was more gray than dark brown and he adjusted the traditional sheriff's hat on his head. "Why don't you stick with me while I finish searching the field? Don't want two people lost out here."

There was no mistaking the scolding in his tone. "I couldn't leave her out here."

The sheriff parted some stalks and motioned with his head for me to go ahead of him. As I passed him, I glanced at his nametag—Rhodes.

"How do you know the driver?" he asked. "I heard you calling out for her."

"Marie McCormick, she's the cousin of a friend of mine." I continued forward, allowing the sheriff to direct me according to which stalks he pulled back. If I was right, we were heading to the abandoned farmhouse. "I'm working with the *Dash Away All* production in Carol Lake."

"When I saw the car, I figured Marie was the missing one. If Luna had crashed, she'd have stayed put. She isn't one to venture away from comfort." We reached the clearing and the sheriff stopped, gazing around. The farmhouse was in the distance. "A deputy is checking with the hospital if someone brought an injured woman in. Nothing so far. Do you know where Marie was going today?"

"Harmony for coffee and mailing something for Ms. Carmichael."

"How about you head toward the farmhouse and I'll head over toward the Parkinsons, which is farther away." He pointed toward the left. "The farmhouse is behind all that overgrown shrubbery and rusted out junk. Do you have a phone on you?"

"Yes." I pulled it from my back pocket.

"Let's swap numbers. If you see anything give me a call, if not wait at the house until one of the deputies and I come for you. The heat is getting brutal out here and you didn't bring any water. I'd hate for you to get heat stroke."

I wanted to argue with him, but I knew he was right. I took a huge risk walking around in the scorching heat, in an area I didn't know very well, without water, or a natural good sense of direction. The last thing the searchers needed was splitting their time between two people wandering around in the heat. I hoped I hadn't diverted anyone's attention from Marie.

"I'll wait there until I hear something." I headed for the farmhouse in the distance. Maybe Marie went in there for some relief from the heat. I kept my phone clutched in my hand. For some reason, it gave me a feeling of confidence, like I could make everything right with a quick phone call.

Carefully, I made my way through the shrubbery, a mix of overgrown weeds and bushes. The slower pace and the shade from the branches and leaves made the area cooler. What if Marie was lying somewhere in the hedges? I stopped and scanned the area, squatting down to peer through the branches. Nothing.

In her condition, she wouldn't have the energy to fight through the overgrowth. I needed to find a more direct path through the mess. I broke through the other side and walked the perimeter of the hedges, searching for an opening, or at least what had been one.

A chill raced through me. On the ground, a hand was reaching out from the hedges a few feet away. I ran, nearly tripping over my feet. I dropped to ground, grabbing and breaking branches out of the way. It was Marie.

Dried blood coated her face. Pressing my fingers against the pulse on her neck, I held my breath, hoping and praying. I was too late. There was none. An image flashed in my head from this morning. Marie had been wearing a gold locket. It was gone. I crawled into the hedges and looked around. No purse. No cup. Had someone robbed the injured Marie?

I fought the urge to move her from the bushes and make her more comfortable. I needed the sheriff. With trembling hands, I scrolled through my contacts and tapped the sheriff's number.

"I found her," I choked on the words.

"How is she?"

"She's dead."

FOUR

It wasn't long after that the sheriff found me. He squatted down beside Marie and repeated the motion I had done only moments before. He removed his fingers from the pulse in her neck and stood. "I really didn't expect this." He heaved out a sigh.

"I don't understand why someone would hurt her. Kill her." Tears burned my eyes.

"Someone?" Frowning, the sheriff stood and hooked his fingers in his utility belt.

"Her gold locket is missing. Along with her cup. Her purse. She had those items this morning and they aren't in her car."

"Are you sure?"

"I spoke to her before she left this morning."

"Can you describe these items?"

"Yes. The locket was round and gold on a thin chain. The tumbler was a twenty-ounce size, stainless steel with a decal on it. Drama It's What I Do. I can't remember much about the purse. Brown leather. Average size."

He nodded, writing down the descriptions.

My phone pinged. With trembling hands, I glanced at the screen, fearing Paul was asking me how things were going. I wasn't quite ready to tell him about Marie. We were at the stage of our friendship where we texted each other a couple times a day.

For a moment, relief flooded through me. I didn't have to tell Paul yet. The message was from Anne. *Guess what? Ebenezer is the new "cat" in the movie. I told the director you wouldn't mind. We're having difficulties getting him into his carrier. Already tried to bite Katrina and the casting director.*

Bite them? Ebenezer was a little particular about people, but he'd never attacked anyone before. Then again, when he started whistling and acting the enraged diva, no one had ever tried picking him up.

The sheriff placed a hand on my wrist. "I'd rather you didn't tell anyone what happened here."

"She's my friend's cousin. I have to tell him." My heart hurt. How was I going to tell him? The sheriff's image blurred as tears rushed into my eyes.

"I think it's best I call. I'm better suited to answer any questions. Do you have the number of her parents?"

I shook my head. "Only Paul's. I don't know how to reach them."

"Give me his number and I'll take care of it."

Sirens drew closer. The ambulance was driving through the dried-out cornfield. My phone pinged again, and I couldn't' stop myself from gazing at the screen. Anne again. About Ebenezer.

Part of me wanted to leave and get to Ebenezer before he hurt someone, or someone hurt him, and avoid dealing with Marie's death. The little guy must be terrified to react so badly to going into his carrier. The other part of me knew the proper thing to do was wait until after the sheriff spoke to me. And I should stay here with Marie—for Paul.

"Go ahead and head out. I know where to find you."

"I have to be here. For his cousin."

He centered a soft look on me and rested a hand on my shoulder. "There's nothing you can do for her."

I shuddered. Responsibilities warred against each other. I felt bad shifting some of focus from Marie to Ebenezer. But he was out of control and might hurt someone. What would happen if he bit someone? Would animal control be called? Would he be taken away?

"Whatever you need to do seems important. Go on. I'll take care of things here."

* * *

Pulling the borrowed car to a stop near my RV, I glanced over at my cell phone. Every minute that passed, I felt more and more like a horrible person and that I made a grave mistake. I should've called Paul myself instead of agreeing with the sheriff. The sheriff's reasoning was logical, Paul would have questions I couldn't answer, but I was the one who found her. More importantly, I was Paul's friend. Friends shouldn't take the easy way out of a situation.

I opened the car door and an exasperated screech flittered past the front door of my RV. I hurried up the steps, clunks and clatters floated past the door and all other thoughts rushed out of my head. I was glad for the distraction and focusing on a simple problem: getting Ebenezer into his carrier. More bangs erupted from the RV. Were they trying to contain Ebenezer or kill him? I yanked the door open and charged inside.

The small tabletop Christmas tree near my crafting zone was on the ground. Some of the plastic balls were rolling across the floor and the star was blinking on and off. The yellow, green, and red lights created a disco-tech effect on the floor. Ebenezer was gleefully chasing a piece of paper across the living room. The little guy was bouncing off anything, including a set of metal Santa Clauses that had been residing on the kitchen counter. He smacked the lilac paper ball and scampered after it.

"No," Katrina squealed and dove for the ball, scattering the Santas around the living room.

Ebenezer perked up. Chase was one of his favorite games.

"What's going on?" I snagged the carrier from the couch and placed it on the floor.

"Your guinea pig stole that paper from my purse." Her voice was growing more frantic. "I need that."

"Since he wants it, put it in the carrier and we can secure him inside."

"He'll eat it." She reached for the ball of paper. Ebenezer hit it with his head away from her hand.

"I can get it out before he even tastes it." I weaved around the boxes of supplies, following after the blur of red, white, and brown fur racing for the back of the RV with his new toy. I squatted down and walked toward Ebenezer, reaching toward the makeshift ball.

He wriggled his nose and zipped past me, carrying his prize with his teeth. I dove for him and missed him by centimeters. Ebenezer zigged while I zagged. A corner of the wadded paper dangled from his tiny teeth. Ebenezer scurried under the recliner, shimmying his backside until his whole body was underneath.

I flattened myself on the ground and tapped on the floor, giving him my best "mom" look. "Come out from under there right now."

He squashed his face up and began to slowly chew on the ball.

"No," I squealed. "Stop it. You're going to choke."

Ebenezer ignored my distress and continued chowing down.

"You'll kill yourself." My voice grew more panicked. "Stop. Now."

I reached under the recliner. My arms weren't long enough. What was I going to do now? Not only was Ebenezer ruining a prized possession of Katrina's but was also likely going to choke on it. I was a terrible pet parent.

There was a knock on the door. I weighed my dilemma: answer the door or retrieve the paper.

The answer came to me as Katrina cried out in triumph. "I got it."

I scrambled to my feet, righted the Christmas tree, and answered the door.

"About time." An irritated Ike stood on the stairs. "Has the guinea pig been contained yet? Edward does not want the pet written out."

Ebenezer zoomed out from under the couch and I scooped his flying body into my arms. "No, you don't, you rascal."

Ike slammed the door shut. The bulbs on the Christmas tree in my RV swayed. The glittered Merry bulb swayed back and forth and clicked against the Bright blub that was beside it.

"Why must you be so difficult?" I placed Ebenezer into the carrier and zipped it shut, tapping my finger on the mesh panel.

"I'll come back and help with the craft projects." Katrina tugged the strap of her bag onto her shoulder. "It's best if I leave my stuff in my room."

The critter wriggled his nose at her.

"Change of plans." Ike pointed at Katrina. "I need you to head up to the main house. Marie hasn't returned from her errands yet. You'll assist Ms. Carmichael until she returns."

My stomach plummeted. The sheriff didn't want me to share what I knew, but how long could I keep it a secret?

"Really? You want me to assist Ms. Carmichael?" Katrina's blue eyes lit up. "Should I head right over or drop off my bag first?"

Ike shooed at her. "Take it with you. Ms. Carmichael is in dire need. First order is going into town and getting her some coffee."

Katrina nodded and raced out of the RV. I couldn't blame her. Even though I loved crafting, I'd also prefer being Luna Carmichael's assistant for a few hours. It wasn't every day one was the right-hand woman for a Christmas icon. But how did Katrina move from being the possible crafter hired for the movie to Anne's assistant? Unless she was local-ish, it seemed strange to have her come all this way for a potential job.

Ike squatted down and looked at Ebenezer. "So, the charming and handsome Ebenezer is finally cooperating."

"He's been forced into it," I said.

"Why don't you go ahead and take him over? The sooner Ms. Carmichael and the replacement pet make each other's acquaintances the better." Ike's phone buzzed. He glanced down at the screen and groaned. "And the sooner the better. Apparently, the sheriff has arrived and is insisting on speaking to Ms. Carmichael. I must now go tell him about his missing cat and that the set is closed. No one but cast and crew are allowed. No matter who."

"With all the pranks happening, maybe it's a good idea law enforcement is hanging around," I said.

"An irritated Ms. Carmichael is not a good Ms. Carmichael to work with. Right now, it's Edward's time for Ms. Carmichael's attention. Sheriff Rhodes can have her attention back once filming is done. Though, not apparent to him, Ms. Carmichael has moved on from Sheriff Rhodes."

"What do you mean?"

He rolled his eyes. "I have worked with Ms. Carmichael long enough that I know when she wants to move on from a man, she finds another to speed it along. Now that Vernon O'Neal has been shooed off, Ms. Carmichael no longer has a need for the sheriff's attention."

"But his cat—"

A devious smiled flittered across his face. "Well, we longer have the cat, now do we."

No, we didn't. I pressed back a frown. Was the man insinuating Luna, or someone on the crew, deliberately lost the cat? I wasn't sure about loaning them Ebenezer. I fiddled with the strap of the carrier. Ebenezer gazed at me with trusting eyes. I was his person. The person responsible for his well-being. Was I doing the right thing letting him become a Christmas movie star?

"Filming starts soon." Ike opened the door and motioned for me to leave.

"I'm not sure..." I trailed off. Sometimes the truth wasn't the best policy. I doubted he'd take it well that I didn't trust handing over my pet to Luna Carmichael.

He heaved out a sign and glanced at his clipboard. "There's no time for hesitation. Just take the guinea pig there. I'm sure he'll behave on the set. All he needs to do is stay still and nibble on snacks."

The nibbling was no problem. It was Ebenezer's favorite pastime. The staying still was a whole different story. "It's not really that."

"He'll be fine. I don't really have another option for the pet, and you do have props to make."

The list. I tugged the list of crafters I took from the car from my back pocket and held it out. "Marie gave me a list of crafters who could possible help. Do you have the contact information for any of them?" I changed the details a bit to protect the information I had to keep secret.

Without even looking at it, Ike responded. "No. Ms. Carmichael and Marie were responsible for hiring the crafter."

"Isn't that unusual for one of the stars to hire the people making the props?"

"Not when it comes to Luna. She wanted control over that aspect since the crafters played a subtle role in the movie. Since she wrote the script, and was helping finance the movie, Edward allowed it." Ike headed for the door, froze, brows drawing down as he frowned. He snapped his fingers. "I do remember Marie and Luna exchanged words about one of the crafters. Something about Luna ghosting the woman. It wasn't the way to treat someone especially when the woman lived close enough to stop and start asking questions. It was right after that Luna hired security guards."

The slight breeze drifted over my skin as I puttered down the road in a four-seater golf cart. I hadn't realized summer was so hot in Indiana. It was already approaching eight-two degrees and the day was just starting. The radio had predicted the weather would be unseasonably warm this week. Not the best time to film a Christmas movie where the cast had to parade around outside in winter coats and boots.

This wasn't the relaxing time I had envisioned. Keeping secrets, avoiding mentioning anything unpleasant to Luna, and coming up with additional crafts for the production, and the worst was waiting to receive a phone call from Paul.

I shook my head and centered my attention back on what I was doing: driving and finding a dirt road. At the speed I was driving, I could've walked faster. The dirt path was bumpy, and I didn't want to risk jostling the box of glass Christmas ornaments on the floorboard of the back seat or Ebenezer, who was safely tucked into his fabric carrier. The small storage area at the back of the cart had a box filled with wooden signs. A bungee cord was keeping that box secured to the cart.

Coming to a complete stop, I checked the written directions Ike scribbled down for me. Go to the end of the row of trailers, after half a mile, make a hard right onto a dirt path and then at the end was the house where today's shooting would take place.

"Well, at least we'll be in shade." I headed down the long gravel path. Every few feet, "Private Property" or "No Trespassing" signs were nailed onto a tree. Whoever had bought the area sure wanted it known they wanted no one venturing into the woods. Kind of surprised they'd allow the old farmland to house the RVs and trailers housing the equipment, crew, and cast on the property.

The dirt road snuck up on me, and I made a quick, hard right, pushing down on the gas to get over the slight incline appearing the moment I turned. The passenger side front wheel bumped over an object, tipping the side up for a moment. A nightmare of Ebenezer, me, and all my hard work splattering onto the ground filled my head. Fortunately, the cart righted itself. I eased off the gas and the cart stopped, taking in a deep breath to settle my racing heart.

"You all right?" I leaned over and looked through the mesh panel of the carrier. Ebenezer was dozing. Nice to know one of us wasn't affected by our near disaster. I slid out and walked to the passenger side, wanting to remove whatever had almost caused us to flip. I'd hate for anyone else to run over it.

Near the tire was a stainless steel tumbler with a Drama, It's What I Do decal on it. Marie's cup. Prickles raced up and down my arms. How did it get here? Why would Marie have driven back to the house before she went into town? Maybe Marie forgot something and went back for it. But how would the cup have ended up here? No one threw an empty Yeti out the window. Had she stopped and it fell out?

Using two fingers, I picked it up, carefully not to plaster my prints all over it. I twisted the cup, examining it. It was scuffed up and some dirt pressed into it, likely from having run over it. Maybe

I was wrong, and it wasn't Marie's. The design wasn't that unusual. Might be something everyone who was part of the cast and crew was given. I put it in one of the boxes. No harm in asking. If someone else had dropped it, I was sure they'd want it back. Those cups weren't cheap.

I returned to the driver's seat and headed toward the house where today's filming was taking place. The shade from the trees kept me cool. Unease drifted through me the longer I drove. Where was the end of it? Had I missed a turn-off? Ike's directions didn't say how long I was to continue before I missed the house. You'd think he'd have us closer. Then again, I was driving in a golf cart, distances likely seemed a little farther away than in a car.

After driving a few more yards, there was the large, two-story farmhouse with a gleaming pond a hundred yards from the front door. Toward the left-hand side, almost one hundred and fifty yards away was a barn. Last night, the golf cart I rode in had come from the back of the house, I hadn't seen the front. It was a beautiful house but there wasn't one indication of Christmas. I had a bad feeling about this. There were a lot of items I made, but outdoor lighted decorations weren't on my list.

On the long, circular driveway there was a line of parked cars and trucks. Cameras and lights were being removed from rental moving vans. I hoped some of the outdoor Christmas decorations were in the vans being unloaded and not in the shed. I had no idea how the director would replace all those items. Stores didn't have much in the way of Christmas yard decorations this time of the year. The gazebo, while beautiful, said "enjoy the lovely summertime," not "gear up for a spectacular Christmas." How could they film anything Christmas in such a non-Christmassy place?

If the items couldn't be replaced, would the movie be cancelled or delayed? With my mom's health issues, I couldn't stay here for an extended period of time. I was already a little concerned about my two weeks away from home, though it was a needed break. And I was excited about Ebenezer's role in the movie and also having some of my crafts appear on the small screen.

I drove past the line-up of cars waiting to unload, looking for a spot big enough for a golf cart. I didn't have that much to unload and had a long list of crafts to make. There was a golf-cart-sized spot between two of the vans. As I parked, a man in an orange vest ran over to me.

"You can't park that here. Crew parking is at the old pond. Near the shed that caught on fire. It's a short walk."

"Nothing's a short walk carrying a guinea pig and boxes of decorations. Once I unload, I'll move the golf cart."

"No animals on the set. And I still can't let you park here. Another truck is rolling in soon and I need to tighten everyone up so it'll fit."

"Ebenezer is replacing the cat someone accidentally freed."

"Well, make sure it doesn't get loose. I don't have time for chasing another animal through the woods. I'll have some of my guys take the boxes right now."

"Did you drop a Yeti cup? I found one a few yards back on the dirt path. Looks like something that was made for the cast and crew." I pointed at it.

He snorted. "I wouldn't carry that around."

"Why not?"

"I'm not a drama guy and we wouldn't have gotten one anyway. Security isn't considered part of the cast and crew. We're allowed access to areas that everyone else isn't."

As he spoke, two helpers removed the box of ornaments and signs from the golf cart. It was like watching a NASCAR pit crew. They reached in, removed the bungee cords, picked up the boxes, then scuttled into the house in what seemed like one smooth motion.

"Like where?"

His eyes narrowed on me and he crossed his massive arms across his chest. "Why are you asking?"

"No one told me. I'd hate to be somewhere I wasn't allowed," I said.

The suspicion in his face softened. "The house, unless it's being used for filming, is off limits, and anything on the property surrounding the house. Also, the director's office and inside of any of the personal trailers."

And yet, someone had found it reasonable to allow Luna and others into my RV.

The man in the orange vest tapped the top of the cart. "Park this on the side of the house. Now."

A security guard in black pants and a navy polo directed me toward the parking area, keeping a close eye on me as if he thought I'd park in the middle of the flower garden.

There was a grouping of trees, long branches with leaves draping down creating a small alcove of shade. The perfect spot for my golf cart. The safest way to get me and Ebenezer out of the golf cart, and not damage the tree, was backing in so we could slip out the driver's side. Since driving the RV, my skills at backing up had improved immensely. It took a lot of practice, but I was finally confident in pulling the RV into spaces, and with my newfound confidence in driving it, it made all other vehicles easy to control. Except for motorcycles. That was one mode of transportation off my list.

"Let's go find out where they want you." I snagged the handle of Ebenezer's carrier and debated about heading to the back door, but decided against hopscotching over the patches of snow that were on the ground.

I walked up the front steps, carefully avoiding the men and women hanging up lights, wreaths, and of course a sprig of mistletoe over the door.

A crew member stared at me and Ebenezer, who was pressing against the mesh part of his cage.

I held up the carrier. "Ebenezer the guinea pig is the new cat."

The woman smiled. "You can take the new cat upstairs. His scene will be in the study, but first take him to the second bedroom on the right and introduce him to Ms. Carmichael. It's her private dressing room."

I walked up the stairs. Keep calm. Don't reveal anything, I ordered myself. Instead of an excited anxiousness tripping through me, it was straight up anxiety. I was finally going to meet Luna Carmichael, my Christmas idol, and I was keeping a secret from her: her assistant had died.

A decade ago, Luna had been *the* heroine in Christmas romance movies. Heck, she had practically been Christmas. There wasn't a week she wasn't appearing in something Christmassy. Over the years, the number of movies she starred in tapered off and she went from being the lead heroine, to the friend of the lead heroine, then the mother of the heroine. The last few years, I hadn't seen Luna Carmichael in a Christmas movie.

Ebenezer whistled from his carrier. Pausing at the door, I lifted the cage to my face and smiled at him. "This will be fun. You get to be in a Christmas movie."

I opened the door to the bedroom and walked right into a rack of clothing.

"Last minute changes," a cool, refined voice said. "Who does he think he's dealing with? I request changes not him. Testing me won't work out well for him."

"It's probably a mistake," A woman said. "Or the work of the prankster. Heard Ike's golf cart had a flat tire this morning. He actually had to walk to get coffee."

"Coffee that didn't exist." There was a delightful laugh. "Couldn't have happened to a worthier foe."

I knew that laugh. I heard it on many Christmas movies past. Luna Carmichael. I fought with a long coat and scarf, doing my best to keep the knitted scarf away from Ebenezer's teeth. Fortunately, he was still confined in the carrier and the mesh didn't allow him to snag an end of the accessory.

"I believe we have a visitor," Luna said.

Hangers screeched as the outfits parted and a young woman stared at me. "Are you lost?"

Behind her, Luna sat in a plush office style chair in front of a mirror, eyes closed. Her face was heavily lined from age. Wisps of gray broke through the deep burnished brunette color of her just-past-the-shoulder-length hair. It was Luna Carmichael. My breath caught in my throat. She was two arm's length away from me.

Luna swiveled her chair, peered at Ebenezer and screeched. "Why is that woman carrying around a rat?"

I refrained from rolling my eyes at the woman who had once been my Christmas hero. "This is Ebenezer. He's a guinea pig and your character's beloved pet. The casting director asked I bring him over for you to meet."

Luna spun back around. "I guess that creature is better than the demonic cat."

"You were the one who arranged for the demonic cat." The young woman returned to Luna's side and began arranging her hair in an updo.

"I hadn't realized its temperament was so horrible. The thing hisses and growls at me constantly. Never imagined such a sweet-looking thing was so evil." Luna flicked her hand, poinsettia berry red nails glimmered in the lights and a big, diamond ring sparkled on her hand. "Have someone set the demon feline free. I have no more use for it."

"I don't think we should do that." The stylist turned her head toward me, rolling her eyes. "It's never a good idea to anger law enforcement."

Luna laughed. "I can handle that man."

No one had told Luna the cat escaped. Ike acted like she was pleased about the situation. Maybe he knew her well enough to know, or her hating the cat might not have been a secret. Would someone let the cat out of the house to please Luna? My thoughts briefly flickered to Katrina. She was thrilled about her "promotion." But she hadn't known Marie wasn't returning from her errand. Though, I'd think she'd have told Luna by now. Then again, Katrina wasn't in the room when Ike told me. She might not know yet or hadn't wanted to start off the new working relationship with "your cat's gone."

"Actually, the cat is gone. That's why Ebenezer was hired," I said. No one told me I couldn't say that. It was also a good secret to test out Luna's reaction. Since she didn't like the cat, it was the easiest "bad" news to give her.

Luna's meticulously plucked eyebrows arched up. There was a hopeful look on her face. "Gone as in..."

"Ran out the door."

Luna laughed, a childlike delighted sound. "How utterly fabulous. The universe must be pleased with me. Make sure security knows that Randolph is not to step one foot inside this house anymore. My need for him has vanished. What a wonderful day this is turning out to be. Be a dear and hand me my script. I can have those changes memorized in ten minutes."

"That'll be hard," the stylist said. "The sheriff trumps the security team."

"Not in my world, and this is my world." Luna snapped her fingers and pointed at me then the script pages.

I picked up the stack of papers Luna jabbed her bright red nail at and handed them to her.

"You're dismissed," she said.

The door opened and the scent of coffee wrapped around me. It was heavenly. I took in a deep breath, trying to identify the other scent mixed in with the familiar smell of coffee. Gingerbread? No. It was a little nuttier. Hazelnut?

Katrina waded through the clothes.

"Took you long enough." Luna snapped. "Thought I had another disappearing assistant. Have you reached Marie yet?"

My heart pounded. I pressed my hand to my chest like I wanted to muffle the sound.

Katrina shook her head. "I've called her personal cell phone and her work phone."

Work phone? Marie had two phones. I only saw one in the car.

"Where is that woman?" Luna studied her reflection in the mirror dabbing at the corner of her mouth with a tissue. "She knows I can't handle her being gone for too long."

"I promise I can do a good job for you Ms. Carmichael."

Katrina smiled. “Ike has told me exactly how you like everything.”

“Considering Ike doesn’t know I don’t drink coffee with a nut flavor, he doesn’t know anything. Take that out of here.”

“I’ll talk with everyone here.” Katrina covered up the spout of the coffee lid. “I’ll make sure I know everything about you.”

“I’d rather you didn’t,” Luna snapped at the eager woman. Katrina’s lips trembled. “Just go.”

The door opened. Before I looked over my shoulder, the stylist gasped and slapped a hand over her mouth as her eyes widened in delight. Luna swiveled toward the door and her eyes narrowed to a slit. I knew who it was without having to look—Sheriff Randolph Rhodes. His sheriff hat was tucked under one arm.

“Did I not say he was banned from this house.” Luna’s hands knotted into fists and she glared at the sheriff. Why was she so hostile toward him? Was it because of the rumors of the affair? Did she think he started them?

“I’m your hair stylist, not your assistant. No one told security not to let him in. And he is the sheriff.” The stylist took the coffee cup and walked out of the room, leaving us to deal with the fall out.

Luna fixed a steely gaze on her replacement assistant. “Why didn’t you?”

Katrina swallowed and stepped back. “I didn’t know.”

Sheriff Rhodes stepped in front of the scared assistant, gaze meeting mine for a moment before he focused on Luna. “I’m here on official business, Luna.” His voice was soft, tender.

Luna tilted her head to the side. Everything in her gaze said she had no trust for him. “Trying to shut down the production again?”

“I’m sorry, Luna. Marie died in a car accident. She skidded off the road and crashed into a baler.” He glanced over at me. “She wandered away from the accident and succumbed to her injury and the heat. We found her a few miles from the accident.”

There weren’t any skid marks. I held back my frown. Why was he lying to her? My mind replayed the scene. The phone was on the ground. Cracked. Had Marie been texting and driving? Was the sheriff trying to save Marie's reputation and not let anyone know?

Katrina gasped and covered her mouth.

Luna swayed for a brief moment before she stood ramrod straight. "Was she coming here or leaving?"

Randolph eyed her suspiciously. "What?"

"Marie. Was she leaving town or returning when she crashed?"

"Is that important?" His eyes narrowed.

"I want to see the car," Luna said. "Arrange for that to happen by the end of the day."

"It was totaled Luna," Randolph said. "There's nothing to see."

I drew in a sharp breath. Another lie. The sheriff fixed a hard stare on me. I eased back into the clothing. He knew someone else had seen the truth. Did he expect me to keep all the details quiet?

Katrina stepped closer to me, crowding into my personal space. With the reddening of Luna and Randolph's face, and the clenched fists, the two looked ready to come to blows.

"Unless the car was blown to smithereens, it still exists. It's my car. I need to get pictures for insurance purposes." Luna opened the vanity drawer and slammed it. Items rolled off the top and fell onto the floor.

"The deputies can send you some." The sheriff nodded at the vanity. "You should be careful. You'll break something."

Eyeing him for a long moment, Luna opened the drawer and banged it closed. The mirror rattled and hit into the wall. More bottles tumbled to the ground. Two knocked into each other and a strong rose scent enveloped the room.

Luna tipped her chin up, doing her best to look down on the man who was a few inches taller than her. "Not good enough. I want pictures of the inside and outside. Today."

"Do you think I'm lying to you about Marie dying?" The sheriff squatted for a moment and scooped an item from the floor, fisting his hand around it. The muscles in his neck twitched as if he was fighting the urge to shoot another look over at me.

Katrina and I knelt down and picked up small bottles and tubes from the floor. He was fibbing about the condition of the car.

Though, it was possible the damage to the front end and engine qualified the car as being totaled for insurance purposes.

She narrowed her eyes. “And if I do, whose fault is that?”

“Marie’s body is at the morgue. You can stop by. I’m sure the coroner will make time for you and show you her body.” The bitterness from the man was undisguised. He placed his hands, still fisted, at his side.

Maybe there had been something going on between them that ended abruptly and without both parties wanting the end. My gaze volleyed back and forth between the two. In the heat of their anger, they forgot there was a witness present during this conversation. Two witnesses. There was no way these two were in a relationship. The rumors were totally off base. Heck, my ex-husband Samuel and I got along better during our breakup and subsequent divorce, and Samuel had dragged it out for months to torment me. A woman had just died, and they couldn’t pull back their anger enough to grieve or for the sheriff to show some decorum to a friend of the deceased.

“I just find it odd, you’re the one to tell me. Why not Carol Lake’s police chief?” Luna asked.

“It happened outside the town’s jurisdiction.”

“How convenient.” Luna stretched out the last word. Animosity oozing out of every prolonged syllable.

Randolph stared at her, tossing the item he held onto the vanity top. Gaze unreadable. “Why do you want to see the car, Luna?”

“Better question is why don’t you want me to?”

FIVE

Ike opened the door. "Ms. Carmichael, we need you in the study for a run-through."

"As they say, the show must go on." Luna turned toward me, quickly averting her gaze. But not soon enough. I saw what Luna was trying to hide. Distrust. "Bring the rodent."

I did the only thing possible at the moment, followed her.

With the camera, lights, camera crew, director, and scene participants, there was no space for me in the study. It was tight. Barely enough room for air for all of us to breath. The space not filled with people was taken by a massive desk and bookcases filled with family photos and decorative books. There were photos of Luna and Garrison Tyler, the actor playing the hero of the movie and photos of younger versions of the pair. I was amazed the production crew was able to find photos of a little boy who I imagined was what a young Garrison looked like. There was even a photo of a mother and young child that could pass off as Luna and Garrison. Whoever was in charge of setting up the scene was incredible. It must've taken them days to find that photograph or create one from old photos of Luna and Garrison.

"Hopefully, after one quick run-through we can get everything in place to shoot the scene after lunch," Edward said, shooing out everyone who wasn't necessary.

I leaned against the wall, keeping myself and Ebenezer out of the way of the mass exodus. The room seemed to expand once some of the people filtered out. On the mantle was the wood pallet sign I made with the words "Family, Home, Cherish." The theme of the movie was the intricacies of family that not only create lasting memories but angst and end with murder. A little bit of a downer for a Christmas movie, but it was a murder mystery.

Luna sighed. "Why can't we just do it now? I don't need a trial run. I can complete this monologue scene in one take. I am a professional." She flickered a hand toward me and Ebenezer. "My new pet is here. I'm sure his mom would appreciate getting this scene done so she can work on everything needed for tomorrow's set."

I schooled my features into a pleasant expression, masking my worry. An image of Marie, holding two Yeti cups, popped into my head. The threats against Luna. Marie was driving Luna's car. What if the fire was a warning? I drew in a deep breath. Had someone tampered with the car and killed Marie instead?

Multiple gazes turned to stare at me. I coughed a bit and patted my chest. Luna's gaze bore into me. A thoughtful and distrustful expression on her face.

"Is there a problem?" Ike asked.

"Allergies," I croaked out.

I had to talk to the police, let them know about the Yeti cup I found. The cup I had put in the box with the Christmas decorations I delivered. If Luna needed protection, they were the best people to know as she didn't trust the sheriff, and he lied about the scene of the accident. Besides, Carol Lake's police department was close by.

Where was Luna's cup? Marie had both. I flipped through my memory, trying to conjure up the console of the BMW. I couldn't envision it.

"I'll take the pet." Luna held out her arms. "We should get acquainted with each other since we're inseparable in a few scenes."

A member of the sound crew walked over to Luna, holding a small mic and a battery pack in their hand. "Garrison is mic'd up and ready to go."

"Garrison?" Luna turned, nearly colliding herself and Ebenezer into the sound guy. "He isn't in this scene."

I stepped forward, readying to save Ebenezer, who was looking rather interested in the battery pack being hooked onto Luna's sweater. Please, don't nibble on Luna's clothes, I silently begged. Ebenezer might have the shortest role in a movie ever. Well, besides the cat who disappeared before his debut.

"Our original suspect for this scene sustained a slight injury hanging up some of the outdoor lights and is at urgent care. Garrison agreed to fill in," Edward said. "It's just the back of him and his voice that's in the scene. He'll change it up a bit. No one will know that the sleuth's best friend and one of the suspects is one and the same."

Garrison stepped into the room, mic'd up and ready for filming.

Luna tapped her lip for a couple minutes, tilting her head to the side as she studied Garrison. She shifted Ebenezer in her grasp and grinned. "That's a perfect idea. The sleuth's best friend being one of the major suspects. Maybe even change it up where he is the guilty party. It'll be fabulous."

"I didn't agree to a role as a villain." A dark expression crossed Garrison's face.

"Come on now, dear, it's common knowledge that during a family dispute it's usually a trusted family member who does in the victim. And you're the only one I trust." There was some malice in the smile she fixed on Garrison. "My character specifically requested her nephew because of the threats she was receiving. Wouldn't it be intriguing if the very person she wanted to save her is the one intent on killing her."

"There's no time for this nonsense," Edward said.

"Shouldn't take any time at all." Luna's predatory grin was now on Edward. "Just a few changes in dialogue here and there. The climax scene will work just as well with exchanging Garrison's character for the current murderer."

"That's a lot of changes for the cast to memorize," Edward placed a hand on Ebenezer's back.

Ebenezer shrieked and tried biting him. Edward drew back quickly.

"Edward is the third person he's tried to bite." Ike evil-eyed my buddy. "He's a menace. Has there been any luck in finding the cat?"

"I'm so sorry. He can be a little skittish. He's not much of a people person," I said.

"Then we should get along fabulously." Luna drew Ebenezer toward her. "Because neither am I."

"Truer words never spoken," Garrison muttered.

"I'm sure the animal is a little out of sorts being dragged here then carried around like an accessory," Edward said. "Let's just get the scene done as previously written. Any other changes can be discussed later."

"Fine." Luna settled herself onto the edge of the desk, placing Ebenezer in her lap. "I'm ready to get this scene over with before I attack someone."

I left, closing the door behind me and fighting back a bit of jealously wiggling its way through me. I should be happy Ebenezer took to Luna Carmichael. A shrieking guinea pig, his usual reaction to displeasure, would have the director on the search for another pet.

There was a noise coming from the dressing room. Either the stylist returned and was putting away items, or the soon-to-be ex was rummaging around in Luna's things. There was one way to find out, and since I had left Ebenezer's travel carrier in the room, I had a valid reason to walk in there. Quietly.

Placing one hand on the door and another on the knob, I eased it open and peered inside the room. Katrina was rummaging through the drawers of the vanity. There was a clink of bottles. She had a small cylinder shaped item in her hand and dropped it back inside the drawer. She closed the drawer and opened another one, finding nothing in there, she dumped out items from a small red purse. Items scattered all over the vanity, some tumbled onto the floor. One object nestled into the carpet.

Voices from downstairs carried into the hallway. Katrina spun toward the door. Shock then anger flashed across her face. I forced a smile on my face.

"What are you doing in here?" She asked, gritting her teeth.

"There it is," I said louder than necessary and walked over to Ebenezer's carrier and snagged the strap. "I couldn't remember where I left it. It'll be hard to get my critter home without it. The little guy is an escape artist."

"Now that you found it, you can go." Katrina knelt and started picking up the items from the carpet.

I paused for a moment, gaze lingering on the items on the vanity. "Looking for something?"

"Nothing for you to know." Katrina shoved the items in her hands back into the purse. "Luna would not like you in her private dressing room. You should leave before she finds out. I don't want to get into trouble because you're somewhere you shouldn't be, and she thinks I allowed you in here."

I had a feeling Luna's irritation would be over the fact that Katrina was rifling through her belongings. I just met Luna and I already knew she was a woman who preferred people remain a safe distance from her and her items. "I'll tell her you didn't grant me permission. What are you searching for?" I crossed my arms and fixed a hard stare on her.

Sweat dotted Katrina's brow. The woman was up to something. Was she having a major stalker-fan-girl moment and was looking for a memento?

"Getting something for Luna." Her tone had too much of a questioning lilt to it for me to buy it.

"What? I don't recall her asking you for anything, and right now she's filming a scene."

"You're the crafter, not her assistant. There's no need for you to know."

Everything about her tone and the way she held her arms tight against her body said Katrina was lying. It was like she was preparing for a physical altercation or was stopping herself from grabbing something. I studied the room, trying to find what she was interested in. All I saw was clothing, makeup, and a framed photo on the vanity that was almost hidden behind the makeup and hair products.

The door banged open. A furious Luna glared at us.

"What are you doing in my private dressing room?" Luna stressed the word private.

"Wanted to get Ebenezer's home away from home." I snagged the strap of the carrier and held it up. "He isn't easy to carry as escaping is his favorite pastime. I knew I left it in here. Katrina, your assistant, didn't invite me in. I didn't think it was big deal to quickly grab it from the room."

Luna fixed an icy gaze on her assistant. "And what are you doing in here?"

Katrina trembled and backed up a few paces. The first few words Katrina mumbled under her breath; I doubted Luna heard them either. She swallowed hard then spoke again, louder this time. "I'm your assistant. I help you."

"Helping me by entering into my private quarters without my permission? The dressing room and bedroom are off-limits unless I give specific permission. Which I did not."

"I brought your coffee earlier." Katrina gazed at the ground.

"Because I told you to bring the coffee in here. Unless I tell you to enter, you don't come in. Ever."

I felt sorry for Katrina and wondered how Marie put up with the demanding woman. How did Luna expect her assistant to do her job properly if she wasn't allowed where Luna was without being told she could come in?

"I wasn't aware of that," Katrina said. "Ike said my main role was making your life easier. Putting things back in their proper place. Making sure no one disturbed you. Making sure no one was where they shouldn't be." She flicked a gaze in my direction.

I pressed my mouth close, not wanting to make matters worse for her by saying Katrina was in the room before me.

"We'll have lunch together later, and I'll fill you in on my rules." Luna smiled. It wasn't an entirely happy gesture but also not a sneer. She took the carrier from me and shoved it into Katrina's arms. "Why don't you put the pet back into his carrier and take him downstairs. I'd like to speak with his mom here for a moment."

Katrina's face brightened at the prospect of having lunch with her employer. She nodded and scurried out the door, likely before Luna changed her mind.

Once Katrina vacated the room, Luna shut the door and leaned against it, tapping her nails against her folded arms. "Now that she's gone, it's time for a little chat. What is the sheriff hiding from me? Don't say nothing. I noticed the quick glances back and forth between you two. You know something he's hiding from me."

Do or don't I tell her? I only debated briefly in my head before I went with the truth. It had a little something to do with the fact I had some questions for her. "I found Marie's car and some of the details he mentioned are different than from what I know them to be."

Her eyes widened. "Why would he do that?"

That was a good question. I ran through some answers in my brain. There was only one reason that made sense—the accident wasn't really an accident and the sheriff didn't want anyone knowing. Someone could've taken the items from Marie and then moved her body. I had only noticed flattened grass for one set of footprints.

"Sometimes things aren't what they seem to be," I said.

Her eyes narrowed. "And what do you mean by that?"

"Maybe the sheriff doesn't think Marie's accident is an accident and he doesn't want that knowledge out. Did Marie usually have two phones with her?"

Her eyes widened for a moment before she schooled her features into a well-practiced boredom. "Yes. I instructed her to only carry her work cell with her when she was on duty. I don't appreciate my employees wasting time on personal calls when they're on the clock. But Marie wasn't one to comply with unnecessary rules. Since her private life never interfered in her duties, I let it slide."

Why had Marie walked away instead of calling for help? She had a back-up phone. Why not use the other one? I didn't know, but I was going to find out. The first thing I had to do was find the phone or get the records from Luna.

Luna frowned and stepped closer to her vanity. "What is this?"

Before I said don't touch whatever it is, Luna picked up the small framed photograph tucked behind the hair gel and hair spray. The picture was a baby, an infant, dressed in a snowsuit. It was hard to know if it was a boy or girl. Dark wisps of hair peeked out from the hood tied tightly around the baby's head.

She dropped the picture into the trash can. The frame pinged against the lip of the metal trash can. "No props are needed in my dressing room."

"Do you pay for Marie's work phone?"

Luna tilted her head to the side and studied me. "Why ever would you ask that?"

"I'm just trying to figure out why Marie left the car and didn't call for help. Her personal phone was broken, so why didn't she use her work phone to call for help. It doesn't make sense."

"And you're not the type who doesn't like when things don't make sense."

"Not in a situation like this."

"Maybe it was broken as well," Luna said. "Or no one answered."

"Had you received a call from Marie?"

Luna let out a bark of a laugh. "Needing a ride isn't something she'd call me about."

"Who would she call?"

"I'm not her secretary." A tinge of anger grew in her voice. "I wouldn't know."

"The phone records would show if she called someone. The records would also help me find the numbers to the other crafters you interviewed." I pulled out the list from my back pocket. "I'm assuming the Katrina listed on here is now your assistant. So that leaves three—"

She snatched the list from my hand. Her eyes widened for a second before she blinked furiously like she was trying to cover up the involuntary reaction. The paper crinkled as her grip tightened. "The crafters. Of course."

I forced back a frown. It almost sounded like she was asking a question. Had Luna not known Marie was the one talking with the crafters? "Ike told me you and Marie were the ones who interviewed the crafters for the movie. He mentioned Marie said one was close by so I thought she might be interested in helping me remake the items that were destroyed."

"Marie gave you this list?"

"No, it was in her car. She had offered it and I went with her to the car to get it. Garrison had wanted to talk with her, and Marie said she didn't have time. She left before she gave me the list."

"Did he now?" A hardness entered her gaze. "It would be a good idea if I found out who Marie has been talking with the last few days. She had been quite distracted lately."

"Was she arguing with anyone?"

"Besides me?" Luna's lips tilted up and amusement danced in her eyes. "You're not that hard to read, Merry. If you plan on keeping secrets, work on our poker face. Sharon Zimmerman is the local person and has a social media account with her business number. Apparently, she wasn't happy with my brush off, as Marie called it. My opinion is once you know someone doesn't fit, you move on."

SIX

There was a tap on the door, and someone called for Luna. Something about a slight issue regarding the pond deck being damaged.

She sighed heavily and turned, wrapping her hand around the doorknob. "That is something Katrina should be dealing with."

Another question popped into my head and I rushed it out before she left. "Did all the cast and crew members receive Yeti cups?"

Slowly, she turned the upper half of her body and faced me. "You sure do have a lot of questions."

"Marie is my friend's cousin. I'm just trying to make sense of her death."

"When you get to be my age," Luna said, "you'll realize life throws out more questions than answers. If you try and answer them all, you'll never enjoy life as you're constantly chasing down answers."

"Sometimes the questions life throws out deserve answers. Marie had a cup with her when she left and then I found one outside. If Marie left with it, how was it here?"

Luna tilted her head to the side. "That is quite a mystery isn't it. I know Marie had some customized cups created for the cast. She wanted to test out a crafter. She might've kept one for herself."

She opened the door and left. There was ruckus coming from downstairs. I walked out and peered over the banister on the second floor, making sure to keep my feet planted firmly on the carpeted floor.

The hallway and first floor of the house were a scene of chaos. Men and women rushed from one end of the house to the other. Bodies weaving around each other. I was surprised no one collided. Everyone was moving at top speed, either carrying something or adjusting a light here, a rug there. There were lights set up all around the living room, and just past the spiral staircase, railing decorated with lighted garland, was the dining room where lights were also distributed about along with boom mics. It almost looked like a store for film equipment.

The sheriff headed straight for the door, ignoring everyone as he weaved in and out of the workers. He'd know if there had been another phone in the car. The big question was would he tell me. As I told Luna, he wasn't the sharing type, but he might be the exchange-information type. Like finding out Marie had a second phone.

"Sheriff Rhodes," I called out.

He paused for a moment, glaring toward the right side, one hand wrapped around the knob. Without a word, he opened the door and slammed it shut.

That wasn't going to stop me. I followed him outside. There was as much hustle and bustle outside as there was inside. It seemed like everyone was behind today. Strings of lights were being tossed down from the roof and other workers scrambled below to catch the ends and wrap them artistically around the front columns.

"We need to talk, Sheriff." I used my mom-isn't-done-with-this-conversation voice. It had always worked on my children. Not so much with a sheriff. He continued forward, not slowing down for a second. I picked up my pace. The man was on a mission, and I wasn't sure if it was ignoring me or he had a police matter needing his attention. I wasn't sure which one I hoped it was. I hated to think someone was in dire need, but it also troubled me that he might be deliberately ignoring me. I jumped down the last step, trying to reach him before he got into the sheriff's car parked in the driveway. "Why did you say that to Luna? It isn't—"

The sheriff whipped around, a tense expression on his face. I stopped talking.

Crew members who were decorating the front porch paused and stared at us before dropping their gazes and pretending to resume working.

"This isn't the place for this conversation." He took hold of my elbow and guided me around the house toward where the golf cart I drove was parked.

It felt a little eerie behind the house. It was quiet and there was no one back there besides me and the sheriff. Off in the distance, a few crew members were carrying boxes out of the shed and placing them on the ground. I tugged away from the sheriff and placed one hand on the frame of the golf cart, readying to jump into it and speed away, or at least as speedy as one could in a golf cart. The last year, or rather my ex-husband's and some town people's murders, had made me a little jumpy and suspicious. I was no longer quite the carefree, all was merry and bright, Merry Winters. There was a slight edge to me now and I realized not everyone deserved a place on Santa's nice list. Some people deserved nothing but coal—and jail time—for the rest of their lives.

I wasn't sure how I liked this new outlook on life. I missed the days where I viewed everything with a childlike Christmas morning wonder. I had truly believed for a long time that everything could work out with enough love, faith, and belief in good.

The sheriff sighed and dipped his head. "I had to twist the truth when I talked with Luna."

I gaped at him. I wasn't sure what I was expecting but it sure wasn't him admitting he lied. "Why?" It was the only thought that fully formed in my head.

He studied me for a long moment then released a sighed. He tugged down his sheriff's hat, shielding his face from the sun. "There is something off about Marie's death. I think you know it too. The less people who know about my suspicions, the better chance I have at getting the truth. The less people who know the details, the easier for me to narrow down the suspect list. Someone will trip themselves up. The only people who knew Marie's plans are the cast and crew. It's best everyone here believes it's being written off as an accident."

My cheeks flushed. I was letting my imagination get away from me. It was a reasonable, logical, law enforcement reason. "I found her cup, or what could possibly be her cup, on the dirt road leading from the cast and crew area to Luna's house."

His eyes widened. "Where is it?"

"I took it inside."

Static crackled over his radio. He tapped his fingers on a button. "I have to take care of whatever is going on. Can you bring it to me? Be careful you don't get too many of your fingerprints on it."

"I found it on the ground. Kind of ran over it."

"No problem. Bring it to me, or better I'll stop by tonight and pick it up. Don't want anyone getting suspicious about you leaving."

"Did you find another phone? Marie usually carried two."

He frowned. "It's not a good idea for you to go around questioning people."

It wasn't the first time I heard that statement directed at me. "I'm just trying to make sense of all of this."

"That's my job. I shouldn't even be asking you to find the cup for me, but the cast and crew and are determined to do what they can to make things hard on me. Wherever I go, they follow, marking it hard for a discrete investigation."

"Likely because Luna requested it."

He snorted out a small laugh. A squawk came from the radio on his vest followed by some garbled words. "I figured that. I have to answer this. Stay safe." He strode away, talking into the radio attached to his vest.

Stay safe. A shudder raced down my spine. Was the sheriff giving me a vague warning or did he have reason to believe my involvement placed me in danger? I had to get the cup, which might be a clue and was in one of the boxes of the decorations I brought.

I hurried inside and froze. Everywhere Christmas decorations were scattered on the floor. The decorations. The box. Marie's cup. Evidence. I had to get it. I scanned the area for any of the items I created. The living room. The main Christmas tree was going in the living room for the party scene. My boxes were in there.

In the large room was a twelve-foot Christmas tree. The Christmas tree branches were being twisted and adjusted, trying to make them just so as the ornaments were being placed on them and then adjusted. Most times by just a fraction of an inch. The white frosted bulbs with black vinyl images of Christmas scenes that also doubled as clues for the mystery would stand out on the massive tree. There were simple green lights on the tree, almost blending into the branches. It wasn't easy for Bright and me to come up with designs that said Christmas and also tied into the murder mystery, but with help from the script writer and the production team, we were able to find the perfect mix.

In the corner were boxes that had been broken down. Where was the cup? I scanned the room, looking for the stainless steel cup. Panic flared. It was potential evidence. I crawled under the Christmas tree, careful not to jostle any of the bulbs or the tree itself. Nope. It hadn't rolled underneath. I shimmied out. If I found a Yeti cup and remembered to move it from a box, where would I put it? The crew knew who the boxes belonged to, so they'd either take it into the kitchen or return it to the golf cart assigned to me.

Relief flooded through me. I loved it when a potentially huge problem remedied itself with only a bit of anxiety, and with a rational idea. Sometimes my mind ventured into the realm of suitable happenings or solutions only deemed possible for superhero movies. I weaved my way through the throngs of people and walked into the kitchen. It was a beautiful space, all white and silver. Sunlight bounced off enormous stainless steel appliances. Every burner on the gas stove had a pot, steam rising from them. The refrigerator was large enough to hold enough food for a basketball team and tucked up against it was a freezer of the same size. There was a line of fresh fruits, vegetables, and condiments on the white marble countertop.

A young man turned away from the stove and stepped into my path, crossing his arms and glaring down at me. "You are not allowed in here."

"Just wanted to check the sink." I took a step to the right. He matched it.

"This kitchen is off-limits to the cast and crew."

"I wanted to see if someone put a cup I'm missing in the sink." Once again, I tried going around him, and failed.

"As I said, the kitchen is off-limits to the cast and crew. No one would've placed anything in the sink."

"Maybe someone from the kitchen staff found it and put it in the sink." I was doing my best to keep my temper. When one wanted a favor, it was best not to yell or get snippy with the only person able to grant it.

"The kitchen staff is comprised of two people: the chef and I. Chef Olivia would not collect cups from the main house. And I know better than to bring anything unapproved into this kitchen." He took hold of my elbow and led me out. "Which includes letting you stay."

Olivia. The name danced around in my head like sugarplums on Christmas Eve night. There was something about it I knew but couldn't quite grasp. I tugged away from his grip, hoping another quick peek into the kitchen brought to mind what I was desperately trying to remember. The space I stood in was a small gap separating the kitchen from the massive area I guessed was usually a dining space reserved for large dinner parties. Currently, it was housing multiple eight-foot-long tables still compressed and leaning against the wall, cloth tablecloths, punch bowls, and boxes labeled "plastic wine glasses." I tried peering over his shoulder, but the doors fluttered close blocking the view from me.

"Can you check the sink?" I asked.

"No. And if I see an unauthorized item in Ms. Carmichael's kitchen, I will pitch it into the trash." He pivoted on his heel and slipped between the doors.

Grumbling under my breath, I headed toward the front room.

Someone must've seen it. Even though Luna said Marie had them made for the cast and crew, I hadn't seen anyone else carrying one around or one laying around the set. Maybe Marie only had one made. Why place a bulk order for an item when you wanted to check out the quality of an item? Unless Marie wanted to test if the crafter was capable of making a large order under time constraints.

"Lose something?" A deep, don't-argue-with-me baritone asked.

I turned and sitting in an ornate rocker, in the other room, was the most unimposing security guard I'd ever seen. He stood, unfolding his body from the chair. The guy was tall, nearly six-foot-three and whippet thin. Even his height didn't make him a commanding figure. No wonder the production was riddled with pranks. No one would take the guards seriously if they all dressed like the one before me.

He was wearing the same navy polo shirt as the rest of the security detail, but instead of black pants, he wore a matching shade of navy cotton shorts with parrots embroidered on them. White crew socks were pulled up over his calves and his canvas shoes were tie-dyed in greens, blues, and reds to match the parrots on his shorts. A pair of mirror sunglasses rested on his head with a tube-like sport retainer attached to the frames.

"A cup. Tumbler. It has a decal on it about drama. A Yeti." I added in the brand, hoping that explained the tension in my voice. Those tumblers were expensive. "I had it in the box with the items I brought in to decorate. It's not in the living room and then I checked the kitchen. Or tried to."

"Luna doesn't like anyone in her kitchen. Except for the chef and her snotty sous chef. Kid thinks he's working for the queen. Did you check the coffee station? I leave my cup there all the time. Get distracted or asked to head somewhere else and my poor cup gets left behind."

Coffee station was another good place. "Thanks. I hadn't thought of that. I know I didn't leave it there, but maybe someone found it and put it there."

"Must be an important cup." The tone of his voice caused me to pause and study him.

"Kind of is," I said.

The man tipped his head down, causing his sunglasses to fall over his eyes. "Then you should've taken some extra time and taken care of your things. Items can disappear. Unfortunately, every workplace, and town, has people you shouldn't trust."

"Like who?" I didn't try to stop the question. I was interested in knowing, even though I was a little suspicious on why he was sharing all of this with me.

"Take a look around. Anyone of them here will turn on each other. For the right incentive. The real truth lurks right under the truth they're willing to show."

"Is that why Luna hired security guards? Because she can't trust anyone."

"It's because someone out there is determined to see her career end. And instead of getting rid of those she suspects, she decided playing a game was the better option."

I stared at the man. "Did you tell the sheriff this?"

An eyebrow quirked above the rim of his sunglasses. He barked out a laugh. "Did you see how he cared about the fire this morning?"

"He wasn't there this morning," I said.

"Exactly." He nodded once and walked to the front door, pausing to gaze down at a spot before heading out the door. "Earlier, I saw the sheriff pick up an item and it glittered a bit. I wonder if it was your Yeti. But why would he want it? Now that I think about it, Luna's assistant, the one who died, had the same type of cup as you. Never saw that woman without her phone or coffee. Interesting the two of you have the same cup."

"Lot of people on the cast and crew had one." I hurried out the excuse.

He tilted his head. "Really. Haven't seen anyone else with one."

The sheriff had been honest with me—a stranger. Too honest if

I thought about it. What if he was trying to throw me off track? An ache developed in my stomach. I didn't like where my thoughts were going. I was basing everything off a feeling. Like not believing Marie, a former police officer, would leave a car after she was injured and head toward an abandoned house, and being suspicious that she didn't her use her work phone to call for help.

"You don't like the sheriff much do you."

"Nope." The man grinned. "Is it that obvious?"

"Yes."

"Makes me a little nervous when two people argue, and one ends up dead."

I swallowed hard. "She died in a car accident. The sheriff wasn't the only one to have words with Marie."

"If you mean Luna, those two always bickered. It was the basis of their working relationship. Luna ordered, Marie argued. Marie corrected, Luna smarted off."

"You sure know a lot about them."

"What can I say, I'm around a lot. I'm like the Three Wise Monkeys. Instead of not seeing, hearing, or speaking evil, I hear it and see it all."

At least he left out the speaking it—unless that was what he was doing now. "Why don't you tell the police about your suspicions?"

"What suspicions?" the guy asked, not even bothering to look back at me.

What game was this guy playing? Ignoring self-preservation in my quest for the truth, I followed after him. With his long legs, and my short ones, I was running to keep up with him. "About the argument between the sheriff and Marie giving you the feeling something evil was going on. Why tell me instead of the police?"

"I was just conversing with you and saying what a shame they fought before she died. It's interesting you used the word suspicion. What would I be suspicious of?"

Heat flickered across my cheeks. He was right. I took his words as him being suspicious of the sheriff, all the guy had said was the sheriff said something impolite to someone. "It sounded like you were suspicious of him. Must be the environment I'm in. The mystery movie."

"Even if I thought something odd was happening around here, they're not inclined to believe me." He stopped and spun around, almost colliding into me. A hopeful look sprang into his eyes. "The chief will listen and believe you. You have no agenda against any of us."

I held back a frown. That was an odd thing to say. Did everyone on the set have something against each other?

"Why won't they believe you?"

"Past behavior." He mimicked drinking a lot of bottles. "Had a few runs in with the police."

"Okay. I'll tell them. First, I need to get Ebenezer then I'll head into town and talk with the police. It would be good if you came also, fill them in on what you know."

"Find your Ebenezer and tell him to hurry up. The chief starts her patrol in an hour. You want to get there before she leaves."

"Ebenezer's my guinea pig. I don't think I should leave him in the house for other people to look after. One pet has already escaped, I didn't want Ebenezer to run off and join the cat in whatever adventure he's on."

"Luna likes yours, so I don't think it'll disappear." He pulled a set of keys from his pocket and held it out to me. Three keys dangled from a sloppily put together paracord keychain. "You can take my jeep."

"The police might want to talk to you."

"They know where to find me. I should stay here. For Luna's safety."

I frowned. "Why do you think Luna is in danger?"

"Why else would Luna hire a PI? Nobody else here has figured it out but Marie wasn't no assistant."

"How do you know?"

"Because she told me."

* * *

The guard's car shuttered and groaned, the jeep looked and sounded like it was pushing out its last mile. The vehicle's body was a mix of blue, red, white, and rust. The canvas top barely existed; it had more holes than fabric. The guard's comment swirled in my head. *She had told him.* I should've had him specify which she—Marie or Luna.

Ebenezer was squished into a corner of his carrier, head facing away from me. I wasn't sure if he was snoozing or hiding in terror. The drive was bumpy. The roads heading into town was more potholes than anything else. Bits of rocks and asphalt pinged against the car. No wonder most of the cast and crew walked into town rather than drive. I swore it was taking me longer having to slow down and navigate around and over all the holes in the road. You'd think the town would fix it up with the movie being filmed.

Fortunately, it was only two and half miles to Carol Lake and the small town—really small town—was now right in front of us. The road evened out and freshly paved roads greeted me. The town must've run out of money before paving the way from Luna's house to Carol Lake, or else they really didn't want to make it easy for the visitors to show up.

The town of Carol Lake was situated around a tiny body of water I'd label a large pond. The shops were around the perimeter of the lake with a few houses scattered here and there among shops and in clusters behind the buildings. At the start of the bend was a local grocery store. The bright yellow and green building had a manger scene attached to its roof. It was hard to tell if the sign saying Carol Lake was to let visitors know if they entered or exited the small town. A walking bridge stretched from one side of the lake to the other. There was a wooden town map a few feet away from the bridge.

I gazed off into the horizon. There was a building with weathered 2x4s over the entire façade. Straining my eyes, I saw that the green windows were spaced evenly apart on the first and second floor of the building. Green columns held up what appeared to be a second story deck in front of the windows. It was the only building in Carol Lake that wasn't near the water. It was set apart from the other businesses in town, on top of a slight hill.

I parked in a spot near the town square. I opened the rear passenger door and retrieved Ebenezer, who was in his carrier. "Let's go see where the police station is located."

Slipping the strap onto my shoulder, I walked over and checked out the wooden map of Carol Lake. The side of the map listed facts about Carol Lake. The lake wasn't very deep, eight feet seven inches at its deepest point. There was a warning on the map about poisonous snakes being in the water and no swimming or diving permitted. I gazed at the clear water. It looked safe and inviting, hard to imagine it wasn't suitable for a nice swim on a hot summer day. But just like other things in life that seemed safe wasn't and at least the lake had a warning. Other areas of life you didn't get a warning before you ventured into danger. You just found yourself in it and had to struggle to get out of it.

I pulled myself out of my thoughts and searched the map for the police station. It was on the other side of the lake, a short walk across the bridge and then five store fronts down from the end of the bridge. Even though it was hot, I opted for walking instead of driving around the lake. I wanted to get a look at the stores and see if any had items suitable for replacing the damaged items, and since I spent most days sitting because of my crafting, I took any opportunity that qualified as exercising.

The smells of Christmas greeted me. Almond. Gingerbread. Peppermint. There was a bakery at the corner and a display unit in front of the window was filled with all sorts of sugar, goodness, and Christmas treats with a large sign proclaiming it was Christmas in December. Might make a stop on my way back to the car. It was hard for me to pass up Christmas cookies.

The town square had piles of wood placed throughout in a semi-circle. I walked through the square, taking note of the bundles. The Christmas bazaar scene was being shot in town and the stacks of wood were likely the material to build the booth. From the stacks on the ground, I estimated at least twenty booths. Of course, with the magic of movies, the supplies for twenty booths might actually turn into forty or more. Attached to the piles of 2x4s were labels. I knelt down and read a few. Pie booth. Cookie booth. Soaps. Wreaths. Ornaments. Personalized signs.

At least the pies and cookies were out of my hands, though I could bake some fantastic Christmas cookies. It was one of my favorite Christmas-time activities. Of course, there was the little issue of all the crafts I needed to make. No cookie baking for me. There was the local crafter who might help out. Hopefully the manner in which Luna told her she picked someone else for the job wasn't too off-putting as Ike's recollection of the words between Luna and Marie suggested.

I took out my cell and searched Facebook for Sharon Zimmerman and found her business page. I scrolled through it. There wasn't a phone number listed. Either Luna was mistaken about it, or Sharon had removed it, and if that was the case, it didn't bode well for my mission of gaining her help for the movie. I sent her a message stating her name had been passed onto me as a local crafter who might have some items available for purchase. There was an issue on the set that had made it necessary to replace some of the crafts. I hoped there was enough intrigue in the message that piqued her interest and made her contact me.

Tucking my phone into the side pocket of Ebenezer's carrier, I took note of the buildings I saw. Across the way there was a toy store, bakery, and a small clinic. There was a lot of Christmas decorations on the backs of the buildings. I paused and looked back over my shoulder, behind me the buildings were blank canvases. Only half of Carol Lake was being used for the film, or the other properties planned on decorating today.

I stepped onto the wooden bridge and tested it. The sun glinted off the smooth water of the lake. The bridge swayed a little under my feet. I gripped the railing with one hand and tightened the other on the strap. Ebenezer whistled a few times then settled down. I didn't want him bouncing around in his cage and adding to the swaying affect. The slats had a few centimeters between each other, giving glimpses of the water beneath. I preferred solid ground, or at least a solid foundation, under my feet, especially when walking over a body of water. I was already a little leery about crossing the bridge. It wasn't too far of a fall into the water, but my swimming skills were basically non-existent, and I didn't want to test them out. I doubted Ebenezer would appreciate a dunk in the pond. Especially knowing there were poisonous snakes residing in the lake. A slight breeze cooled the air. It didn't take long to cross to the other side.

The Carol Lake Police department was one of three offices located in a brick building that resembled a townhouse. There were three separate white awnings over the doors of the different establishments. The police department was the first in line followed by the health department office and the town bank. There were four parking spots in front of the building, and all were taken.

I placed the strap of Ebenezer's tote on my shoulder and walked into the police department. There were two desks and chairs in the front room and in the back, there was one private office with large windows to see out into the area.

A nearly six-foot-tall striking woman wearing a police uniform stood near the desk, flipping a calendar with her left hand while her right was cupped to her ear. She looked through the window and spotted me. With a nod, she held up a finger, and shifted so I saw she was on a cell phone.

She ended the call and walked out of the office, eyeing the pet carrier. "Let me guess, the director Edward Yale sent you over to file a formal complaint about my officers' handling of the situation this morning. Tell him Chief Quinn handled the matter."

I'd ask how she knew I was with the production, but in a town this size, and one that didn't seem to have much of a tourist business, I was either employed by Yale or was a visiting relative. I was sure she knew everyone who lived in Carol Lake and their relatives. Was it better to go with the truth from the start and ease my way into it? I placed the tote on a desk, positioning it to where the mesh part faced the chief.

The woman heaved out a sigh and picked up a set of car keys, glancing at the clock on the wall. Right. She had patrol duty in an hour. Now, less than an hour. Our police chief never went on regular patrol duty, but then again Season's Greetings had more than two officers on the police force.

"No. Luna Carmichael might be in danger and I thought the police should know. Keep an eye on what's going on at the movie set."

"Why would you believe that?"

"Her assistant died in what appeared to be a car accident."

Quinn shot up from the desk, body rigid. "The person killed in the accident was Luna's assistant, Marie?"

Ebenezer drew back quickly, smacking the back of the fabric carrier and almost skidding it and him off the desk. I grabbed the handle and placed him on the floor.

Should I tell her the sheriff was investigating it? What if he suspected someone in town? "I was the one who saw her car and called 911. Something felt off about the scene. Like her wandering away and not calling for help."

"I'm sure it's being investigated."

"Yes. The sheriff showed up at the scene."

"Then the case is in the sheriff department's hands and they wouldn't appreciate another law enforcement department butting into their investigation."

"Someone told me he heard Sheriff Rhodes and Marie having words sometime before her death."

"Bringing that up now sounds like an accusation, Ms..." She trailed off, voice hardening with each word.

Ebenezer whistled. The sharp noise had the chief staring at him.

"I'm Merry Winters. This is Ebenezer. I don't like spreading rumors, but I'd feel horrible if something happened to Luna and I hadn't told the police what I know and heard. Marie was driving

Luna's car."

Chief Quinn leaned against a desk and motioned for me to continue. "I'll hear you out."

I wished the security guard had come with me to tell her what he saw. In this situation, two were better than one. "The sheriff came to tell her about Marie's death. Luna wanted to see the car..."

Quinn tilted her head to the side and leaned forward. "That seems a little odd."

I swallowed hard, starting to regret my decision to speak to the chief as my words might turn Luna into a suspect. "Luna mentioned needing information for insurance purposes."

Leaning over, the police chief tugged a pad of paper and pen toward her and scribbled on it. "You saw Marie drive away from the set? Did the car make any unusual sounds? Was there anyone else at the scene of the accident? Besides you, the sheriff, and the victim?"

I shook my head and held in a groan. I was turning Luna into a suspect. "No."

Chief Quinn looked up and met my gaze. "I keep tabs on what's going on in the neighboring jurisdictions. I heard about the car accident with a fatality. There was no mention of a witness."

"Would there be?"

"It would help to reconstruct the scene and know what happened. Why was that kept quiet?"

"I didn't see it happen. I came across it later," I said. "Marie had left over two hours before I did. She was going to Harmony to get coffee for Luna and mail out a manuscript to Luna's attorney."

The chief paced around the room. "Anything else you think I should know?"

"I found Marie's cup, or one that looks like hers, near the sharp turn leaving the area where the cast and crew are living. It's a design Luna says others on the set have, but I haven't seen another one like it. Yet."

"I'll follow you back to Luna's and pick it up. I'll get it to the sheriff. Best not leave possible evidence in civilian's hands and for him to send out for prints. We don't have the proper equipment here." She stretched out her arms as if giving a tour of the department. Quick tour. Two desks. Two files cabinets. At the back of the room was a small refrigerator and a coffee pot.

I drew in a fortifying breath and braced myself for a reaction. "It's gone."

"Gone." She sat on the edge of the desk, fingering her handcuffs.

I had a bad feeling she thought I was toying with her. "I put it in a box with the craft props I made for the film. When I went to get the cup and turn it over, it was gone."

Something in my expression told the chief I was holding back because she frowned and leaned forward, almost eye-to-eye with me. "You have a person in mind who took it."

I squirmed. "Someone else does."

"Someone saw who took it."

"A guard on the set hinted the sheriff took it."

Her shoulders slumped forward, and she covered her face with a hand, shaking her head back and forth. "Let me guess, six-foot-three. Skinny. An odd taste in shorts."

I nodded.

"Merry, the best advice I can give you is to ignore any opinions that man has about Sheriff Rhodes. My cousin, Vernon O'Neal, is usually a good judge of character except when it comes to Rhodes."

"Why?"

"Why?" Her voice grew weary. "Because before Luna recently invited, and then disinvited, Sheriff Randolph Rhodes from her life, she was married to my cousin. Luna's three loves in life are acting, trouble, and men, and which takes the top spot changes from day to day. If I were you, I'd keep a nice distance from Vernon. It's best not to follow him on his tangents. He's been trying to prove the evilness of Randolph Rhodes ever since the man caught Luna's eye over forty-six years ago. It's best for you to stay away from the pot Vernon is stirring and planning on throwing Rhodes into."

SEVEN

With my mind whirling with information, I wandered out of the police station. The humidity clung to my skin as I walked down the sidewalk of the picturesque town. The guard, Vernon, deliberately kept the fact he was Luna's ex-husband and the police chief's cousin quiet from me. What game was he playing?

Matter of fact, what game was Luna and the sheriff engaged in? For all I knew, everyone here was playing a game and I wasn't sure how they saw me fitting into it.

Though I hadn't walked very far, I already felt drained and Ebenezer grew heavier with each step. Maybe I should hitch a ride back to the car, not for my sake as exercise was good for me as my job usually consisted of sitting for long chunks of time. Nope, I was thinking about my furry companion. The heat was probably getting to him. I lifted up the carrier. He was snoozing away.

I paused in front of the toy store. I smiled, a feeling of goodwill toward all washed over me as Christmas spirit filled my heart. The front of the building reminded me of my house, gingerbread trim and soft colors. The door was bright red with white trim framing it and a wreath filled with toys hung on it. White vinyl in a script font filled the top portion of the large picture window: Visions of Sugar Plums. The open sign was in the window and next to it was a sign reminding customers of the store closing for the day except for those customers who were selected as extras for today's shooting, regular hours resumed tomorrow.

A cheerful tinkling announced my entrance. I hoped she didn't mind animals coming inside. Walking into Visions of Sugar Plums was like stepping back in time, and into someone's home rather than a store. Each area of the room was divided by the paint color on the wall, soft shades of primary colors, and tables and chairs designed for playing and curling up with a book to read, or to talk with a friend. There was a large wooden train table with an elaborate city set up. Different train pieces were in boxes stored underneath. This store alone was a good reason to film the Christmas movie here. The place spoke of Christmas magic and love.

The area to the left of the door was dedicated to trains, cars, planes, anything with wheels or that could get a person from one place to another. Across the room was the animal section. Stuffed animals, veterinarian toys, plastic figurines, Breyer horses.

Each section of the toy store was painted in a different pastel color and set up for shopping and playing. Toys out of boxes were in children's reach along with small tables and chairs strategically placed out of the way of shoppers yet perfect for little ones to sit and play or snuggle with a baby doll. The cabinets were wooden, the bottom opened with mesh storage boxes for the toys and above were wooden shelves for the products available for sale. Every shelf and piece of furniture was bolted to the walls in case a child decided mountain climbing was their area of interest.

"Welcome to Visions of Sugarplums." A woman said stepping out from the backroom. She was dressed like Ma in her kerchief. She wiggled her fingers at Ebenezer who woke from his snooze and was pressing against the mesh fabric. "You must be here with the film crew. Everything is in order and we made the few adjustments to the store that were requested. Our customers know that for the remainder of the day, the store will have limited access. A few of our regular customers are scheduled to arrive in thirty minutes for the scene."

"I'm not on the production team," I said. "I was hired to create the crafts the heroine makes. I just couldn't help wanting to see the inside. I promise to go before the filming begins. Hope you don't mind I brought my friend along."

"I don't mind him at all. He seems well behaved."

"He's on his best behavior right now, though he does have his naughty moments."

She laughed. "Don't we all. I'm Abigail. My husband is Ernie."

"Your store is amazing. You must also be excited about the film. You're store screams 'we love Christmas.'"

Her bright smile faded. "If it helps bring tourists to our area or interests a company to set up shop here, I'm all for it. I prefer keeping our small-town small. But small means lack of jobs and more of our young people move away. Hard to have a town if the new generations all move away."

"Hopefully, the movie and Ms. Carmichael moving here brings some new opportunities."

"I'm not counting on that, but I know others are and that causes hard feelings. Let's just say your Ms. Carmichael isn't known for embracing the small town where her family came from, then again she did inherit that attitude along with the summer house."

A summer house. That must be where the basis of the animosity toward the production, and Luna, was coming from. Seemed the wealthiest residents were only summer-time locals and hadn't seen how they could help beyond their little parcel of land.

"Ms. Carmichael grew up around here?"

She waved off my question. "I've said more than I should. It's not kind, or Christmassy, to gossip."

"How long have you owned the store."

"Visions of Sugarplums was one of the first stores built when the town was conceived in the late 1920s. The owners had wanted a place for children to dream, wish, and play with toys. Most of the residents were poor and had lost money during the Depression and hoped to start over in a new town with a fresh outlook, new opportunities, and away from the feeling of failure."

In the back of the store, tucked into an alcove on the right-hand side was a Christmas tree with ribbon tied onto the branches.

"That's our wishing tree." Abigail pushed her wire-rimmed glasses back up to the top of the bridge of her nose. "It stays up year-round."

"A wishing tree?'

"It's not just Christmas when parents struggled financially and nothing breaks a parent's heart more than not being able to fulfill a simple wish for their child, especially for birthdays. Those that can, will take a ribbon off the tree and make the purchase, leaving it at the counter for the parent to pick it up."

A commotion erupted at the door. A flood of people carrying camera equipment and lights walked into the building. Filming was about to begin. Shifting the strap of Ebenezer's tote higher onto my shoulder, I tugged out my phone and jotted down a note to come back later to fulfill some wishes.

Edward Yale walked through the crowd of cast and crew members and roved his gaze around the area, a smile growing on his face. He squatted down to get a better view of the train track set up in front of the large picture window. The display reminded me of a miniature version of Season's Greetings, all ready for the holiday and time warped back to 1955. "Luna was right. This town is perfect."

"It would be better if more shops were already prepared," Ike said, making check marks on the list attached to the clipboard in his hands. "Do you know how much it's costing to spruce up some of the stores?"

"Authentic places add to the heartfelt atmosphere a Christmas movie requires. A studio set just can't quite replicate it." Edward said.

Ike sighed and headed toward the back of the store. "The town could've prepped the Christmas bazaar area. We still have to build booths and fill them."

"We'll put up some flyers around town and get some donations. Besides, our Christmas crafter is handling all of that for us."

I wished he had notified me of that before I left Season's Greetings. I'd have prepared a lot more items and sent out a call for help to all the crafters I knew to borrow and buy a few items. Or I'd have just pilfered items from my collection at home. I had enough personal Christmas decorations to decorate a small town.

Anne waltzed by me as she took in the store. "This place is pretty perfect."

"We're already running behind," Edward said. "Hurry and get everything set up. Garrison and Anne get in your places for the scenes. We'll do a quick walkthrough while the crew is stationing the lights and cameras."

Garrison weaved his way through the crowd looking like he'd rather be anywhere else. He probably was still upset about Luna's attempt at changing his character's role. It couldn't be good, getting your first starring role and finding out your hero status was revoked and you're now the murderer. Hopefully his father talked sense into Luna, the scriptwriter and the big name in the movie.

I tucked Ebenezer behind the counter and stayed near the register, watching all the preparation. It was amazing how fast the crew was moving, there was little talk among them and yet they moved in harmony. In no time at all, the equipment was in the proper place.

The bell tinkled and a group of men, women, and children walked into the store wearing Christmas garb.

"Your extras are here," Abigail said.

"Fantastic." Edward waved his arms over his head. "Extras pay close attention. I need everyone to mill about the store, don't congregate in one area but stay as quiet as possible without it seeming like no one is talking. We want this to be natural but not pick up a lot of background noise. Abigail, stay at the cash register. When Garrison and Anne move toward the counter with purchases, I need..." Edward trailed off and looked around the room.

"What about our crafter Merry." Ike pointed at me.

Edward grinned. "Perfect. Merry, you stay close to the back room. As Garrison places the items on the counter, Merry you run into the backroom and open the door and let it slam shut. You'll be portraying someone fleeing from the store. Anne and Garrison's character have no idea who it is, just that someone in the store left in a hurry."

I nodded. Simple instructions. I was excited I had a small role in the movie. Granted no one would see me, but I'd always know I was the one to slam the door during one of the tense scenes.

"The rest of the extras shop with purpose. Read packaging, pretend you're calling home to get advice, compare items. Children play with the toys in the play centers but do so quietly."

A few of the mothers caught each other's gazes and rolled their eyes. Kids playing quietly in a toy store wasn't an easy accomplishment. Some of the little ones were toddlers. It was hard to keep toddlers relatively quiet in general. Add in toys and friends and it was likely an impossible mission.

"Setting the scene so the extras know the mood I'm creating here..." Edward paused and once all eyes were on him, he continued. "The heroine offers to help the hero shop for his nephew and niece and as a means to pump him for information about the murder of his mother's agent who she threatened to fire. In retaliation, the agent threatened to reveal a dark secret of the hero's mother."

"Nephew," Anne corrected. "And that is not what the scene is about. Or at least not in my script. The characters we play are best friends."

Even the director himself couldn't sway Luna. It was becoming obvious who was in charge of the film.

Edward frowned and flipped through a script. "Are we sure? Didn't Luna have that changed? Nephew to son? Acquaintances instead of best friends because of her bright idea of switching up the murderer?"

"I'm not the killer," Garrison said through gritted teeth. "And no, the script I have says I'm the nephew, best friend of the heroine, and today we're scoping out the store and buying toys for nieces and nephews as our cover."

"Mine matches Garrison and Anne." Ike showed Edward a sheet of paper. "I even wrote a brief description of each scene. Sleuthing friend duo at toy store tracking down a lead."

Edward threw his script over his shoulder and took Ike's. "When I find out who swapped my script with that new drivel, I will fire them."

"Sir, there's a car driving up and down the road. Gone past three time so far. It's going to ruin the shoot," a cameraperson said.

"Probably a local wanting in the movie. Ike, take care of that. Give them some money to eat at the diner or let them be an extra during a different scene."

"You know—"

"I know, it will encourage more of it. Right now, I don't care. We're behind. Wasting time and money."

Ike walked out.

"Roll," Edward said.

"I'm feeling that Christmas shopping wasn't the reason you came here." A young woman flipped her long blonde hair over her shoulder and jammed her hands onto her hips.

"Of course, we did." Garrison flashed a flirtatious smile onto the clerk and pulled out a wallet. "See, niece and nephew. Being a bachelor without children, I wasn't sure what toys children liked nowadays."

While Garrison spoke with the clerk, Anne, as her character, was sidling up to the empty counter and placed some toys on the counter. She leaned over and—

"Santa Claus is Coming to Town" blared throughout the store. Anne stopped and spun toward the sound—me. I wished the floorboards turned into quicksand and sucked me down. It was my phone. Paul's ringtone.

"Cut," Edward yelled.

"Sorry." I hurried out the backdoor. It shut behind me, a lock clicking in place. I was no longer a sound effect in the movie. The phone continued to ring. Had the sheriff spoken to him yet? A breath hitched in my throat as I answered. "Hi, Paul."

"Why didn't you tell me?" Paul said in a broken voice shaking with anger.

Marie. The sheriff had notified him. "The sheriff asked me not to."

"And you always do what law enforcement tells you to do." His anger grew stronger with every word.

I worked on keeping my temper in check. I didn't deserve his hostility, but his cousin had just died. Under the same circumstances, a friend withholding information like that, I doubted I'd handle it much differently than him.

"Of course not, I'm not going to let Scotland order me around, police officer or not. He'd have me moving to Morgantown so he can keep me safe." I hoped my attempt at humor calmed him down some.

My son was starting to think that Season's Greetings wasn't the nice quiet, little town he wanted his mother living alone in. Two murders in nine months shook him up, and reminding him that the first victim, my ex-husband Samuel, had been found in the RV when I arrived in Morgantown hadn't helped my case. Because, as my son pointed out, Samuel had been killed and shoved into the RV in Season's Greetings.

"I'm not talking about Scotland. I know Orville asked you, at least once, to stop interfering in the Wilcox murder investigation."

"I wasn't—" I stopped myself from arguing. He was right. I had been told by Season's Greetings' officer Orville Martin to let the police do their job, and in my quest to preserve what little good feelings our community had for a man I had once been married to, I involved myself and put my life in danger. "I learned a valuable lesson last time and thought it wiser to listen."

"I have a feeling that's not the truth." Paul sounded weary. Broken.

"The truth is I didn't want to give you the news. I was afraid you'd ask questions I didn't want to answer."

"What didn't you want to tell me?"

"I wasn't up to talking about it. I took the coward's way out. She had left the car and when I found her..." my voice trembled, "...she had already passed. There was nothing I could do to help her."

"I know you would've done everything in your power to save her. Don't beat yourself up because of that," Paul said.

Tears filled my eyes at the compassion in his voice. The more I learned about Paul, the more I cared about the man. He was kind. Strong. Considerate. And always was able to think of someone else no matter what he was going through. I wish I could say the same about myself.

"That's not what I was most worried about telling you."

"What were you afraid of telling me, Merry?" His voice dropped to a whisper.

"I think someone killed her."

"What? The sheriff said she crashed into a hay baler and died from injuries and the heat."

"That's the official word. He doesn't believe it either. I talked to him a few hours ago about my suspicions."

"Merry, what are you doing?" His tone was a mix of anger and worry.

"When I found Marie, I noticed she wasn't wearing her gold locket. She had been wearing it this morning when she left it. Also, the cups she had with her weren't in the car. Where did they go? There are some weird things going on here."

"What weird things?"

I told him about the shed fire, the coffee prank, the released cat, and what Vernon had said. "I don't know if Luna told him or Marie. Had she told you she was doing PI work for Luna?"

"No. She told me she was her assistant, but I had a feeling something else was going on."

"Marie mentioned Luna had received a note about someone revealing a dark secret." The basis of the *Dash Away All* plot. That truth unsettled me. Why was the plot of the movie and the threat so similar? Had someone in the movie sent them...or was it a ploy of Luna's? Why?

Paul drew in a sharp breath. "She didn't tell me that. If I'd known, I'd have talked you out of going. I can't believe Marie asked about you knowing what was going on. I told her it sounded like a dream opportunity for you. There was no way you wouldn't jump at the chance. She said good, made her job a whole lot easier."

"She probably didn't think anyone was in danger. But now I know something sinister is going on and has it to do with the secret."

How did that make her job easier? Was it because she was desperate for a crafter or something else? I tugged the list of names from my pocket. Desiree Young. Olivia Highman. Sharon Zimmerman. Katrina Emerson. Merry Winters.

Olivia. Olivia was the name of the chef. Was it the same person? What were the chances the cook was also a crafter? Or this wasn't just the list of crafters but of the people Luna wanted control of hiring. It made sense she'd choose her personal chef.

There was a simple solution for settling the matter, search Marie's room for evidence of what she was working on that might have led to her murder.

EIGHT

After returning from my disastrous attempt at being a sound effect, I worked on some crafts and waited for evening when I had a better chance of getting into Luna's house. One, I had been hired for crafting not sleuthing and didn't want to fail at my job, and two, I didn't think anyone would let me upstairs if Luna wasn't home. Now that the dinner hour was approaching, it was the perfect time for a visit since Luna preferred dining at home.

I took the golf cart over rather than Vernon's jeep who still hadn't stopped by for it. Probably wasn't a good idea showing up in Luna's soon-to-be ex-husband's vehicle. Taking in a deep breath, I knocked on the front door. The front of the house was now decked out from top to bottom in Christmas finery. The wreath and garland looked like real evergreen wreaths. Across the way, the gazebo and the deck were also decorated with greenery and lights. At night, the lights would twinkle off the lake. It was beginning to look a lot like Christmas at Luna's house and around Carol Lake.

The door opened and Katrina smiled at me, the gesture seeming forced and not all in good nature. "Hi, Merry, how can I help you?"

What had I done to irritate her? "I was hoping to speak with Luna."

"She's not available right now."

"I can wait." I took a step forward to walk into the house and Katrina blocked me with her body.

"She won't be available at all today." Katrina blushed. "I'm really sorry. She made it clear no visitors regardless of who they are."

"Marie had told me, before she died, that Luna wanted to talk with me. There wasn't time earlier."

"Now is not a good time." The reddish tone to Katrina's face deepened. The nervousness was turning into anger.

"It's really important."

"You are a persistent one, aren't you?" Luna's cool voice flowed from behind the door. She stepped into view and studied me.

I fidgeted, not sure if the coolness in her gaze was from admiration or annoyance. "I'm sorry to disturb you, Luna."

"I highly doubt that." One eyebrow quirked up and she rolled her wrist. "It has been a trying day and you're delaying my plan of retiring early with a bottle of wine."

"I was wondering if I could see Marie's room."

Luna drew back. Katrina's eyes widened.

"That's a rather bold request," Luna said.

"As you are aware, a friend of mine is Marie's cousin. I'd like to pack up her items for the family. I assumed Marie stayed in the house with you, since she's your assistant."

"One should never assume anything." Luna clicked her nails on the doorframe. "Yes, Marie's residence was inside my home. I slept better knowing she was here."

Katrina ping-ponged her gaze back and forth between us.

"Would it be all right?" I asked.

"No," Luna said. "But when her cousin arrives, with proof of their relationship, I'll allow him into her room. Now, I'm retiring for the night."

"Is now a good time for us to get acquainted? Marie had said you wanted to meet me."

"Didn't we do that earlier?" Luna drummed her nails on the doorframe.

I knew I was pushing my luck. "Since what we discussed had to do with Marie's demise, I don't think that was what Marie meant."

Luna looked me up and down. Something about her gaze was unsettling. It was searching, almost judging, but I wasn't sure what she was judging. After a few moments, she let out a loud, dramatic sigh. "I have no idea why Marie said that. Katrina finish up the tasks I've given you then you may leave. I'll see you in the morning. I prefer not having strangers in my home tonight. It's been a trying day." Luna spun on her heel.

Glaring at me, Katrina shut the door.

Well, I tried. I had hoped looking through Marie's items would give me and Paul a clue into what she was doing. Luna admitted she felt better with Marie in the house. That sounded like Luna was scared of being alone at night. Had Luna hired Marie because she had law enforcement experience? Did Luna find the threats upsetting, even though she decided against telling the sheriff or the police chief about them? Matter of fact, it didn't seem like anyone except Marie, Luna, and Vernon knew about them. Wait. Edward. Almost forgot he had received the note.

Why share it with her ex-husband? Or maybe everyone on the security staff knew. I continued down the dirt path, keeping an eye and ear out for anyone driving a car down the dirt road. The remains of sunlight were getting less and less and the lights on the golf cart weren't bright, and I'd rather not get run over. The day was already bad enough. Vernon's jeep was still parked near my RV, the keys placed in the glove compartment. I hadn't been able to find him, not that I had looked that hard, my priority had been getting into Marie's room which was a bust.

I reached the RV and trudged inside, plucking Ebenezer out of the playpen and placing him on the floor. He zipped around, burning off some bottled-up energy. I watched for a few seconds, letting his frolicking bring some happiness into my spirit before I started working.

Pulling out a spiral notebook, I inventoried the craft projects I had finished today. Considering how little time I spent creating today, I had a large number of projects completed. It helped I "cheated" by leaving some of the painted ornaments blank instead of adding a decal to all of them. The blank ornaments could be used in one of the bazaar booths, placing them in the back to fill out the booth and have some decorated ones up front. For the ones needing a design, I'd use some of the simpler ones I'd done for orders. No sense designing something new or too elaborate when most of the items were background pieces. I still had a large backload of projects and I had a feeling Katrina was no longer interested in helping me. Not that Luna was one to share her employees.

I tugged my phone toward me, tapping on the Messenger button. With my finger poised over Bright's icon, I ran through other options besides contacting my partner, coming up with none. We'd been business partners for the last ten going on eleven years because we worked well together, stepping up to fill in when the other was falling behind or over their head in their craft area that was their specialty. I hated asking as the last nine months, mainly November and December, I was the one requesting an abundance of help because of my ex-husband Samuel's murder and then taking on the role of Christmas parade organizer and finding myself once again tracking down a murderer.

Was it fair asking Bright for help? Her genealogy project was important, and with her family reunion coming up, her time was limited. Some of the branches of her family tree had grown apart and Bright was working on drawing them together. I had offered my help a time or two and Bright declined, wanting to do it herself.

I understood her need to track down her family. Over the last few months, my mother's illness had progressed and there were more days that she no longer knew me and her grandchildren than she remembered us. It was heartbreaking for all of us. I'd never envisioned my mom smiling at us with anything other than her bright, loving smile. I, and then me and my children, had been her world. Everything had centered around us. Now, most days I visited, she offered me a polite smile and had trouble remembering my name.

For the first time in my life, I wondered about my birth parents. The people who left me on the front steps of a church on

Christmas Eve. I never gave them much of a thought, either they were desperate people doing the best for me, or self-absorbed, uncaring people doing the best for them with no regard for me. While my adopted parents were alive, I didn't care. I knew they loved me. Wanted me. It was more than enough for me. I didn't want to risk hurting myself or them by looking for my birth parents.

It wasn't until the last few months, especially hearing Bright talk about everything she was learning about her family, I wondered about them. The biggest question in my head was why they left me, and I feared that answer the most. Did I really want to find out they left me on the church steps because I meant nothing? I always imagined them as scared teenagers doing what they believed was best for their baby and I'd rather still hold onto that fantasy than face reality.

I wanted a tie to someone. I had my children, but something in me yearned for a little more. More family. Bright filled part of that need. We were connected to each other. While my children knew me as their mom, Bright knew me as Merry. Crafter. Worrier. Insecure mother of two. A woman who tried to stand on her own and do right for her family. A woman who loved everything about Christmas especially the spirit of it. A woman who loved to feel needed and felt lost when those who had needed her most—children and mom—either no longer did as they're venturing out on their own, or because they couldn't remember her.

The rambling thoughts froze in my brain, one highlighted more than the others. Needed. I loved—thrived—in being needed. Felt lost without it. It was why I adopted Ebenezer. Was that why I involved myself in two murder investigations? And also, why I was obsessing over Marie's death?

What I *needed* to concern myself with was how I'd complete all the crafts for the movie. There was only option: back-up. With Bright's help, we'd knock these out within a day and a half, and I'd love having someone here. For the first time in my life, I was truly alone somewhere, and I wasn't liking the feeling.

Fire destroyed some of the Christmas props. The director

wants me to make replacements. I need some massive help in getting these done. Been trying to stay on top of it all day. I fibbed a little not wanting to admit I spent a large portion of the day being suspicious about a death. *The to-do list keeps getting added to. Could use some help.*

I sent the message and sat back, picking polish off a fingernail. Bright couldn't say no now. Right? I wasn't sure why my stomach flipped and flopped, or why it had become so important that Bright see me in person. I'd been happy with our friendship for the last eleven years. We messaged. Texted. Emailed. It was the basis of our relationship and I couldn't think of another person, besides my children, who I was closer with. But lately, there was something in me requiring a little more and I wasn't sure why. When had I become so needy? *When your children grew up*. The thought slammed into me.

No more moping and wallowing. Work time. I checked the list again and started plotting out a battle plan. I'd complete half of each item needed and then restart at the top of the list and finish the rest. It was better to have a little of each than all of one item and none of the other. For the fabric items, I'd ask the locals for advice on handcrafters. There had to be somewhere I could get those items, and if there wasn't any fabric critters or people dressed for Christmas, I'd heat press a decal onto a tiny shirt or hat. Tonight, instead of eating in the RV, I'd venture out into town and have dinner at the eatery. It would be fun to hang out in a saloon and I might even find a local crafter who could help me out. I still hadn't heard back from Sharon, which made me think the answer was heck no.

My phone pinged. Bright responded. Drawing in deep breath, I swiped my finger over the screen and pulled up the message.

How horrible. I hope no one was hurt. Whatcha need, darling? I can overnight some product. The sentence ended with a kissy face emoji.

A brilliant idea came into my head and I typed it out before I talked myself out of it. *No injuries, besides to the craft products.*

Don't know if mailing is the best option. It'll cost a small fortune to overnight the items. Cheaper for you to fly out. I have two machines in the RV and supplies. Just bring your laptop.

Bright replied, *It'll be less of a fortune to mail completed items than buy a plane ticket and rent a car. I'm sorry about the predicament you're in but leaving home isn't an option.*

I was about ready to offer to pay for one then stopped myself. I was being pushy. She couldn't make it. She had her own priorities and they weren't mine. *I'm sorry. I can get a little me-me-me sometimes. Getting a little antsy with everything going on around here. Forgive me.* I added an anguished face emoji.

Aww, honey, don't give it a second thought. I know how well you deal with stress. Had some family issues come up. Nothing earth-shattering but if I head out there, it'll make things a little complicated.

Off the top of your head, can you think of anyone in our network that has any of the following items and can deliver within the next two days? I typed out the list from the prop department.

I know a couple of crafters in the vicinity. I'll message them and get back with you. I'll overnight some items. Have a few wooden signs that'll work and can get some tulle wreaths from a friend of mine.

I typed in Luna's address, using the overnight delivery as a great way to get into the house, and just maybe sneak upstairs and check out Marie's room.

Have you checked the items in questions? Some might be useable in their current condition or you can upcycle what is there.

It was a simple solution. Why hadn't I thought of it? I knew exactly why I hadn't, complicating matters was becoming a new hobby. I was turning back into a teenage girl and morphing everything into a drama of the century. Though, the items had already been gone through. Did I really have time to waste trying to reuse the unusable? Did I really have time then to poke around in Marie's death? The snarky question jumped into my head.

That's a brilliant idea, I replied to Bright. *The prop department said everything's ruined.*

Who's to say they're right? They don't know what you're capable of restoring or repurposing.

You're right. Off to check. I signed off.

I accepted this job not only to work on a Christmas movie, a dream I hadn't known was inside me, but also to have less angst for a few weeks. I loved crafting. It was calming. Yes, there were a lot of projects on my plate, but I could do it. Been doing it for ten years. We had lots of last-minute orders every Christmas, some because there were the shoppers who knew no other way to shop than last minute, and those that had no concept on how long it took to create a handcrafted, original item.

Pausing for a moment, I stared out the window into the dark, contemplating the smartness of searching the shed in Luna's backyard. The shed was a good distance away from the house. It wasn't like I would be lurking right behind her windows or breaking into the house. I was just checking out the items in the shed, or possibly outside the shed. The crew had been working there earlier, clearing everything out. I doubted they put everything back inside.

Luna's house was far enough away I wasn't comfortable walking there in the dark. Vernon still hadn't picked up his vehicle, so I'd borrow it again. I grabbed a flashlight from my RV and after making sure Ebenezer wasn't up to any mischief, I headed outside. Hoisting myself into the jeep, I hoped Vernon didn't mind I borrowed it again. I was a little surprised he hadn't stopped by to collect it before now but maybe he was laying low in case his cousin was visiting the set.

Despite its rundown appearance, the jeep started right up, and I slowly drove toward Luna's house. The headlights blinked on and off as I drove over the rough road and I hoped they didn't go out. The flashlight I brought with me rolled off the passenger seat onto the floorboard. The sky was overcast, not many stars in the sky and the moon was half-hidden behind clouds. The area didn't have many lamps, making it slow going and not as safe as I'd like it.

Maybe this was a bad idea. I hummed "White Christmas" hoping it would calm my nerves.

I spotted a handmade road sign directing crew members to their parking lot, which was a little distance behind Luna's house and near the shed. Perfect. I'd take it instead of driving around Luna's house. It was a more direct approach to the shed and I wouldn't be announcing my presence. I reached the empty dirt parking lot and exited the jeep.

The area around me was quiet. I shivered a little, wrapping my hand tightly around the flashlight, swinging the beam back and forth across the ground as I walked. The silence was a little unsettling after all the hustle and bustle during the day. In the distance, I spotted a soft glow of lights from the house, either from someone still being up or the Christmas lights were left on. It was a little creepy with the fading pinpoints of light in the distance and the lack of sound. Almost like I was about to take part in a horror movie rather than a Christmas movie.

There were two plastic trash cans outside the shed along with boxes piled up with items, some spilled onto the ground. Either the crew was in a hurry or hadn't cared about preserving any of the items. I took a look in the boxes. If the items were placed neatly inside the box, I could consolidate the mix of paper, clothing, and crafts into half the number of boxes the crew was using for the trash.

Shining the beam of the flashlight into the trashcans, I evaluated the items inside. Most of it looked like trash: half-burned and soaked magazines, wrinkled and stained clothing, disposables cups, and discarded food. Not digging through that bin. The other trash can was half filled with garbage. Using a stained piece of material in a box, I squashed down the trash, giving me room to put in some of the unusable items from the boxes.

I dumped out the items from the least filled box and laid my flashlight on the ground, aiming at the mess I had just created. From my quick scan, I identified a dozen items suitable for repurposing. There was a box of ornaments and a few mesh wreaths I placed in the save box. The wreaths smelled like smoke, but since they were for the outdoor Christmas bazaar scene, the scent was manageable. No one was actually taking the wreaths home to hang up.

"Merry, what are you doing?" a feminine voice called out from the darkness.

Thankfully, it wasn't Luna, but I still didn't like someone spying on me. I picked up the flashlight and shone the beam in the direction of the voice.

Anne shielded her eyes with one hand. "I saw some light and thought I should see what's going on."

What was she doing near Luna's house? "What are you doing down this way all by yourself? In the dark. Doesn't seem safe." The scolding came out before I thought too much about it.

Anne laughed. "I could say the same to you. We finished filming a scene fifteen minutes ago and I was sitting at the gazebo enjoying the cool night air and lights. Saw some headlights heading back here and thought I should check it out."

My cheeks heated. That was good reason for her being here, and she had a point. She was an adult perfectly capable of taking care of herself. "Sorry. I have a habit of treating people like they're my kids to worry about."

"It's better than not caring about people. Everyone can use one more person who cares about them." Anne glanced into the boxes in front of me and groaned. "Please don't tell me Edward now has you clearing out the shed. You have enough to do right now without him using you as a cleaner, especially when the only time you have available is at night." There was a tinge of anger in her voice.

"No, this was a mission of mercy for myself. There are a ton of items that need to be redone because of the fire. I came to see if there was anything I could recycle for another project."

"In the dark? Be easier during the day."

"I hadn't thought of it earlier. I was afraid if I waited until morning, everything might've been thrown out."

"I understand. Must've been exciting being in the movie. Ike hadn't mentioned you were also an extra. Said you were the crafter Luna picked. Apparently, it was between you and a Sharon somebody and Luna decided on you after speaking with Marie."

I wasn't sure how I felt about people asking about me. "I wasn't actually in the movie. I was a sound effect and a lousy one at that."

She picked up an item and held it out. "The director should've reminded everyone to turn off their phones. He had a lot of new people on the set today. Repurpose or toss?"

The stuffed snowman was still wet, and the bottom was charred. He must've been close to the firepit. "Toss."

"How did you get into Christmas crafting?" Anne asked.

"Christmas has always been my thing and I loved crafting since I was little. I enjoyed making Christmas items and had a house full. I didn't need any more for myself or friends, it seemed a great business for me. I needed some extra income and didn't want a job that left my children alone in the evenings, so I decided on opening an Etsy shop for my Christmas items. Me and my partner."

"You have a partner? As in..." Her eyebrows quirked up.

I tossed a few more items into the trash pile. "Business partner. Brighton Lane. The bright of Merry and Bright Handcrafted Christmas."

"You're not married?"

"Why do I feel like you're interrogating me?"

She blushed. "Sorry. Garrison was asking questions about you. He's extremely interested in you and I thought I'd help him out. You wouldn't know it, but he's more of an introvert."

I stopped myself from rolling my eyes. Not that she'd see me in the dark. I secured the top on the keep-item box. "Probably wondering who the woman is who ruined this afternoon's scene."

"That would be Luna. He is not happy about the hint of the movie changes. I have no idea why she's tormenting him like that. It's bad enough what others are saying..." she trailed off.

"What are others saying?" I couldn't help asking. I was nosy.

"Wondering about him and Luna. He spent a lot of time

talking to her. Someone even said arguing with her."

"Who said that?" My voice was sharper than I meant, and Anne drew back.

"Vernon."

"He didn't mention that." I tossed another item onto the get rid of pile.

"You talked with Vernon? Why?"

I squatted down and tested the weight of the box. "I was going into town and he offered me his car. It was too hot to walk." Everything in me said not to really tell her anything. It was like she was pumping me for information.

"The police chief stopped by the set and the house and was asking questions about Marie's death." Anne knelt down beside me, hooking her arm through the mesh wreaths I set aside. Her voice dropped to a whisper: "I noticed she didn't ask you anything. Makes me think she had already talked with you. Like during your visit into town."

Uneasiness danced up and down my spine. I didn't like that Anne had been watching me and I hadn't known. "I was a little worried about all the pranks and wanted to know if the chief knew about all of them. Someone might get hurt."

After placing the flashlight into a small opening in the flaps, I stood with the box in my arms. This wasn't my brightest idea. I wasn't sure if I meant sharing my thoughts with Anne or juggling a box I could barely wrap my arms around in the dark. I hoped I made it back to the jeep before it slipped from my gasp.

"I was thinking the same thing. There's something not so innocent about..." Anne trailed off and jerked upright, gaze scattering around the area, eyes widening as she grabbed hold of my arm.

Did she mean something about Marie, or the pranks weren't quite so innocent? I started to speak then held in my breath, trying to pick up the sound again. Footsteps crunched over gravel. The sound stopped for a moment then it came again. A soft shuffling before ceasing again.

Anne drew closer to me. My mind warred with the most important item right now: finding out what Anne knew or who was lurking out in the dark. We could either pretend like we didn't hear anything or send out a challenge.

I opted for the latter. "Who's there?"

The gravel rattled. The person was still coming toward us.

Anne drew in a harsh breath and shifted the wreath, holding onto the frame and raising it above her, ready to bring it down on someone's head.

"We know someone is out there. If you're trying to sneak up on us as a prank, think again. We're not scared." I was proud that my voice didn't shake. I sounded angry. Murderous even. I was tired of people thinking I was an easy target. Having run-ins with murderers was giving me a stronger backbone than I ever believed I'd possess.

"You should be," a voice whispered from the dark.

Anne screamed, a horror movie-worthy sound, nails digging into my arm.

I dropped the box, the items scattered to the ground, and stepped in front of Anne, fists clenched. I scooped up the flashlight and shone it in the direction of the possible attacker and gripped it so I could use it as a club if necessary.

Sheriff Randolph Rhodes, in civilian clothes, stood a few feet away.

"You're not allowed here." Anne's grip loosened from my arm. "Security will throw you out."

"Why are you skulking around here?" Anger sparked through me, forcing my words out in a rush. "Luna Carmichael will have you strung up if she finds out you're here."

"She's not the only one trying to do that," the sheriff fired back, his anger matching mine. "Turn that dang thing off."

"No," I said.

Using his arm as he a shield, he blocked the light from his face and stepped closer. "At least move the light from my face."

I wasn't sure I wanted to do that either but wasn't sure it was a good thing to keep doing it. He was a sheriff and had the ability to arrest me. I didn't know if shining a bright light into a sheriff's face was an arrestable offense and thought it best not to chance it. "I'll move it away as long as you don't come any closer."

"Keep it on him, Merry," Anne said. "The man is here for no good."

"I'm here to make sure everything is okay," the sheriff said, gaze flickering toward me.

"You didn't care when the trailer was on fire," Anne said. "Besides, Luna has hired security."

"Right, one of them being her ex-husband who threatened to hurt me...and her," the sheriff said. "I received a call that there was an item that I should pick up. Might be related to a case of the sheriff's department."

That was another piece of information Vernon hadn't shared. Why would Luna hire him if the sheriff was telling the truth? I could see Vernon threatening the sheriff but not Luna. The man seemed a little scared of her.

"What case?" Anne asked.

"Can't say." The sheriff fixed his gaze on me. It was clear I was the one he came to see.

Anne spun toward me. "You found something? Is it about the fire?"

I shook my head. "Nothing besides the fire starter Deputy Paugh took with him."

Sheriff Rhodes frowned. "Must've misheard the message."

"Anne!" someone screamed. A light shone in our direction.

"Garrison, over here!" Anne sent a smug look toward the sheriff. "Rhodes snuck up on us and is acting a bit creepy."

Garrison jogged over and tucked Anne against his side. Even in the dark, the scowl he aimed at Rhodes was unmistakable. "Stay away from her and Luna." The tone he used wasn't lost on me, the simple statement was a threat.

"Luna...really?" Rhodes stepped closer to Garrison and smirked. "Still playing that game?"

"It's not a game, and you'd be wise to remember that." Garrison tucked Anne's hand into the crook of his arm.

"And you should remember the truth always comes out. Be careful who you trust, Ms. Winters, pretty much everything you're seeing here is fiction." Rhodes pivoted and faded into the dark of the night.

"What did he mean by that?" I asked.

"Nothing." Garrison shot a look over at Anne causing her to press her lips together.

"No, that meant something," I said. "What's fiction?"

"The animosity between him and Luna. It's the way she is. Two days from now, she'll likely want him back," Garrison said. "Luna always runs hot and cold with the men in her life. And Vernon isn't someone you should take at face value. He likes to tweak the truth just enough to where he's not lying but also shows himself in a much better light than the reality."

And liked withholding important details. "I'll keep that in mind." Wait—how did he know I spoke with Vernon? Had the chief mentioned it?

"Let's get you back to your trailer, Anne." Garrison tucked Anne's hand into the crook of his arm. "Would you like an escort?"

The more I interacted with people working with the movie, the more I was certain there was trouble lurking in the background. I wasn't so certain the pranks were, well, pranks. "No, I'm good. I drove over. I also have a flashlight. Good for knocking someone out."

Anne started to say something and stopped when another voice joined us.

"Who do you need to hit?" Paul's voice came from the darkness.

"Paul." His name came out a little more breathless than I liked. It was just a huge relief knowing someone I trusted was nearby. I spun toward him, smiling. The happiness was short lived as my mind reminded me why Paul was here—his cousin died.

"Looks like Merry will be fine," Anne said. "We should get

some sleep, Garrison, filming starts for us tomorrow at five in the morning."

The pair walked off, leaving me and Paul alone.

I wrapped my arms around Paul's waist and hugged him for all I was worth. "How are you doing?"

"Okay." He untangled my arms from his waist, draping an arm around my shoulder. "I was around front when I heard some commotion back here. Thought I should check it out. I had wanted to talk with Marie's employer, but all the lights are out. I'll wait until morning and talk with her. What are you doing out here?" He nodded at the boxes and piles of items.

"Sorting through the damaged items. I can repurpose some."

"Since I was coming here, I called Cassie and told her about your craft emergency and she agreed to go over to your house and help me get some of the crafts you had completed for the vending event you were attending until you got this job. I hope you don't mind."

I smiled briefly. What reason had he given her for coming to Indiana? It couldn't have been the truth that his cousin who worked on the movie was killed, because Cassie would've been on the phone to her former stepbrother and stepsister, and the three would've shown up here. The only other thing was Cassie was led to believe I asked Paul for help. With him working for his parents, he'd have no trouble getting the time off, but I didn't want Cassie thinking there was something more between me and Paul. Her best friend was Paul's baby sister, and Cassie's father and I had only divorced a few weeks before he died. I still didn't think she was ready for me to move on from him. Especially with her grandmother in the final months of her life.

Grief and shame rolled through me. I really shouldn't have abandoned everyone and come to Indiana, even for a "dream come true." Cassie was excited for me and insisted I come, but right now I felt like I should've ignored her and stayed home. It was easy listening to someone when they encouraged you to do what you really wanted to do.

"She's doing good, Merry," Paul said softly, rubbing a circle on my back.

"How did you know what I was thinking?"

"I know that worried look of yours. It always involves your friends and family, and knowing you, you were torn coming here even though the break was good for you. Helen is hanging in there and is thrilled that her girls are off living their lives. Helen doesn't want everyone hovering around until she dies. Life is short. Unpredictable. She knows that more than anyone with Samuel having been killed. The best thing you can do to honor her is follow your dreams and come home and tell her all about it."

I drew back and looked up at him. "Please don't worry about me. I should be comforting you. Are Marie's parents on their way?"

"My parents are having a hard time locating them. They know they went on a cruise but can't remember which line and the destination. I told them I'd come and handle things here."

I couldn't even imagine how I'd feel knowing something happened to one of my children and no one could reach me. "I hope they find them soon. Let's head over to the RV and I'll get you something to eat and drink. I went to Luna's house to get your cousin's items, and Luna said she'd allow it once you were here and proved your Marie's cousin." I held his hand and headed for the jeep.

Paul stopped walking, the cease of movement bringing me to a halt. "Proof? Who asks for proof?"

"Luna Carmichael. The woman is..." I stumbled around in my mind for a fitting word, "intensely controlling. How did Marie hear about the job?"

"It's one of my many questions." Paul continued holding my hand as we navigated toward the jeep in the dark. "Being someone's assistant doesn't fit. Months before, Marie told me she was setting up her own PI firm. Going from a business to an assistant of a television star is a huge change. It's what I found odd. Thought maybe she decided on a more relaxing and less dangerous job for a change. But Marie never dreamed of working in the film business or around a Christmas theme. That's your thing. Not hers. She wasn't much of a holiday person. What was she working on here?"

And had it resulted in her death?

NINE

The next morning, I woke up feeling groggy and had a headache. My mind had refused to turn off and played hundreds of scenarios theorizing the reason for Marie's death. I shuffled into the living room holding back a yawn as Paul handed me a cup of coffee. I had let Paul sleep on the pullout couch last night after convincing him I was not being put out by having an unexpected guest. There weren't any hotels in Carol Lake, and I hated the thought of Paul, tired and grieving, trying to find a hotel in a neighboring town late at night, not to mention all alone with his thoughts.

"What are your plans for the day?" Last night, I had finally heard back from Sharon and was picking up some items at her house in a few hours.

"I'm heading into Harmony and plan on talking with the paramedics and the emergency room doctors. I'm not waiting for the sheriff to decide I deserve the truth on the cause of my cousin's death. I'll also call some of her old work colleagues. She might have contacted one of them about what she was working on for Luna."

"I'll eat breakfast with the cast and crew this morning. Maybe someone knows what Marie's been doing for Luna. The times I saw Marie, Luna wasn't anywhere around though Marie was in constant contact with Luna through the phone. The first night I was here, a woman named Katrina was angry about something Marie did. She told Marie she had no right. I interrupted the argument before either of them mentioned what was done. Katrina was an assistant to one of the actresses and was then supposed to help me with creating more items but was reassigned as Luna's assistant. I'll head up to house and ask about borrowing her or dropping some items off for her to work on when Luna's filming. I'll pry a bit and find out what Katrina was upset about."

"Be careful, Merry." Paul left the trailer.

"You too." I wasn't sure he heard me as the door shut while I was speaking.

I yawned and headed toward the food pavilion. I had everything I needed for breakfast in my RV, but I wanted to sit among the cast and crew and get to know them a little bit better. Or more truthfully, hear what the gossip was among them. There were so many secrets swirling around and I couldn't help worrying they were dangerous ones.

What had Anne wanted to tell me, and why had she changed her mind when the sheriff appeared? I yawned again. I had stayed up late googling for information about Luna Carmichael, Garrison Tyler, Sheriff Rhodes, and the movie *Dash Away All*. The articles about the cast members were ones I had already read and nothing new about the movie.

After I was hired, I read up on everything I could about the directors and the cast members. I had wanted to tailor the crafts to the movie and cast members as much as I could. The only thing missing from Luna's biography was about her marriage and pending divorce from Vernon O'Neal. It seemed no one had the information about it. The marriage, along with the divorce, must've been recent.

In a gossip blog dated four months ago, there had been a two-line mention of Luna and a man from a small-town, a former high school basketball star, which I presumed was Vernon. Said they met at a fishing tournament where Luna had been gathering information for an upcoming role. The last movie Luna Carmichael had starred in was three years ago and nothing I found talked about why Luna had taken a break from her movie career and was now venturing back into it.

I also searched Sheriff Rhodes, hoping it gave me a clue into the animosity Luna showed toward him. Rumors said they had been in a relationship, but her reaction seemed a little over the top considering she was a love them, dump them, move on quickly kind of person. The sheriff's only online presence was a Facebook page. The man's setting was on private though, and it probably was not a good idea to send him a friend request.

The line for breakfast was short, and the coffee urns were fixed, the liquid coming out at an appropriate pace and stopping when the lever was pushed up. It wasn't until after I filled up my cup and picked up my tray that I realized the problem with my plan. Who was I going to talk to without it seeming suspicious? I didn't know any of the other crew members.

My gaze fell on the leadman, the man in charge of all the props. Except for him. We chatted briefly when he dropped off the list of damaged items for me to recreate. It was polite to give him an update and let him know I had rescued some items from the trash. The man was hunched over a script, flipping through it and jotting down notes on a tablet. Please don't let it be more crafts.

"Mind if I join you?" I asked.

"Sure," he answered, sneaking a glance at me before returning his attention to the script. "We're not formal around here. Sit wherever there's an open seat, no need to ask."

"The cast members won't mind either?"

"Ms. Carmichael is the only one who would, but she doesn't eat with the staff. And according to the Queen of Christmas, everyone is staff."

"Luna does live in Carol Lake. I can understand why she prefers to eat in her home rather than eating at the pavilion."

He fixed an odd look at me and shrugged his shoulders as if to say he was willing for me to continue believing whatever I wanted, he had no desire to change my mind. "I have a list of crafters available to help you. Vernon dropped it off last night to me, said you were in the middle of something."

Uneasiness wiggled through me. Maybe Anne and I blamed the wrong person for lurking, and it was Vernon spying on us and Sheriff Rhodes had actually been patrolling the area—in civilian clothes. Of course, Vernon might have just been tracking down his jeep.

"He must've seen me sorting through the items taken from the trailer. A few of them I can repurpose."

"We were wondering who went through everything. Ms. Carmichael wasn't happy seeing the mess in her yard. You really should've put the items back in bins. Crew isn't happy they have to pick everything back up." The man swallowed a forkful of scrambled eggs. "The director wanted a list of everything in the bins. I'm guessing as a write off."

"I sorted everything into different trash cans and boxes."

He shrugged. "Was all over the ground this morning."

"I can give you a list later of the items I took. Hopefully, Vernon patrolling the area last night stopped anymore pranks."

He rolled his eyes at Vernon's name. "My bet is Vernon is the one who caused all of them. Could also be the one who dumped everything out. There's been nothing since..." The man dipped his head and continued eating.

"You think Vernon stopped because of what happened to Marie?" I asked. I wasn't sure the guy stopped talking because he thought it would sound like he was blaming Marie or the fact that it was possibly a prank turned deadly and that made the person stop. Had the prankster turned into a murderer?

He sighed and put down his fork. "It's possible. Vernon said Rhodes would rue the day he took away his woman. Or it's simply whoever was doing the pranks lost their joy in them. Someone we all knew died."

I hadn't given any consideration to the fact people here knew Marie and considered her a friend.

A woman plonked her tray onto the wooden picnic table. "Vernon liked Marie. If he was the one responsible for the pranks, he wouldn't have the heart for it anymore. He loved that she had a backbone with Luna. Most people back down when Luna demands something."

"No one has seen the prankster?" I asked. "It takes time to set up two firepits in the trailer. It's not a usual item to be carrying around."

"They were already in there," the leadman said. "The fire pits were being used in a later scene."

Whoever was responsible for the pranks had a copy of the script. That narrowed down the suspects. "Would Vernon have a copy of script? He wouldn't know there would be firepits in there."

"As a security guard, he had access to the keys for all the buildings. He could've seen them in there and came up with the idea," the woman said. "He and Luna were married. Likelihood is she gave him an early read of the script or asked his opinion on some of the scenes."

True. "Why would he start the fire? Seemed it irritated Luna more than the sheriff." The police officers and the volunteer fire people hadn't been happy at dealing with the prank. Which likely meant his cousin wasn't happy either. And one of the officers had mentioned the chief said it was a waste of time. Did Chief Quinn suspect her cousin was the prankster?

"The man is heartbroken that Ms. Carmichael left him for the sheriff. Probably not thinking right or thought he'd come and save Luna. I have no idea why anyone thought he was security guard material."

"Because his being here would antagonize Edward Yale," the leadman said.

"The director doesn't like Vernon? Why doesn't he fire him?" I asked. Did anyone really like anyone? "Has anyone seen Sheriff Rhodes' cat around?"

"I haven't. Edward has never liked any of Luna's husbands. He won't fire the man because Luna is likely the one who wanted Vernon hired and what Luna wants, Luna gets," the woman said. "My guess is Luna is the prankster and wants Vernon to take the fall. Why else would she have her ex-husband here?"

"My money is still on Vernon," the leadman said.

The woman waved off his words. "He wouldn't hurt Luna. Plus, I heard Vernon's attention was drifting toward someone new.

Luna wants Vernon here to irritate the man she no longer wants. Luna is a great actress but not so great of a person."

I squirmed on the bench. Even though it was my intent to pick up gossip, now that I was hearing it, I was uncomfortable. I wasn't sure if it was because I knew what it felt like being the subject of it and was now remorseful for my willingness to turn rumors into fact, or because the gossip was about Luna. Someone I idolized and really wanted to like.

"Who's everyone betting is going to be the next Mister Luna Carmichael?" one of the newcomers asked.

The woman who defended Vernon leaned forward, motioning for everyone to come closer, her smile growing broader. "There's one man she's been spending a lot of one-on-one time with." She paused dramatically. "Garrison."

At least I knew what Rhodes was alluding to. Was that what Anne wanted to tell me? Had the secret she planned on sharing last night been about Garrison or Sheriff Rhodes? Or something not related? Had Anne changed her mind because of the sheriff showing up or Garrison? There was one way to find out—ask her.

I wiped my brow. The sun was unbearable. I felt sorry for the poor actors and actresses who'd have to shoot today's "winter" scenes during the melting heat of the summer. Why didn't they film in January or February? The weather would be more suitable for wearing winter coats and gear, and they might even get some natural snow rather than having to make it. I was sure there was a reason a layperson like me didn't understand.

Walking into the main cast area of the house, I read the name tags on the right side of the doors. I recognized most of the names, other actors and actresses who regularly appeared in television Christmas movies. There were two trailers larger than the rest labeled with Garrison Tyler and Anne Lindsey. The trailers were so close together, you could look from the window of one trailer to the next. The curtains were drawn tight in both trailers so no peeping going on—or at least not right now. Had Garrison left his curtains open and Anne saw something troubling?

Raised voices floated from Anne's trailer. I stood near her trailer, trying to look like I wasn't eavesdropping while doing just that.

"You have to stop it," Anne said.

"There's nothing I can do," Ike said.

"Then I'll tell Edward."

"I don't advise that."

Silence filled the air for a long moment before a loud bang from Anne's trailer ended it.

Without knocking, or thinking, I opened the door and charged inside. "Anne, are you okay?"

Two startled gazes settled on me. Anne stood in the small hallway, the bedroom door opened and a blow dryer in her hand. The couch Ike was sitting on was flat on the floor, having collapsed underneath him.

"I'm okay." Her cheeks reddened. "I guess you heard us. I'm used to projecting on set, sometimes I forget about using my indoor voice."

"Sorry for busting in." My complexion matched Anne's. "I thought you were in trouble."

"It's nice to know some people around here care about possible threats and are willing to do whatever is necessary to stop them." Anne fixed a disgusted look on Ike.

He scrambled to his feet. "That was not a threat. It was a warning. You should know how Edward will react to that rumor about Ms. Carmichael. Once he hears it, there will be a major problem."

I had a feeling I knew what rumor they were discussing: the coupling of Luna and Garrison.

"Garrison is important also." Anne clenched her hands together. "He shouldn't put up with what's being said about him. He is not sleeping with Luna."

Ike turned red and shot a look over at me then turned the glare to Anne. "You shouldn't say that in front of crew members. We don't want it getting around."

"I heard it already," I said. "From the crew members."

Anne pointed the hair dryer at Ike. "See. What did I tell you? You can't just hope it goes away on its own. Stop the cast and crew from gossiping. It's bad enough we have to deal with everything coming from the locals."

"I'll talk with the cast," Ike said.

"What about the crew and Luna's staff?"

"I'm sure Luna can handle her staff without my help." He crossed his arms and looked up at the ceiling. "She'd maim me if I spoke with them. She, and she only, is allowed to tell them to do anything. And Garrison wants to be treated like everyone else on the staff. He doesn't want privileges because Edward is his father."

"Privileges?" Anne shrieked. "This isn't about a privilege. He's being gossiped about. Edward needs—"

"To ignore it like he does all the other rumors he's heard over the decades," Ike said. "Director Yale going on the warpath will not help his son's career if Garrison decides acting is his future plan rather than returning to behind the camera."

"Is that what you wanted to tell me last night, Anne?" I asked.

She spun away, heading back into the bathroom. "Just be careful wandering around by yourself at night. Some of us have been here since the beginning of the week, and we've had a prank every day. Though things got worse yesterday with the fire, coffee, and Hercules' escape."

"I think Hercules was Luna's doing," Ike said. "She likely took advantage of the fact there were pranks and let the dang cat loose."

"Hercules?" I asked.

"The sheriff's cat."

"I'm guessing it's still missing," I said.

Ike nodded. "The sheriff comes by every morning and night and looks for it. No luck so far. Not that Luna wouldn't have it chased off."

That explained what the sheriff was doing last night. Poor Hercules. I'd grab some tuna in town and leave it out in case the cat was around. I'm sure Ebenezer wouldn't mind giving up his carrier for the cat once I caught it. "I don't think it was her. Maybe one of her staff. Luna had seemed surprised when I told her the cat was missing."

"Right, she didn't know a cat who lived in her house and followed her around was missing," Ike said, his voice telling me exactly what he thought of my opinion. It was worth nothing. "Luna is a great actress. Of course, she looked and sounded surprised. She was acting."

"Sheriff Rhodes wasn't the only one who ignored everything." Anne strolled into the living area of the RV. She walked over to the couch and sat down cross-legged on it. "Chief Quinn hadn't shown any interest in what was going on until yesterday afternoon."

The tone of Anne's voice told me she knew exactly why that was—I had spoken to the chief and whatever I said had piqued the woman's curiosity and the need for an investigation.

Not many people knew about my secondary hobby, as my daughter Raleigh called the two times I found myself immersed in a murder investigation. Now, it appeared I was on my way to being involved in a third.

The phrase "the third time's a charm" drifted into my head. I wasn't sure if that was a good thing to dwell on or not. Because the last two times, I found my life in danger and was able to get out of it. Was my brain trying to warn me getting involved this time might just be the death of me?

Ike flipped through the sheets of paper attached to his ever-present clipboard. "It's nice knowing something is going right. I'll mark that all the needed crafts are complete. Since you have time to listen and repeat all the gossip."

"Actually, I'm looking for a car to borrow. I want to drive into Harmony and pick up a few things. After I inventory what I saved from the trash pile by the shed."

The slight breeze and the RV awning helped ease some of the heat bearing down. It was ten in the morning and I feared I'd melt soon.

How in the world would the cast handle doing a daytime Christmas scene tomorrow afternoon? According to the weather app, the heat wasn't expected to let up for a week. The poor cast would roast tomorrow in their winter finery.

Swiping a bead of sweat from my brow, I stepped away from the boxes of handcrafted Christmas decorations. There hadn't been enough room inside the RV to sort out all the items I saved last night and the new and borrowed creations of mine into categories.

On scraps of wood, I wrote the categories I read on the signs for the Christmas bazaar booths and also the types of decorations still needed for the movie scenes. I needed some more Christmas ornaments and hoped Katrina had found some time to make some more between errands for Luna, or maybe one of the stores in town had some ornaments or something I could use.

I finished sorting out the items and jotted down the scene locations where the crafts belonged. Hopefully, someone from the casting department picked up the boxes. I didn't have time to drive them around the lot, especially when I wasn't sure where a few of the scenes were being filmed. I had to get to Harmony today to pick up the fabric elves.

"Merry, I need to speak with you," a frantic voice called out to me.

I turned and saw Katrina running to me, clutching a cell phone in one hand and a notebook in the other. Must be her list of errands for Luna. The woman's excitement from yesterday at being Luna's assistant had faded. Today she was frantic. Her hair was in disarray and her gaze held a panic bordering on terror look. Either Luna was a grinch to work for or the job was a little more intense than Katrina had the stamina for.

"I have a few questions for you," I said. At least now I didn't have to find Katrina. The harder part was finding a natural way to broach the subject of why she was angry with Marie. I smiled, hoping to ease her tension.

She stopped near me, trying to catch her breath as she flipped through the notebook. "Ornaments. Luna wants more ornaments with words on them for the Christmas tree in the living room. She said there isn't enough. You have more right?"

There just wasn't enough time to make a slew of new ones, especially with being distracted with the pranks and Marie's death. I'd loan out the ornaments I was using for decorating my tree in the RV. They were some of my favorites, the first ones I made, and while I hated letting them out of sight, it was a simple solution. Besides, they were going in Luna's home. They'd be safe there. "Sure, I have some inside the RV. Come in and I'll give them to you."

"I'll wait out here." Katrina dropped her gaze from the window. "I don't think he likes me."

I glanced up. Ebenezer was laying on the back of the couch, sunning himself while the air-conditioning blew tufts of his fur around. Leave it to Ebenezer to sunbath in the bliss of the cold. Lucky critter.

"He's harmless," I said. "He's just a little standoffish at times."

"He bit the casting director."

I cringed. Oops, forgot about that. "Almost bit. He's not overly fond of men." I had a feeling Ebenezer's time as a movie star was going to be short lived. No one would hire a star that bit directors, or anyone for that matter.

"He wasn't very nice to me either," she huffed. "He snapped at me the moment I walked in the door."

I drew in a breath to settle my growing temper. I wanted to scold her for taking Ebenezer's behavior personally and yet I was taking her distrust of my pet personally. Some people just didn't get along with animals. "He's moody and protective at times. You know how people can rub you the wrong way at times and make you snap."

Her eyes narrowed. There must've been something in my tone telling her I was saying more than I was. "What do you mean by that?"

"The other night, I saw you and Marie arguing. Seemed rather intense."

"It was just a small disagreement." She forced out a smile and waved like my comment wasn't important. The shaking of her hand said otherwise. "Apparently, wanting an autograph from Luna wasn't appreciated. I might have taken it more personally than I should. Now that I'm working for Luna, I know why Marie said no. Luna doesn't like giving autographs out to anyone. She's very private. Kind of like your pet. He probably didn't like a stranger in his home and was bothered by Anne being in your bedroom."

In my bedroom? Why was she in the bedroom? How many people were in my RV that morning? Ike had said Garrison brought Luna over and I remember seeing Katrina and Anne there that morning as well. "Was Luna here also?"

Her eyes widened. "Not when I was here. I was looking for Anne and heard she was in the Christmas-themed RV. It was just Anne. Craft supplies were all over the place. I started tidying up when your pet snarled at me."

I hadn't left craft supplies everywhere. Either Ebenezer found a way into the cupboards or Anne had been poking around. Plain nosiness, or was there another reason? The past had taught me not to write off people's weird behavior, it was usually a sign of hiding something huge.

Like murder.

"You probably startled him," I said, tugging open the door and walking inside. The cool air was heavenly. I stood still for a moment, eyes closed, and let the cold wash over me. I walked to my bedroom and pushed up the door, leaning into the frame as I studied the room. I hadn't noticed anything out of place yesterday, though I hadn't been looking for signs of someone searching my stuff.

I opened up the dresser drawers. Everything still folded. I heaved out a breath. Katrina must've been mistaken. Why would Anne search my RV? She did have a lot of questions for me yesterday. But the only thing Katrina mentioned was craft supplies being on the floor. Her character did own a craft store and what better way to get the feel of owning a mobile crafting studio than checking one out and also being more familiar with the items a crafter used.

After I talked sense into myself, I emptied out a cardboard box and placed the ornaments from my tree into it. I hated the idea of loaning out my prized possessions but hated failing my clients even more.

"I'm sure they'll be fine." I placed them into a box, lovingly touching each one and telling myself there was no way anyone would damage something in Luna's house. No one, beside the sheriff, wanted an angry Luna.

When I walked back outside, Katrina was pacing back and forth, phone to her ear and nodding back and forth. She blinked rapidly. "I understand." With a heavy sigh, she ended the call and gazed at the ground, looking like her world was about to end.

"Is something wrong?"

"Luna has items needing to be picked up in Harmony from the sheriff's office. He's giving her back things that were in the car and she's afraid he'll change his mind if I don't go now." She had a panicked look on her face.

"I'm sure someone will lend you a car."

Katrina swallowed and lowered her chin, hair now shielding her face. "I don't know how to drive. And it's not like I can just call an Uber here. What am I going to do? Luna will fire me."

Well, maybe that was for the best. Apparently, being able to drive was a needed skill for the job. "You should tell her."

Katrina shook her head, hair swinging back and forth. "I don't want to give up this dream so soon. I can always learn to drive."

In a couple of hours? I doubted it. "Not soon enough to pick up Luna's personal items."

"Could you do it for me? I know how to craft. I can work on some of the projects you need done while you pick up the items for Luna. It's only right I do your job if you're doing mine." Katrina fixed a hopeful look on me.

Well, I was going into Harmony to pick up fabric elves from Sharon and check out some of the items in the local stores. No sense both of us heading into Harmony. Luna wouldn't assign another task to Katrina because she was in town picking up the personal effects from the car. Sounded like a win-win.

And it gave me the opportunity to take a look at what as in the car.

TEN

Flipping the visor down then flipping it back, I squinted as the sun played havoc with my driving. I should've grabbed my sunglasses from the RV. One of the problems of being five-foot-tall was that visors didn't help block the sun. I had bought a pair of sunglasses that fit over my glasses and forget them. I should buy a second pair and keep it in my purse.

My cell phone buzzed from the cup holder. A text. Glancing to the shoulder, I found a spot a few yards ahead perfect for pulling over. I wanted to check it in case it was Paul with important news. It was also a good idea to let him know my change of plans. I didn't want him worrying about me when he got back. He knew me well enough to know I'd do everything in my power to help him find the truth about Marie's death.

I plucked the cell from the cup and swiped my finger across the screen. It was Paul. *There's something going on. Not sure what yet. The paramedics are acting a little weird. Heading to the coroner for information.*

Be careful. I'll be in Harmony soon. Picking up crafts. I can delay the meeting and meet up with you.

No. Get your crafts. I got this.

I dropped my phone back into the holder and eased back onto the empty road. There was no other traffic, pretty much like yesterday when I left for Harmony. Was this the usual traffic for the road? No other cars. No witnesses. Had the killer known?

Sweat coated my hands. I was nearing the scene of the accident. With the SUV being higher off the ground, I saw the corn baler over the corn stalks and weeds while I was still about a mile away. Yesterday, I hadn't noticed until I was almost at that point. Sadness welled up in me. The sun glinted off the top of the hay baler that was hidden by the weeds and the corn.

I slowed down, fixing my gaze on the road. There weren't any skid marks. For Marie to hit the half-hidden baler right in the middle, it meant she was distracted and veered off the road, at a high rate of speed—at the exact moment she was passing the baler. A second or two sooner or later and she'd have driven through the weeds and dried cornstalks. Why hadn't she tried slowing down? Was it too late? Or hadn't she realized she was off the road?

Convenient. The word bounced around in my head. I no longer believed in spontaneous convenient timing, especially when a death was involved. I pulled off the road, flattening a section of the weeds. I exited the car and carefully walked to the area of the accident. The corn stalks were pressed to the ground. There was a slight dip in the ground level between the road and the grassy patch. She'd have felt the car going off and nothing indicated she slowed down. Then again, I didn't know what to look for.

Even with the heat in the air, a shiver worked its way up my spine. I rubbed my hands over my arms, warding off the chill. Marie had died here. I stared at the spot for a long moment, trying to make sense of what happened and how it happened.

I walked on the flattened portion of the stalks and weeds, getting as close to the baler as possible without touching it, in case Chief Quinn opened her own investigation into Marie's death. There was a dent in the side of the baler. I frowned, stepping even closer. The dent on the baler wasn't large enough, to my untrained eye, to cause the damage to the front of Luna's car. Or at least from what I was remembering.

But why would someone damage the car more? The answer was obvious—to make the accident seem worse and be given as the cause of Marie's death. What were they covering up? There had been dried blood on her forehead and cheek indicating a head injury. It would be easy to believe the injury combined with the heat resulted in her death. Had someone not followed Marie and killed her, taking her locket and the cups? Had someone taken the cups—and Marie—from the car? I shuddered. I walked over to the pressed grass I spotted yesterday that sent me into the cornfield. I sighed. There were now tons of down patches of weeds. The sheriff's department and ambulance crew had swarmed the area. There was no way I'd know which was the spot I saw yesterday and if I was remembering correctly that there was only one spot.

I slipped my cell from my pocket and took some photos of the area and the baler. Now I only needed pictures of Luna's car. If the sheriff wasn't at the station, I might be able to convince one of the deputies to allow me to get pictures for the insurance adjuster.

Yards away from me, the cornstalks rustled. I froze, waiting for the feel of a cool breeze. There wasn't one. I inched back toward the car, my eyes on the area where there had been movement. I didn't know if a potential killer was hiding nearby watching me, now knowing that someone was questioning the findings of the accident. I wasn't safe here. I ran for the car, throwing myself inside and locking the door.

Without buckling my seatbelt, I pulled out only securing it once I put some distance between me and the spot where Marie was murdered.

The road to Harmony was miles of farmland occasionally broken up by a glimpse of a farmhouse in the back part of the land. There had been one town about ten miles, but it didn't look like a town "You can't miss," as Anne described it. The town I drove by was smaller than Carol Lake. I had spotted a convenience store, a bait shop, and a bar. Of course, that might have been the end of town and had I turned down the dirt road, I'd have seen a larger town.

I should've turned on the Waze app on my phone and not trusted how "easy" it was to find the town. I'd at least know how many more miles "just down the road" was the town of Harmony. A small housing development was a few miles ahead, followed by a small gas station with an attached convenience store. Right after it, the two-lane road turned into four lanes and the traffic picked up.

A wooden arch with a maroon sign saying "Welcome to Harmony" splayed over the four lanes. Anne was right, it was hard to miss. I drove under the archway and felt my tension melt away at the sight of the town. Golden lights hung from nearly every building. There was something old-fashioned, yet modern, about the wood paneled buildings with a hint of mountain chateau. Large trees lined the brick sidewalks and there were bike racks at each block.

The town was spotless. Windows gleamed. No trash on the street. People ambled down the sidewalks, smiles on their faces. Harmony seemed true to its name. The town was a quintessential Christmas town by the appearance of the buildings and the friendliness of the people on the street. Why hadn't Edward chosen this town for the movie? There were more stores to choose from and enough hotels for room for the cast and crew rather than staying in trailers.

Toward the middle of town was one building that seemed out of place. The sheriff's department was a one-story brick building, a more contemporary design with large windows across the front of the building and a metal and glass door rather than the quainter style of the other businesses, two-story brick buildings with residential-style windows framed by wooden shutters. Everything about the sheriff department building and the outside grounds said modern and functional. Even the landscape was functional with no-fuss plants and two-inch high Kentucky bluegrass.

I pulled into a parking spot in front of the building. I walked inside and was hit with a blast of Antarctic cold air. Wrapping my arms around myself, I held back a shiver. Someone in the building liked it cold. I blew out a puff of breath and was surprised a cloud didn't form in the air. The floor was a smooth tile surface and gleamed under the florescent lights. I stepped carefully in case the floor was freshly mopped.

A deputy sat at a large desk boxed in on three sides by a tall partition, alternating her gaze from a mammoth computer screen to me.

"I'm here to pick up Luna Carmichael's personal effects. Sheriff Rhodes called and said they were available for her." My heart picked up speed. I tried pushing down my nervousness not wanting her to question why I was sent. It was likely the deputy wouldn't hand over Luna's private items to a third party. Then again, she might not care.

Moving her chair away from the desk, the deputy scanned the area. "I don't see anything here. When did Sheriff Rhodes call you?" The deputy stared at me, something approaching suspicion flickered in her eyes.

"I was only told he insisted Ms. Carmichael pick up the items as soon as possible," I said. "And since she wasn't able to run down here at his request, I was sent in her place."

"The sheriff said the items were in the reception area?" She drummed her fingers on the counter.

I shrugged. "I'm not aware of how many details he gave Ms. Carmichael. All I know is he wanted her to pick them up and she believes there was a time limit to the request, which is why I'm here instead of completing my own work." I filled my voice with as much annoyance as possible. The deputy was less likely to think I was up to something when I acted like this was the last thing I wanted to do today.

The deputy leaned over and opened up a few desk drawers. "I don't see anything in here. Do you know how much stuff he was holding for her this time? A sweater. Books. Our receptionist should be back in a few moments."

"They do this a lot?" I asked.

The deputy rolled her eyes. "It's been a daily occurrence for the last week. Fighting one day, making up the next day. Usually Luna comes herself."

"Filming is in progress. From what I've overheard, I thought the rift between Luna and Rhodes was new," I said. "This sounds like it's been going for a while."

"It's what they've always done. Argue," the deputy said. "From what I've heard, been arguing or thick like thieves since high school. Do you know what items Luna sent you to pick up?"

"Just what was in her car. The car was totaled in an accident yesterday. The one where Marie died."

"It's likely in the evidence room. Let me call Deputy Paugh."

"Do you think there's any chance I could take some pictures of the car for Ms. Carmichael?"

The deputy's eyes narrowed.

"It was the one topic that really had her and Sheriff Rhodes arguing. He said no. She insisted. Needs them for insurance purposes."

"I'm not sure the car is still here. I'll ask Deputy Paugh about that as well." She picked up the phone at the desk and jabbed a couple of numbers. She eyed me for a long moment, then lowered her voice and turned away from me.

I eased away from the reception area and browsed the pictures on the wall. There were photos of the town throughout the years. It started as a small town and grew into a city that still held the charm of a farming town. On the opposite wall were pictures of the past sheriffs. Starting with the first sheriff, I walked down the row. I paused at the photo of the sheriff from seventy years ago, Hancock Rhodes. I leaned in closer and studied the features of the man. There was a resemblance between Hancock and Randolph Rhodes. Twenty-five years after Hancock, there was another Rhodes as a sheriff, that man having an even stronger resemblance to Randolph. It seemed being sheriff ran in the family.

"Thought you were the craft person," a low rumble said from behind me.

I turned and faced the disgruntled deputy from the other night. He held a box in his hands and, once again, eyed me suspiciously.

"Double duty today." I reached for the box.

He stepped back and turned his body sideways, blocking the box from me. "Luna's assistant is picking this up."

"Right now, that's me. There wasn't much of a pool of people to choose from and the replacement assistant doesn't drive. I'm it."

Reluctantly, he handed me the box.

Placing the box on the ground, I searched through it. Wallet. Sunglasses. Umbrella. My fingers felt papers. I pulled out the sheets. A script with notes about the scenes. I flipped through the clipped stack then put them back in the box. Sticking my hands in further, I parted the items carefully looking for the manuscript Marie was taking to the attorney. It wasn't in there. It was possible the papers got detached from each other.

A shadow loomed over me. "Something missing?" Deputy Paugh asked.

I closed the box up. "Just seeing if Marie's wallet was in here."

"Right." He stretched out the word.

I gathered the box into my arms and scurried out the door. The tone of the deputy's voice was clear on what he really meant—liar.

ELEVEN

Sitting in Ike's vehicle, with the air conditioner blasting, I completed a more thorough search of Luna and Marie's personal items. I pulled out the items and placed them in stacks. Papers. Clothing. A gold locket. Marie's necklace. Gently, I picked it up and cradled it in my palm. I smoothed out the delicate chain and spotted the broken clasp. Had it broken during the accident? I tucked it into my purse, afraid it would get lost amongst the other items in the box.

I gathered the papers onto my lap and flipped through them slowly: a script with Luna's scenes highlighted and notes scribbled on it, drycleaners receipt, and a sheet of paper with Katrina's and three TV actresses' names on it. Must be people Katrina was an assistant for.

I started the search from the beginning and cataloged everything in the box. No manuscript. What happened to it? Why would the sheriff think it was needed for the investigation? Unless there was something written in there he believed tied into Marie's death.

The beginning of a headache worked itself in my temples. I turned up the air-conditioning and directed the vents at my face, then leaned my head back against the seat and rubbed my temples, my phone on my lap. What I should be doing right now was picking up craft items for the job I was hired to do—making, or buying, handcrafting items for the movie. Not proving that Marie was murdered and who did it. That was the sheriff's job. I've given him all the information I knew and had to trust he was capable of doing his job.

But that didn't mean I wouldn't get the pictures of Marie's car for Luna.

In the rearview mirror, I saw a tow truck pull out from a side street beside the sheriff's office. On the bed of the truck was a silver BMW with the front smashed in. Luna's car. I was sure of it. Where were they taking it?

There was one way to find out. Follow it. I backed up and kept a few car lengths distance behind the truck. The driver was heading down the main road, in the opposite direction from where I entered. Looked like I was seeing the whole town today. We passed by some large brick office buildings.

The truck picked up speed as the part of town we entered was sparser. There were a few buildings but most looked run down and empty. It didn't take long before I spotted a large white building—Rhodes Collison and Detailing Center.

The sheriff owned the business where the car was being taken. The good feelings I had toward the sheriff dwindled. There was something odd about taking the car there rather than leaving it at the sheriff's department. Especially after Luna insisted on having pictures of the car and the sheriff refusing the request.

The driver parked in front of a tall, locked fence and got out, heading into the building. There were a few spots in front of the building and I quickly parked and jumped out, making sure I took my cell phone with me.

I ran over to the tow truck and stood by the driver's side, snapping a few upward angle photos of the front end. What I needed was close-ups and from the front. It was hard getting them when I was on the ground. I stepped sideways a few feet and peered through the glass door. The driver was leaning on the counter, drumming his hands on it. There was no one else in there.

I might have enough time. I braced my hands on the truck bed and jumped, straining my muscles and hooking my right leg onto the flatbed. After a few moments of wiggling, I finished pulling myself up.

Carefully, I walked along on the edge of the bed, holding my arms out to maintain my balance. I knew it was a bad idea to get my fingerprints on the car. Or at least any more of them. When I reached the front of the car, I leaned over and snapped a picture of the front. Too blurry. Holding my phone out further, I tried again.

"What are you doing?"

The deep rumble startled me. I windmilled my arms, gripping my phone tightly and trying not to drop it or tumble off. It was a bit of a ways down and explaining how I broke my leg was not something I wanted to add to my to-do list.

A hand pushed on my back, holding me up and nearly squashing me against the car.

"Getting photos for my boss." I reached back and grabbed hold of the arm, steadying myself. "Anyway, can I get a look inside the car. There's something in there she needs."

"Nope. Now, get down from there before you fall. I don't think my insurance covers that type of injury."

"But—"

"I can't have you up there. Want to get me fired?"

I shook my head and inched my way to the back of the truck. The guy kept a hand on my back, either to stop me from falling or making sure I didn't disobey and climb into the car. I sat on the edge of the bed then hopped off.

"Let the attendant know you left items in the car. Maybe he'll let you look."

The gate opened and the driver climbed into the cab of the tow truck and drove inside. The gate closed after him.

I peered through the chain links. There were tons of cars with various damages, some near destruction while others had some dented bumpers and smashed windows. I rose on my toes, clutching onto the fence and craning my neck, trying to find where he was putting Luna's car. Sunlight glinted off all the cars. I shielded my eyes with my hand and took another look.

"The auction isn't until next week," a voice said from behind me.

I spun around and saw a disgruntled looking man with long gray hair and an equally long beard glowering at me, though the laugh lines around his eyes and mouth softened his anger quite a bit. He tugged up the jeans slipping from his narrow hips. The oxford shirt with the name of the collision company stitched on the pocket was stained with grease and dirt. He shoved up the sleeves, crossed his arms, and intensified his stare, trying to be more intimidating.

"No pictures allowed. Don't want anyone getting an unfair advantage."

"I was taking photos of the car for my boss. It's her car. Needs them for insurance purposes."

"Right. For the car picked up from the sheriff's department that I was told not to let anyone near." His eyebrows rose and he tilted his head slightly to the side. "Just snuck on up there without asking. Maybe I should give him a call and let him know."

I gave him my most winning smile and discretely swiped away a trickle of sweat from my brow. With each minute, the sun was more intense. "Just need a few shots of the damage."

"He said it's evidence."

"I understand. I won't touch anything. She just wants some more photos of the front of the car where most of the damage is." I held out my cell phone. "Can you take them for me? I have to get these, or my boss won't be very happy with me. She can't get the paperwork rolling for a new car without the pictures."

"I'm not sure my boss will be pleased if I do that for you."

Who was his boss? Sheriff Rhodes might've kept the business in case the sheriff thing didn't work out for him. I doubted his employee would go against his boss who was also the sheriff. Darn it all, I should've told the guy I was the insurance adjuster and needed photos for the claim.

"He has to let us get the pictures." I worked on keeping the panic out of my voice. There was no way the guy wouldn't start thinking something was off by me being too desperate for photos of the car.

"Tell your boss to have the insurance adjuster come here."

"She wants me to take the photos. Doesn't trust the insurance adjuster will get the correct ones because they don't want to pay out for everything. She's not a very trusting soul."

"Yet, she sent you rather than come herself." The man grinned at me.

"That's because she picked me. She's not allowed to pick the adjuster herself. Just whoever the insurance company assigns." I let out a dramatic sigh. "She does not like relinquishing control or wasting her time. So, I'm here to satisfy her need for control and not wasting her time."

The man's face softened with sympathy and he held out his hand, palm up. "I know those types. I'll take the pictures for you. I can't get in trouble for letting anyone back there if you stay out here."

I unlocked my phone and handed it over. "Thanks. Can you also look for a stack of papers left in the car? She's working on a book and left her draft in there."

"You can wait inside the office. It's hot out here." He pointed to the office door then headed into the area marked service.

I stepped inside the office and basked in the cold air flowing around my body. Already, my arms were a little pink from standing outside in the sun. My left arm a little more so from the sun shining through the window when I was driving over. Stopping for sunscreen was going on today's list of errands.

In the corner, near the only desk in the area, was a water cooler. I got some ice-cold water, my eyes drifting over to the paperwork on the desk. The top sheet was for Luna's car. From the corner of my eye, I read the document. It was a form detailing the tow of the vehicle.

The name of the customer was Randolph Rhodes, rather than the sheriff department, and the tow pick up location was listed as the road where the department was at. No building number to say it had been at the department, just on the street.

The door opened. I diverted my attention to the water cooler, refilling the paper cup with water.

"What are you doing here?" The familiar voice startled me, and I almost dropped the cup. Paul. I turned and caught him eyeing me in a critical way.

I inched backwards. Paul had never looked at me that way before, as if I was doing something wrong...distrustful. It hurt. "Luna wanted pictures of the car damage and I came to get them since I was in Harmony."

He kept that unsettling gaze on me.

I wasn't liking this new-to-me Paul. I crossed my arms and tilted my chin up. After having lived with a critical man, I refused to stand by and allow any man to treat me like that. Especially one who claimed to be my friend and wanted more of a relationship with me. "Why are you here? You were talking with the coroner. Has an autopsy been done?"

"The information led me here."

His lack of response threw me off. What was he holding back from me and why? Was he not comfortable sharing the information here—or with me?

The worker walked back in. "Here's your phone. The lighting—" He stopped talking, staring at Paul for a long moment before shoving my phone toward me. "Is not very good back there. Took me a while to find your phone in the car you dropped off. Should be ready this afternoon."

I was a little envious of the tech's ability to switch truths on a moment's notice, and a little concerned about it. Did Paul know the tech was lying about the reason he had my phone? I was certain Paul was here for the same information. How to stop him? Or was it better for the employee to know something was up with what his boss was trying to do? I tapped on the screen of my phone. Without even looking at the pictures, I sent them to Paul. "Thanks for finding the phone for me. Have an appointment today and the address is on here. I'd be lost without it."

"No problem. Seems nowadays most people's lives are in their phone."

Where was Marie's work phone? Was it locked away in the sheriff's office as evidence or did the killer have it?

TWELVE

My phone rang as I got into my car and I glanced at the screen. It was Sharon Zimmerman, the crafter I was supposed to meet—a half an hour ago. Doing everything in my power not to look at the car photos, I answered the call.

"Merry and Bright Handcrafted Christmas. This is Merry speaking. How—"

"You're late," the woman snapped at me. "Do you want the items or not? I have better things to do than wait for you. I should've listened to my friends who said this was all a trick. Ms. Carmichael didn't hire me. I shouldn't be helping you."

I couldn't blame her for the attitude. I was late. I prided myself on my professionalism and I stood the woman up. Not being reliable, either on the selling or buying end, ruined a business's reputation. It wasn't just me at risk, it was Bright also. She didn't deserve it.

"I am so sorry. I definitely need the items and have brought cash to pay for them. I'll be there in about fifteen minutes. Had to stop at the sheriff's department for a quick errand for Ms. Carmichael."

"The sheriff's office?" The harsh tone of her voice softened into a questioning tone. An interested, questioning tone. Potential gossip. There was my way to forgiveness, offer up some information.

"He insisted she send someone by and pick up some items for her." I dropped the most innocent of statements that was attention grabbing enough but not really giving away anything.

"You could have texted me to say you'd be running late."

"I was told to stop as I was leaving this morning. It slipped my mind with how insistent she was that I pick it up now. Looks like I'm needed again. I promise I'll be there asap."

The woman hummed and hung up the phone. I bet she'd be on the phone to all her friends, telling them how Luna Carmichael was now having me waste her time. I just hoped she kept it to a private rant and not regal her tales of woe on the internet. The last thing I wanted was Luna finding out about my hints of gossip about her.

Paul strode out of the collision center, slipping his sunglasses on then paused for a moment and switched his gaze from his truck to the car I was sitting in. After a moment, he walked over and tapped on the passenger window and pointed at the lock. I hit the unlock button on the driver's side door and Paul opened the door and slid inside.

"I'm concerned Luna Carmichael has you involved in whatever Marie was doing." Paul stared straight ahead, jaw tense. "I don't want you getting hurt. The sheriff lied about the cause of death. She didn't die from the head injury and heat stroke. Or rather it might've been the cause but resulted from a car accident likely caused because of the heavy dose of a sleep aid in her system. Marie was killed. She wouldn't have even taken one, much less multiple ones, and then drove."

The cup. It was gone. Whoever poisoned Marie stole the cup because there was residue in it. They likely followed Marie and made sure she ran off the road near the baler, then lured her out of the car or carried her away, so it appeared she died from the trauma of the accident and heat.

"I bet her work phone is the answer. It's not with the items the sheriff returned." I pointed to the box of Luna's—and Marie's—items in the backseat. "The manuscript she was mailing to Luna's agent isn't in there either. From what I know, it was a tell-all autobiography."

Paul frowned. "The sheriff might have the phone. It's evidence. I'll go by and ask him about it. Let him know I heard about the sleep aid and Marie never took any. Maybe he'll share some details with me since I'm her family member."

"He wasn't buying the accident either but doesn't want anyone else knowing."

"Since none of us are buying this accident, I'll keep the box with me. Let whoever sent you for it know that Marie's cousin picked it up and has her personal effects. As far as anyone will know, you didn't look through it."

"Paul—"

He shook his head. "That's what you'll say."

"But—" I tried arguing with him again. Still didn't work.

"I'm not wavering on this, Merry. Someone killed Marie and I'd rather you're not involved in it."

"It's too late for that. I was the first one on the scene of Marie's accident. At least that's what the police report will say. The only one who knows differently—"

"Is the murderer," Paul cut in. He dropped his head against the seat rest.

"What if the killer had been after Luna and not Marie? Luna wanted pictures of the car and the sheriff didn't want her to have any. He might be trying to protect her. The mechanic said no one was allowed in the back and I talked him into snapping a few shots for me. Well, for insurance purposes. I'm thinking someone forced Marie off the road at that spot. Someone who knew the baler was there."

"The killer is local and knows that road really well. I'm sending the photos to Orville and get his take on the damage."

"I can always send them to him."

Paul shook his head. "It's better Orville doesn't think you're up to something. He'll call your children, and your son and daughter will come and drag you back to West Virginia. There's no way they'll want you involved in another murder."

I'd been involved in more murder investigations than my son and he had been on the police force for eighteen months. "Fine. But at least let me have the paper with Katrina's references on it. I can call them later and see what they say about her. I'll fill you in on what I learn."

"All right." Paul tipped the box toward me and I fished it out, placing the paper in my purse. "Whatever you're doing, please be careful. I have to meet with a crafter. The fire took out some of the craft items needed for a few scenes. I'm already behind."

Paul opened up the door taking the box with him. "You be careful also."

Fifteen minutes later than I had told the crafter, I finally arrived at my appointment. As I pulled into her driveway, a large dog jumped at the window, banging into it and baring its teeth. It appeared to be a cross between a German shepherd, poodle, and a Labrador. Slipping my phone into my back pocket, I cautiously approached the house, not wanting to set the dog off anymore. Had the woman left? I deserved it. Should I wait for her?

The dog barked, throwing itself against the window. I leaned toward the side and glanced in the window. No movement. I pulled out my phone from my pocket and debated texting the woman. If she needed to run an errand, I'd happily wait in my car for her to arrive. I didn't want my presence causing the enraged dog to hurt itself or break the window. Which it seemed capable of doing.

"Lay down you crazy beast," a woman's voice floated through the closed door. "Don't make me banish you."

Please banish the dog. I'd rather not meet the crazy beast.

"Go on now. I don't make idle threats." The door opened.

I fixed my most apologetic smile onto my face and stepped back a few feet, just in case the beast rushed out the door. "Hi Sharon, I'm Merry Winters. Again, I'm so sorry for being late."

"Come on in. My friend will be arriving soon. We have a thrifting outing planned." She motioned me in.

"I'm sorry my unexpected emergency errand has affected your plans. I know I hate running late and I feel so bad I'm causing that for you."

"Stuff happens." She motioned to a small room down the hallway. The beast was sitting at the far end of the hallway, gaze fixed on me. A low rumble echoed through the space. Sharon waggled her finger at the dog. "No scaring my guest. You're just upset it's not Lenny, she'll be here in a few."

The dog thumped its tail on the floor.

"The fabric elves are in here. I also have some Santas and Mrs. Claus plus other animals wearing winter gear."

I stepped inside her home office and was transported to a world of fabric beings. It was breathtaking. Instead of the stuffed animals and people sitting on shelves against a wall, the room was divided into motifs. There was a winter wonderland with a North Pole mural painted on the wall, another wall was divided into a forest and jungle, another wall was a city. The last wall had a castle mural with a rainbow and stars stretching from one side to the other, on those shelves were fairies, dragons, and elves.

"Your work is amazing." I touched a penguin wearing a Santa hat. It was sewed from the softest fleece. "I love this little guy."

"I have a few of him if you'd like to take them with you."

I did need more craft items and all of the fabric would fill up a booth. "They are planning on having a fabric-themed craft booth for the Christmas bazaar scene. How much for all of them?"

Her eyes widened. "Are you sure you want all of them? There's about three-thousand-dollars' worth of product.

"Yes." If the production decided they didn't have a use for the items, I'd take them back home and donate the items. Or, I'd leave them with the owner of the toy store in Carol Lake. She'd find a home for all the stuffies.

"That's a relief. I don't have the space to store them until Christmas. I made so many because I was certain I was being hired for the film and I wanted some done so I could enjoy the experience of being on the set of a Christmas film. Last week I called, and they told me they found a better fit." She struggled to maintain her cheerfulness while she told me the story.

Around the time I was told I was perfect for the job. I felt bad for Sharon. It had to hurt. No wonder Marie was upset about the way Luna handled it. She hadn't even called Sharon herself with the news, instead Sharon had called and asked. "I'm sorry."

"It is what it is," she said. "I just got my hopes up because Ms. Carmichael had sent her assistant to interview me and even insisted I refer to Ms. Carmichael as Luna."

Interviewed? I only sent pictures of my products and links to my Facebook page. "What type of questions did she ask?"

"About my family. If I was born and raised here. I told her I was adopted and wasn't sure where I was born, there were discrepancies in my record, but I had lived in Harmony since I was two. I thought they wanted a local person but..." She trailed off.

I knew the end of sentence—they hired me, a non-local crafter.

The dog ran out of the room barking and heading for the front door.

"Lenny must be here. I'll box everything up for you."

"I'll put these boxes in the car and come help with the rest." I stacked the two boxes then hoisted them onto my hip. They barely weighed anything, a positive of working with fabric and batting, easy to load and unload by yourself.

The dog jumped at the window, nails scratching at the pane as it barked. The dog was frantic. Who was out there? Standing a few paces behind the dog, I leaned to the right and peered out the window. The front passenger door of Ike's car was opened. A figure was hunched over.

I dropped the boxes and ran to the front door, yanking it open. "What are you—"

The slight figure yanked the collar of their oversized t-shirt over their head, holding it tight around the face and ran hunched over. I sprinted, casting my gaze toward the car to see the damage. My purse was on the ground amid the broken glass. Ugh. I had left it on the passenger seat out in the open. The dog bounded after the person, barking and snarling.

"Heel, Potter, heel." Sharon raced out of the house.

Marie's necklace. It was the only thing of value in my purse I couldn't replace, and I had a couple hundred dollars in cash left in there. In case Paul called, I took my phone with me. I couldn't think of anything else besides Marie's locket that held any value. There were some craft tools but those were easily replaceable. The person reached a white sedan and jumped in. I took out my cell phone and aimed it at the license plate as the person sped by, nearly hitting a navy truck. There was a piece of cardboard over the plate.

I froze. This wasn't a random car break-in. It was targeted. A shudder hit my body as I remembered the corn stalks rustling. Someone had followed me since I stopped at the scene of the accident. Slowly, I picked up the items, putting them back into my purse. The dog sat near me, whining and butting its head into my arm.

"Goodness, thieves are getting bolder every day. You shouldn't have left your purse on the front seat." Sharon rubbed the dog's head. "Such a good boy. Chased that bad man away."

A truck pulled up behind mine in the driveway. A young woman with bright pink hair slid out of the truck. Large, dark tinted sunglasses blocked her eyes from me. It was always easier to judge a person's attitude when their eyes were visible. "Did anyone get the license plate of that jerk? Sped right past me, almost sideswiping me."

Potter galloped across the driveway and the beast flung itself into the woman's arms. Large paws were on her shoulders and the dog licked her face over and over. She laughed and scratched the massive head.

"Went by too fast," I said, not wanting to admit the license plate was covered. No need scaring them as I knew I was the reason the person was there. I should tell Ike about the damage, or at least his insurance agent. I opened the passenger door then the glove compartment. Taking out a plastic envelope, I flipped through the documents inside. Insurance card. Registration. A business card. Vernon O'Neal, esquire.

What was going on? Why was a lawyer working as a security guard on the movie his ex-wife was starring in? And why did Ike have the man's business card in the glove compartment of his car?

"Now that's a way to greet a woman. How's my favorite boy?"

"I swear sometimes Potter likes you more than me," Sharon said.

"Of course, he does. I never take him to the vet." Lenny tipped her sunglasses to rest on top of her head and gently lowered the dog's paws from her shoulders. "Ready for a day of thrifting? I have some great upcycling ideas."

"Sure am, Lenny. Merry bought the rest of the Christmas stuffies, let me help her load them and sweep up the glass," Sharon said.

Lenny frowned. "I wouldn't sell her those. Not after how they treated you. Luna Carmichael turned you down."

Sharon blushed. "I couldn't make everything she needed."

"Neither could she." Lenny tilted her chin at me. "That's why she's here buying your fabulous creations, and yet Luna hired her. The woman could've hired a couple of local crafters, instead she brought in someone from out of state. Why? I'm sure she's not the only person who focuses on Christmas crafts."

I started to speak during the slight pause, but Lenny continued on with her rant.

"It's because Luna Carmichael enjoys giving people the run around and now this woman is doing it for her." Lenny's eyebrows quirked up as a challenging smile stretched her brightly colored lips. The red lipstick was too bright for the woman's skin tone but was a nice shade of Christmas red. Perfect for a Christmas in July outing. "Just be glad you're not wrapped up in that debacle of a movie. The chances of it being picked up is slim."

"What?" The word choked out of me. I was under the impression the movie was a done deal.

"Lenny's hobby is Christmas. There isn't anything about it she doesn't know. Or at least it seems that way." Sharon grinned at her friend.

"Some people are into sports, traveling, crafting. I'm into Christmas. I keep tabs on all the new Christmas movie releases.

Television and theater. I hadn't heard one word about *Dash Away All* until Sharon mentioned she was contacted by Luna Carmichael's assistant. The woman had seen some of her items on Etsy and was wondering if she was interested in working on the film as a crafter. There's nothing about it. Only name I know of is Luna Carmichael and that's because her name was used."

"There are a few details out there now about it," I said, keeping the facts I knew about the cast to myself. The heroine of the film was Anne Lindsey and until now she played secondary characters, and Garrison Tyler was behind the camera. *Dash Away All* was his first movie role. Luna Carmichael had taken on the role as the victim for this movie, a part she had never played before.

"There wasn't any six weeks ago when I looked."

"Maybe they were still waiting on contracts or wanted it a secret. What do you know about Edward Yale?" I asked. "He's directing the movie."

It seemed everyone tangled up with *Dash Away All* was holding something back. I still needed to find out what Anne had wanted to tell me the other night. While I was pretty knowledgeable about Christmas, I didn't keep up on the gossip. All I was interested in was the titles of the new upcoming movies and who was playing the key roles, not about who the actors and actresses really were who were playing those parts.

"He took a few years off from directing. I read in an interview he regretted never making time for family and was spending some time reestablishing relationships he let slip away."

"Then why did you talk me into doing the crafts for this film?" Sharon directed a frown at her friend. "I wasted my time making all of these Christmas-themed crafts. I could've made other items that would've sold better during the summer."

Lenny blushed and dipped her head. "Once they passed on you, I started researching the movie more. I wanted to know why they didn't pick a local crafter. Wasn't that what they had told you? They wanted someone local."

Why were Luna and Marie vetting the crafters anyway? Unless

that wasn't what the names on the list represented. Olivia was the chef. Katrina was an assistant. Sharon and I were crafters. Who was Desiree Young? Ike said that Marie and Luna were responsible for hiring the crafters. Why would she also choose Anne's assistant? But if they weren't crafters, why was Luna looking into them—me? The piece of paper with Katrina's names and the celebrities. Had Luna or Marie suspected something about the woman and called some of her former employers? There were two ways to find out: search the internet or contact the actresses myself.

"Thanks for your help." I held up the box of crafts and hurried for the door, without showing I was hurrying. I placed the large box on the floor of the front passenger side and searched my purse for the list. The list was gone. Why would the person steal that?

THIRTEEN

I parked in a space right in front of the only mechanic shop in Carol Lake. Outside, a young man was wiping down a steering wheel before closing the car door then cleaning off the handle. I got out of Ike's SUV and walked over, hoping it wouldn't take long to replace the window.

The young man smiled at me. "How can I help you, ma'am?"

"The passenger side window was busted out when someone tried stealing my purse." I tweaked the details just a bit for brevity.

"I'm so sorry." The young man looked shocked. "I've never heard of that happening here in Carol Lake. Did you report this to Chief Quinn?"

"No. It didn't happen here. I was in Harmony."

"Do you have a copy of the police report? If not, I can call the police station and get one. Your insurance will take of the damage." The guy smiled at me. "I should be able to have it replaced by this evening."

"I didn't report it. Nothing was taken. The person ran off when I came out of the house."

"Someone did this at your house?" The guy frowned. "I wouldn't want a thief lurking around my house. They might come back."

"I was picking up items from someone. I had to get back here as I'm behind on work." I was getting flustered. I hadn't expected so many questions from the mechanic. And truth be told, I was also feeling a little bad that I hadn't called the police. Hopefully whoever searched the car didn't show back up at Sharon's house. "I'll just pay for the damage in cash. It's a borrowed car so I'm not even sure who's insurance would pay for it. It might take weeks for the insurance companies to argue it out."

"Let me go inside and call around about the window. I'll let you know how long it'll take." He walked inside and picked up a phone on the desk.

I leaned against the car and checked the Merry & Bright Handcrafted page on Etsy. Bright had put the shop on vacation mode. Probably a good thing while she was helping me round up some more craft items. Between my job here and her genealogy project, there wasn't much time for creating orders, and it wasn't like this was a busy time of the year for our business.

"All set." The guy smiled at me and handed me a clipboard with a drop off form. "I'll have the new window in before we close up tonight. You can either pick it up or we offer a drop off service."

I quickly filled out all the information. "Drop off will be great. I'm staying in the cast and crew area for the movie."

"I'll just give you a call when I'm on my way over it. This way I'll know where to meet you." He ripped off a portion of the sheet with a written estimate for the repair work.

"Great. I can pay now."

"Let's wait until we know the actual cost. You can pay either tonight or stop by tomorrow. Folks in this area are a trusting bunch." He smiled at me.

"Thanks." Much different attitude then people working with the movie.

I headed for the bridge. Might make a stop at the bakery before heading back. With the day I was having, a sweet treat was well deserved. As I walked past the police station, I glanced through the front window. Chief Quinn was sitting on the edge of a desk and talking on the phone. She flipped through some papers on the desk, stopping abruptly and looking up. She must've sensed someone staring.

She hung up the phone and crooked her index finger, gesturing for me to come inside. The expression on her face was not a happy one. Had I done something?

Taking a deep breath, I squared my shoulders and walked inside, clutching my phone in my hand. "Good morning or almost afternoon, Chief, what can I do for you?"

Quinn settled herself into a rolling chair. "Is there a reason you were over in Harmony—"

"Picking up crafting items for the production."

"At Rhodes Collision Center. Was that why you were poking around? Looking for crafts."

"I wasn't poking around."

"Climbing up on a tow truck is normal behavior?"

Who ratted me out? "No. Luna wanted pictures of her damaged car—"

"So, you just took it upon yourself to get them. Contaminating evidence in the process."

My face flamed. I hadn't thought about that. "I'm sorry. It was important Luna had those pictures."

"Right." Quinn sat up and picked up a sheet of paper from the desk and read it. "Only for Luna. Has nothing to do with you picking up a secondary career as a volunteer police officer."

I gaped at her.

"In case things are different in your town, I want to explain that here in Carol Lake we don't have or use volunteer police officers. Fire personnel, yes. Officers, no. Am I making myself clear?"

"I don't think I'm in law enforcement or acting like it, I just want justice for Marie."

I brought the photos up on my phone and slid it to her across the desk and told her everything that happened that morning, from stopping at the scene, my misgivings about the coincidence of the timing of Marie driving off the road, what Paul discovered, the items in the box the deputy gave me, the sheriff having Luna's car towed to his mechanic shop, and the plans to scrap it.

Instead of the concerned interest I expected, Quinn gripped the sides of the desk and stood, her fury barely contained. "You're not acting like law enforcement? Almost everything you've done proves you're doing that. Examining the scene of the crime. Questioning people. Discovering what you think is evidence and taking it rather than returning it."

"The sheriff called Luna to pick up her items that were in the car," I said. "I was doing her a favor because Katrina doesn't drive and asked me to run her errand while she worked on the crafts. Since I was meeting a crafter in Harmony, it made sense that I'd stop and collect the items rather than both of us leave and go into town."

"I'd like you to bring the box and its items here. Since you think it's evidence in Marie's death, I'll keep it here."

I cringed. "I don't have it. Paul does."

"Paul?" Her eyes narrowed.

Oops. I forgot about mentioning him in my retelling of the day's events. "Marie's cousin. He's a friend of mine and how I heard about the job with the production company. He's the one who talked with the doctor at the ER and the coroner and found out about the sleep aid."

"There are two of you going around acting like law enforcement? I don't know how things work in West Virginia, but that's not how it's done in Indiana."

"That's not what we're doing." I had a feeling my words, contrary to my actions, weren't convincing her.

"What you and your friend are doing is dangerous. Police are trained to handle these types of matters. You aren't. Someone broke into the car you were driving. There was a reason for that. It's better you leave the police work to the police."

"I don't have a personal car here, so I borrowed Ike's and after the window was broken, I looked in his glove box for his insurance information and found a business card of Vernon's in there. Why is Vernon working as a security guard? He's an attorney."

"Again, with a question. But I'll answer it. Hopefully, it'll make you rethink chasing down what you think are leads in a murder investigation." Her smile was tight with little humor in it.

I remained quiet, knowing the chief would explain, and probably sooner, with no additional input from me.

"My cousin was suspended."

"For what?"

Her lips twitched and a light sparkled in her eyes for a moment. "For punching Sheriff Rhodes. During court."

When I returned to the crew quarters area of the filming lot, it was practically a ghost town, even the food pavilion area was empty. I headed into my RV and frowned as I touched the door handle. It was quiet. Too quiet. I'd expected to hear the Cricut going or Katrina arguing with Ebenezer about something. The little guy had a way of bringing that out in people. He was just too nosy for his own good. A characteristic my daughter and son would say my furry companion shared with me. There was also the option that Katrina was wondering what I was up to and was digging through my stuff. She had mentioned Anne was rummaging around in my personal space in the RV, but Katrina might have said that to cover up her own actions.

There was one thing my sleuthing taught me: whatever information people shared, it was usually for their best interest, not someone else's, and Katrina supplied the information offhandedly.

Slowly, I eased the door open and slipped inside. My heart rate accelerated. Where was Ebenezer? He had super hearing when it came to a door opening. Escape attempts were his major exercise routine and quite the hobby for him. This would be the first time I recall him not trying to run out a door. Unless he was locked up or not here.

The silence in the RV was ominous. There was no one in the main area of the RV. The Cricut was off and there wasn't one completed craft project. Everything was just as I had left it. Clean. Not one thing out of place. No scraps of vinyl or backing sheet in the garbage. I turned my head to the left. The bedroom and bathroom doors were shut.

Where was Katrina? Had she taken Ebenezer? Anger and fear curled in me. Stay calm. Don't think horrible things. Maybe she was in the bathroom. She could've put Ebenezer in the bedroom. I had trouble crafting with Ebenezer as he either wanted my undivided attention or to play with whatever I was crafting.

I knocked on the bathroom door. "Katrina?"

There was no answer. I searched the RV for a note, anything to tell me where Katrina or Ebenezer had gone. I peeked out the bedroom window. The golf cart was gone. Maybe Ebenezer was needed for a scene and she took him. A license wasn't required to drive a golf cart, though I wasn't sure how I felt about Katrina driving around the set with my buddy. But it explained their disappearance in a way that didn't require me to go on the hunt or call the police. Not that the police would come charging over because a guinea pig disappeared.

There was a tap on the door. I peered out the small window. Edward. Shock ran though me. Why was the director on my doorstep? With a shaking hand, I opened the door and stepped aside for him to enter. "How can I help you?"

Edward made himself at home on the couch. "It's time for a chat."

The anger spiking in his voice made me think just the opposite. "I don't have time now. Ebenezer is missing.

"You'll make time. Ebenezer was needed at the house and Katrina took him over."

That explained, quite rationally, the disappearance of my pet. Katrina must've won him over or bribed Ebenezer into the carrier. But I still wasn't comfortable with talking with the director. "I should still go. The critter can get into quite a bit of mischief."

"Kind of like his owner." Edward crossed his leg, one foot on top of his knee, and leaned back into the couch. "We can make this a private conversation, or I can invite your new friend, the police chief, to join us. She might be interested in what I've learned about you."

"Why does that sound like a threat?"

He smiled at me. A similar one to the Grinch when he thought of his brilliant plan of ruining Christmas for the Whos. "Have no idea. What could there be troubling about you or your past that makes my comment a threat?"

I had no idea, but I was certain the words were a threat. Why else would he bring it up after I tried ending this chat session?

"You've been spending a lot of time off the set, considering all the crafts needed for the scenes."

I dipped my head. Okay, I was spending time doing something other than crafting, but some of it was movie business. "It was hard picking up items for Luna from the sheriff's office and crafting. I figured it was best doing what Luna wanted."

"That's always the best option. But why did she ask you?"

Drat. I walked into confessing Katrina's secret all by myself. Thought, I couldn't let him think I was unreliable. "Katrina asked me. She doesn't know how to drive."

His brows drew down and he hummed. "That's interesting as I'm sure I saw her driving onto the set a few days ago. Someone's lying. I wonder who."

Why would Katrina lie about that? Maybe it wasn't either of us who were lying. What was the director up to?

"Well, it's not my concern. Luna can deal with her assistant how she sees fit. My only concern is your time isn't tied up doing Luna's assistant's job. Or the sheriff's. I've heard you've been asking a lot of questions and making the cast and crew a little uncomfortable."

I held back a frown. No one had seemed upset about me talking with them. Except for Katrina. I didn't see her running to the director and telling him. Unless Vernon talked with the director to explain why the police chief showed up. He didn't want the blame, so he put the target on me. Since the director knew I was asking questions, might as well ask him a few.

"Why was Luna's ex-husband, a lawyer, hired as a security guard? From what I've heard, he has quite the temper." And you don't really get along with him.

"My hiring decisions are none of your concern, but I'll go ahead and answer as long as you reciprocate. A question for a question. An answer for an answer."

Even as apprehension danced through me, I nodded. It was fair.

"I hired Vernon to keep an eye on Ms. Carmichael. He's one of the few people she tolerates hanging around her house even with the impending divorce. She's known him for decades and trusts him. Since he was taking a short sabbatical from his business—"

"A forced one after hitting the sheriff," I cut in.

"The man has a temper and is protective of Ms. Carmichael. Plus, he'd never believe anything negative about her."

"Why is she divorcing Vernon if she trusts him and wants him around?"

"Luna has her reasons for wanting a cease in the relationship and starting one with Rhodes."

"And now she doesn't want Rhodes anymore."

"It appears that way doesn't it." Edward lowered his leg and leaned forward, bracing his hands on his knees. "The count so far is three questions from you, three answers from me and none in reverse. It's my turn. Who's the man you brought onto my closed set?

"Paul. He's a friend of mine and Marie's cousin. Luna knew. I had told her."

Surprise flashed across his face. "You knew Marie."

"Not really. I know her cousin and it was his recommendation that got me the job."

"What does Marie's cousin do for a living?"

This time, I didn't hold back my frown. "Why are you asking that?"

"I answered your questions without any argument."

"I didn't ask any personal ones."

"I'm sure Luna would find the questions about her quite personal. Why are you so interested in her?" Edward asked.

Should I trust the director with the truth or make up an

excuse?

"Part of my responsibility is discerning if you're friend or foe," Edward said. "Right now, I'm leaning toward foe."

"Marie told me before she died that Luna had received threatening letters."

"Now you're trying to protect Luna. Why?"

"It's more that I think Marie was killed by whoever threatened Luna. It wasn't a car accident."

"You think it's tied into the threats Luna received."

"Yes. Why else would someone kill Marie. She either figured out who it was—"

"Or she discovered the answer." He scrubbed his hands over his face.

"What answer?"

Edward sat up, dropping his head back against the headrest. "I might as well tell you as you're likely tied into this. It's about an anonymous message I received about an exposé coming out regarding Luna giving away an infant."

"Giving away?" I stared at him. "Why would anyone even think it's true? I've never heard anything about Luna giving a child up for adoption."

"It's true. The problem is it's not as altruistic as placing a child for adoption. More along the lines of abandoning a baby girl about forty-six years ago."

For a moment, the world tilted as my head felt fuzzy, the image of my name on Marie's list running through my mind over and over again. No. No. It couldn't be. That wasn't what the list was. Right?

"Is everything okay?" Edward's voice broke through the voice in my head screaming not possible.

I nodded. "Did you share the letter with anyone?"

"Luna, of course. She shared it with Marie who I'm sure you know by now wasn't just an assistant." Edward pulled a folded piece of paper from his shirt pocket. He unfolded it and handed it to me.

"Are you sure?" I pressed back a frown. Why was he sharing it with me?

He nodded. "You deserve to know."

Trying to hide my confusion, I read the letter. It was handwritten and a mix of print and cursive. Everything in the letter was vague except for the fact that the baby was thrown away. No indication of where the baby was found, the age, or the time frame. Whoever wrote it only knew that one detail. Which sadly was true. "Has the sheriff or police chief seen this?"

"Luna prefers keeping this matter quiet as possible considering there's no proof of what happened to the newborn once Luna left the child." Edward held out his hand and I reluctantly returned the letter.

All the information was running through my brain and my stomach roiled. "The child might've died."

"It's one of the sad possibilities. Luna said the newborn was left in a safe place in a town they were traveling through."

A safe place. Church steps? "How old was Luna when the baby was born?" My parents hadn't ever learned anything about the woman—or girl—who had left me.

"She would've been seventeen."

A scared teenager. "It's never been easy being a teenage mother and I'm sure it was harder back then. People won't judge her harshly because of it. I wouldn't." My last statement was barely above a whisper. I swallowed hard. I meant it. I would forgive her.

"People will feel compassion toward a distraught, confused teenager dumping a baby but not a sixty-three-year-old woman who has lived a pampered, privileged life and until recently had never told the father. Especially if the abandoned child had a troubled one. Or died."

My heart hammered. I rested a hand on my chest, hoping it calmed down the beat. I couldn't fathom that possibility. "I'd think Marie wouldn't have had a hard time discovering that. It would've been in the news."

"That's the hope I've held onto." He clasped my hands and

gazed into my eyes. Brown eyes. Similar to my eye color.

I swallowed and gently pulled back, scared of the thoughts swirling through my head. This wasn't something I had ever contemplated for very long. I was happy with my life. My parents. Never before had I yearned for more than them. More family than my parents and children. But now...I couldn't go down that path. It felt disloyal to my mom who was still alive, even if she didn't remember me much anymore.

"Are you the baby's father?" I asked.

"It's possible."

Luna and Marie weren't interviewing for the crafter—they were searching for Luna's daughter.

"And me?"

He smiled and blinked back some tears. "It's possible."

Edward left. I collapsed on the couch, mind whirling with too much information. Marie's death. Luna's secret. Name's on a list. My name on the list. Possibly being Luna's daughter. Edward's daughter.

There had to be a way to find out. I knew my mom didn't have any more details about my birth besides what she had told and was in the newspaper articles. Bright. Over the last few months, she'd become a bit of an expert on genealogy or at least finding out information. She was a member of quite a few genealogy forms and had subscription services.

She'd help me. I grabbed my phone and with shaking fingers quickly typed out a message and hit send before I chickened out.

I think Luna Carmichael is my birth mom.

While I waited for a response, I distracted myself by reading the script that was dropped off earlier. Fortunately, the script I had was marked with the days the scenes were being filmed and I checked it against the list of changes the leadman handed me. How in the world were the actors and actresses able to pull off their scenes when nothing happened in order? The reveal of the murder was happening today before a late dinner break and the murder wasn't happening until tomorrow evening.

I scanned the script for the roles needed for the evening scene. Pretty much everyone was required at the house. Ebenezer was also in a scene filmed this afternoon. I wondered how Luna's private chef felt about an animal in her kitchen. She sure didn't like people, and I had a hard time believing she was okay with a guinea pig running around. Though, he'd have the time of his life.

At least I knew where Ebenezer was and chances were when Katrina took Ebenezer over, Luna wanted her assistant back and was now wondering where her items the sheriff had were at. My eyes were drawn to the words, "I killed her," on the page. I found the spot in the script where the murderer and the heroine started their showdown.

A few lines down and the killer confirmed the heroine's suspicions about his evil doings. The man killed the people who believed were a threat to his family. A somewhat noble reason, but the killer labeled everyone a threat to his family. *You should've left it as an accident. Everyone knew that woman was an inattentive driver.*

My breath caught in my throat. One of the victims in the movie died in a car accident. A staged car accident. Like Marie. Jumping up from the couch, I retrieved my phone and snapped a picture of the line, texting it to Paul before I thought too much about it. Was someone in the movie using the script to commit crimes?

Pacing around the room, I speed-read the script searching for a fire. There it was. At night. A shed that was filled with property taken from the killer's second victim's house. The description for the items was photos and memorabilia of Luna's character's children. The second husband had been trying to erase them from his wife's life.

What about the pet in the script? Had it escaped? Apparently, the cat in the film disappeared and reappeared randomly. It wasn't until toward the end of the movie that the heroine discovered the animal was sneaking in and out of the house through an old laundry chute in the bedroom hidden behind a dresser in the closet.

My phone rang.

"That line was in the script?" Paul asked.

"Yes. There's also a lost cat and a shed fire. The murderer, the second ex-husband of the victim, was trying to wipe out proof of others in his wife's life by destroying photos and other family documents."

"You're thinking the movie and Marie's murder are tied together."

"As far-fetched as it sounds, yes. I think someone is using the script as a blueprint for the real crimes."

"Are there any other deaths in the movie?"

My stomach tightened. "Yes, Luna's character. The scene where she dies is being filmed tonight."

"How?"

"I don't know yet, but I'll read the script and know before then."

"I'm heading back. Don't go anywhere until I arrive. We'll talk to her together."

"Ebenezer is at the main house. I'm going to collect him."

"Merry—"

"There's a whole crew over there. I'll be fine. Besides, no one knows we're connecting Marie's death with the one in the movie."

After I hung up, I realized I hadn't shared with him about the possible motive for Marie's death. I wasn't quite ready to share that my possible birth parents had arranged a "meeting" between us.

FOURTEEN

The sky had darkened, and the wind whipped around. There was a storm brewing and I wanted to get back before the sky unleashed. Pressing the accelerator to the floor, I forced out every inch of get-up-and-go the golf cart possessed, and it wasn't much. Hopefully, there was enough time for a quick search of Marie's room before the rain delayed any filming and I was kicked out of the house.

I parked the golf cart then ran into the house, stepping into a scene of chaos. Men and women rushed from one end of Luna's house to the other. Everyone was moving at top speed, either carrying something or adjusting a light here, a rug there. There were lights set up all around the living room and just past the spiral staircase, railing decorated with lighted garland.

"To the left. No, too far. Not enough."

"Can you give us a hand?" A security guard stood at the top of the stairs, fighting with plastic sprigs of berries. "The Christmas party scene was moved from tomorrow to tonight."

"Sure." Dread filled me. The party scene was when Luna's character died. If Paul and I were right, Luna was in danger. There wasn't enough time to find out who killed Marie and was targeting Luna. We had to protect her. "Let me just send a quick message. Let my assistant know what I'm doing."

After I was done with the decorating, I'd snoop around and find out more about tonight's scene. With my top half over the banister, I added berries on the banister while the guard ensured I didn't topple over and handed me the items. For whatever reason, the set people wanted the berries tied around the wooden plats of the railing not just on the top rail.

"How did you get roped into this?" I asked the security guard. I wasn't the only one leaning over with their derriere almost pointed at the ceiling. There were also three extras being directed how to make the garland camera ready.

"What Luna—"

"Wants she gets." I finished the statement for him. My arms ached. If I'd had known I'd be halfway up the stairs, leaning over ready to fall headfirst over the rail, I wouldn't have jumped at the chance to offer my Christmas decorating skills.

Had Luna asked for the change in filming the scenes? I doubted Edward changed it without any input from her. She had a lot of power among the film crew and the community. Anger and something more sinister twisted inside me. The last woman I knew who commanded so much devotion was blackmailing people.

"There's not much security needed. Not that it was ever needed but..." He flashed a grin. "It's easy work and the pay's great. I get to spend all day inside an air-conditioned house."

"You only work the dayshift."

"There's only dayshift."

I frowned. Why had Luna wanted security during the day and not at night? Nighttime seemed the more appropriate time for security. There weren't as many people wandering around, and it was easier to commit mayhem and crimes at night than during the day. *Was that why?* Was Luna responsible for the antics happening at night? The fire. The cat escaping.

Marie's accident. Dizziness swept through me. I grabbed the railing, pushing myself up. Having all the blood rushing to my head wasn't a good thing. I needed to think properly. There was something important I was forgetting. Vernon. His job.

"Are all the security personnel taking a leave of absence from their jobs to work on the movie. This job can't last for long. What is it? Two weeks?"

"A month," the guy said. "A week before the crew arrived and then a week after. My family owns a farm and the money I'm making here will help tide us over while my wife is on maternity leave."

"And the others?" I asked.

The friendliness slipped from his face. His brows and mouth drew down. I was pushing it.

"I'm nosy." I pushed out the first excuse, and very much a truth. "I like knowing what I'm getting myself into and this has turned into a lot more than making crafts."

The man's face softened. "I guess this is overwhelming. I can promise you, Carol Lake is usually quiet. It's why Ms. Carmichael moved here."

"Why doesn't anyone call her Mrs. O'Neal?"

"Because she's her own woman and has never taken the last name of a man." The guard said almost like he was reciting something he heard over and over.

With as quickly as she married and divorced, there wasn't much time for a name change. I never officially changed my name from Winters to my deceased ex-husband's name. Of course, we'd only been married a few weeks before I knew I made a terrible mistake. The best thing about the marriage was gaining a stepdaughter.

"At least she still gets along with one of her exes. Nice of her to hire Vernon as a guard. Kind of an unusual part-time job for an attorney."

"How do you know that?"

"People talk," I said, hating myself a little for the lie.

"Don't let Ms. Carmichael hear you. One thing she doesn't abide by is gossip about her past."

There was a screech from down the hall. An outraged Ebenezer. "I should take care of that. That's my pet." I rushed off.

There were three doors on each side on the right-hand side of the hallway and just as many to the left. The house was like a mini mansion. A mansion in rural Indiana.

I stood in the hallway, listening for the sounds of my angry pet. He was likely contained in a room while he wasn't needed and no longer pleased with his accommodations. There was a tap against the bottom of a door on the right-hand side of the hallway. Ebenezer. Squatting down, I opened the door and snagged the little guy before he raced out and created havoc.

A breeze drifted across my skin. I stepped inside. It was a nice sized bedroom with a twin-sized bed, dresser, and a desk. The curtains behind the desk rustled and a small slip of paper danced across the top and fell to the floor. Other papers littered the floor. Christmas lights were hung on the window and a four-foot Christmas tree tucked in the corner was knocked over. Small stuffed beings were on the floor, some under the branches of the tree. In the corner was Ebenezer's carrier, the top unzipped enough for the critter to squeeze through. In the distance, there were lines of white coming from the sky. The rain would soak everything. Including me and Ebenezer if we didn't leave soon.

First, there was cleaning up the mess he made. I turned Ebenezer around, so we were face-to-face and fixed a stern-mom gaze on him. "What did you do?"

He wiggled his nose at me. Tucking him against my side in a football hold, I stepped into the room and shut the door, surveying the mess caused by the open window and Ebenezer.

"Stay out of trouble while I clean this mess." I placed him on the ground and started cleaning. I hoped whatever scene was being filmed in the bedroom was complete because the place was a disaster. The comforter was shoved onto one corner of the bed, and the pillows had been slung onto the floor.

I shut the window before anymore of the papers fell onto the floor and gathered the ones near the desk, placing them back on top in a neat pile. There was a crinkling sound from the corner of the room, near a mini fridge. Ebenezer was gleefully munching away on a piece of paper. Ugh. Not even one minute on the floor and more destruction.

I pulled the small slip of paper from his mouth. The word "Will" was now in my hand. "What did you eat?" I waved the tiny piece of paper at him.

Or at least chewed to bits as shredded paper was all around the room. It looked like it had snowed in the room and it wasn't like that was meant as part of the scene. This wasn't the type of movie where snowing indoors was possible.

"You sure were busy." At least it was only paper. I could reprint everything for them. "You're lucky if you're not fired from your first acting job."

Ebenezer whistled and plopped over, glaring at me with his dark eyes. A guinea pig temper tantrum.

"Paper isn't on the food pyramid." I stood, rescuing the other papers from my pet's teeth. At least Ebenezer left some of them alone.

Quickly, I flipped through the other documents. Half of them were related to movie-victim Luna and the other to real Luna. I sorted the papers into two piles, movie and personal, and stopped halfway through. Maybe it wasn't a good idea for me to do this. These were Luna's personal papers. Why were they in a spare bedroom? My gaze caught a name on one of the documents. It was the employment contract between Marie, Second Chance Private Investigations, and Luna. We were right, Luna hadn't hire Marie as a personal assistance. Was this Marie's room? Why the Christmas décor?

I flipped my gaze to the window. The open window. Dread crawled across me. Had someone snuck out the window? What had they been looking for? Had they heard me and fled?

Carefully, I tugged out the slip I placed in my pocket and smoothed it out. *Will I.* I smoothed out the jagged edges. *By Lu.* Was this the coversheet for Luna's manuscript? Had Marie accidentally left it behind? Had the person who broke into Ike's SUV been searching for it?

The rest of it had to be around here somewhere. There was no way Ebenezer ate a whole manuscript. I walked over to Ebenezer and placed him inside his carrier. "Can't have you eating anything else."

I knelt on the floor and looked around for more pages. None. I hadn't missed anything. But where was the sheet that the torn and nibbled scrap came from? Or did Marie only have the cover sheet in her room?

Who had stolen the rest of the document? I approached the window and peered out. Right outside the window was a small roof, a sliver of patch over a portion of the porch, I stared at the dry ground below. Wide enough for someone to stand on to get into or out of the room. The drop to the ground was about twelve foot. Survivable. But with all the cast and crew dashing around, decorating the outside for tonight's filming, no one could sneak out.

Of course, with everyone decorating, someone could use it as an excuse for why they were climbing or jumping off the roof. I studied all the people on the ground. I recognized Ike, Chef Olivia, and Vernon. Ike and the chef were in an intense conversation, both gestured wildly at a delivery truck parked on the backyard near the kitchen door. Their loud voices carried up to me. The sky had turned an even more ominous shade of gray.

"Ms. Carmichael will lose her mind. Her garden is being destroyed." Ike pointed at the boxy truck. A few feet away, the sheriff's car was parked in the shade of a tree.

"He had to park somewhere." Olivia planted her hands on her hips. "We have to be close to the house, the rain is coming."

Vernon stood nearby, peering into the truck and ignoring the brewing battle in front of him. Either he knew the enraged man and woman wouldn't come to blows or he didn't care. He was more interested in what the people in the truck were delivering.

Olivia continued her rant. "You're responsible for this. I had no choice but ordering from a local company."

"I didn't move the scene up. Edward did."

"That's not what my assistant told me. You handed him the changes." Olivia crossed her arms. "I believe him over you."

"I thought Ms. Carmichael didn't eat outside food."

"She's not. It's the props for the cast and crew during the scene. Anything left they can take. She won't touch what I haven't made."

Vernon climbed up the ramp and inspected the trays. A man in a green chef's coat headed down the ramp.

"The food is fine." Ike said, voice filled with exasperation either for Olivia or the security guard who seemed more interested in the food delivery than in guarding the premises. "Your assignment is stopping unauthorized vehicles from entering. Like this truck. Not inspecting them once arrived."

"Just following orders," Vernon said. A horn blared and a siren blipped on and off as Vernon started down the ramp. He lost his balance and knocked into the guy pushing the cart.

The cart slipped from his grasp and rolled down the ramp, hitting the lip at the bottom and tipping over. The metal cart clanged against the small walking path and food scattered everywhere.

Olivia screamed, an anguished sound, and fell to her knees. Rain splattered the ground and she remained kneeling.

"Sorry about that." Vernon righted the cart and picked up some items and placed them on the cart. The poor guy from the delivery service gaped at the mess before him.

"Those were for tonight," Olivia raged at the darkened sky, appearing like she was avoiding looking at Vernon so she didn't harm the man. "There's not enough time to replace them. Where will I find more appetizers for tonight's scene? I only have three hours."

I felt for the chef. Why the last-minute change when it put the whole production into pandemonium? The original scene for today was the reveal scene, and it was in a building. Unless the shooting was rearranged because part of that scene was outside, and the storm was worsening.

"I'll fix this," Vernon said. "I can get chips and dips from the grocery store."

"Chips and dip. Chips and dip." Olivia sprang to her feet, hands fisted as she stalked toward him.

Ike jumped in front, blocking the woman from throttling the man.

I backed away from the window and continued my search. In the distance, a bolt of lightning arced from the sky. I found it unusual there wasn't a dresser in the room. Though, there was the room in the script where the dresser was in the closet and hiding a laundry chute. I opened the doors and on the right-hand side was Marie's hanging items and the left was her dresser.

A twinkle of light on the floor caught my attention. I squatted down and froze, hand reaching for the object hidden half behind the dresser. It was a stainless steel cup. Reaching over, I tugged one of the dresser drawers open and pulled out an article of clothing. I used the t-shirt to ease out the cup and turned it over, revealing the design. It was Marie's cup.

My hand shook. How did it get here?

Thunder rumbled and Ebenezer let out a shriek. I turned toward him, and the bedroom door opened. In a moment of panic, I flattened myself to the floor and scurried under the bed, the cup still in my hand. Two sneakered feet tiptoed into the room then eased the door close. Ebenezer squealed.

"Shut up," a woman's voice harshly whispered.

A sharp whistle filled the room. Ebenezer decided to up the noise factor.

"You know I can free you too," once again the voice was harsh.

I fisted my hands.

The papers on the desk rustled. I took a risk and wiggled forward, stretching out enough to peek out. The woman leaning over the desk and pawing through the papers had long blonde hair. A page fluttered to the floor and landed on the carpet near the bed. I scuttled backward, holding my breath. Fingers grazed the carpet and picked it up. A sharp gasp filled the room followed by a crumbling sound.

Shirts and jeans were thrown onto the floor followed by socks and shorts. Whoever was rifling through Marie's belongings was frantic. Those items belonged to Marie. Paul's cousin. Anger churned through me. I no longer cared if I was caught. It had to stop.

I crawled from underneath with the t-shirt-wrapped cup still in my hand. I pushed myself to my feet, leaving the bundle on the ground, and prepared to knock the woman down. I'd use any means necessary to stop her from destroying any of Marie's items. "How dare you!"

The woman gasped and spun around, her hands clutching a slim binder. Katrina.

"How did you—I didn't hear—" Her gaze flew to the door then returned to me.

"Put that down." I pointed at the binder. "Carefully." I added, fearing she'd toss it at my head.

Lightning flashed along the sky, followed closely by a clap of thunder. Katrina dropped the binder to the ground. Using my foot, I brought it toward me, keeping an eye on Katrina in case she decided it was a good time for a quick attack and escape.

"Why are you searching Marie's room?" I asked.

The woman's eyes narrowed, and she crossed her arms, acting the aggrieved party. "Why are you in here? You don't belong in this house."

"And you do?" I snapped. Whenever I was feeling I was being backed against a proverbial wall, I either was angry or stuttering nervous. Right now, I rode on the anger rolling through me.

"I'm Luna's assistant. I live here. Just like her other assistant did. This will be my room." There was a ton of anger in her voice when she mentioned Marie, even though she refused to use her name.

"Did Luna offer you this room, if so, you're clearing it out rather haphazardly. Marie's family will want her belongings. You're damaging her items by throwing them all over the place."

Katrina blushed a deep red. I wasn't sure if it was from shame or embarrassment, though I hoped it was the former. She dipped her head, staring at the binder still under my foot, and her blonde hair curtained her face. "People are pretending they're me. I was hoping to find out who."

"People are pretending they're you?" I leaned down, eyes on

her, and picked up the binder. Was she accusing Marie of stealing her identity? Why would Marie want to be Katrina? "Did you think Marie was stealing your identity?"

"Yes." Katrina eyed the binder.

She thought Marie was an identity thief. Why? Had she killed Marie? "Why would she want to be you? From what I know, Marie had a great life."

"She didn't want to be me. She was telling Luna I wasn't me." She snagged the hem of the t-shirt and lifted it. The cup rolled out. There was a strange glint in the woman's eyes. "What were you planning on doing with this?"

The "crafter" list. Was it a list of women who were possibilities of being Luna's daughter? I backed up and gripped the binder to wield it as a weapon.

The door slammed against the wall, an accompaniment to another round of lightning and thunder. Katrina let out a yelp and jumped. I edged backwards, still holding onto my makeshift protection. Rain beat against the closed window and raindrops splattered onto the desk from the open one. The wind whipped into the room.

A furious Luna stood in the doorway. "What are you doing in here?"

All of the scary mannerisms and confidence left Katrina in that moment. Her hands shook and she sent a pleading look in my direction, almost like she was begging me to save her. I didn't know what from. Katrina pointed a shaky finger at Ebenezer. "Getting the pet for you. Ike said he was needed for the next scene."

"This room was locked. No one was permitted in here. You knew that." Luna's eyes narrowed.

"She was in here." Katrina nodded at me.

Luna's gaze switched over to me for a brief moment before returning to Katrina who was the main subject of her ire. "Who's responsible for this mess? I know it wasn't like this a few hours ago."

Sorry, buddy, I have no choice. I pointed at Ebenezer. "He's a little mischief maker. I heard him squealing in here. The carrier wasn't zipped all the way and he wiggled his way out."

"Very talented guinea pig. Being able to open up desk drawers and get himself into a locked room." Luna's brows quirked up, gaze drifting to the binder I still clutched. "Is he also responsible for putting that in your hand?"

"I think a lot of the items were on the desk. The window blew them onto the floor and Ebenezer believed they were snacks." I refrained from mentioning Katrina tossing out the items. It was information I felt compelled to hold onto for a bit. There was a thick tension between Luna and Katrina, and I was leery of dropping that tidbit. Katrina had remained quiet, squishing her arms against her side and making herself as small as possible. I tucked the binder under my arm.

Plus, I wanted answers on Katrina's theory of Marie lying about her and figured she'd share if I didn't throw her under the bus.

"The window shouldn't have been opened." Luna frowned and crossed over to it and peered outside. "I told my staff no one was allowed in this room."

"Someone else was in here before me," I said. "The window was opened when I entered. I heard Ebenezer making a fuss and came into the room."

Slowly, Luna turned and fixed an icy stare on Katrina. "I presume it was you."

"I told you, Merry was in here first. Ike told me the guinea pig—"

"And when was this?"

"After filming this afternoon's scene." Katrina's voice shook.

"That's interesting because he's been busy running errands for me since you weren't around."

"Vernon put him in here. He said it wasn't wise to allow just anyone into your room so the animal shouldn't be left in there alone." Katrina was practically pleading for Luna's understanding. "That's why I came in here. I thought it was what *you* wanted." She stretched out the word you.

I had a feeling she used Ebenezer's presence the same way I did, as an excuse for being in the room.

"You've been having a bit of trouble with the truth, Katrina," Luna said. "It's why I requested Chief Quinn stop by and ask you some questions. There are some important things we need to clarify. Like your inability to drive, when you drove yourself here. The chief also looked up your driving record. You have quite the lead foot and get a little aggressive behind the wheel."

Katrina blanched.

She had lied. Was it so no one suspected she ran Marie off the road?

A smile slowly spread across Luna's face. "Why do so many forget that I know everything that happens around here? Did you free the cat to get on my good side or to distract Randolph the night of the fire?"

Chief Quinn stepped into the room decked out in full police gear, expression on her face all business. There wasn't a hint of friendliness in her. Utility belt. Revolver in the holster. One hand slightly over the cuffs attached to the back of the belt. "Ms. Emerson, I have some questions—"

Katrina's eyes widened, the scary glint returned, gaze scattering around before locking onto me. As Paul stepped into the room, I inched back toward him, knowing it was prudent to put some distance between me and Katrina. The woman was about to snap.

Katrina ran to the window. Without a backward glance, Katrina gripped the frame with one hand and the other still clutching the cup, slung one leg then the other over the sill and jumped.

FIFTEEN

Chief Quinn cursed and ran down the stairs, shouting into the radio receiver attached to her bullet-resistant vest. Another clap of thunder echoed through the house and the lights flickered.

I leaned out the window, watching the figure running toward the main road, rain pelleting the ground. I glanced down. Two stories was a long way to jump down. For me anyway.

"Move, Merry." Paul placed a hand on my waist and gently pressed me away from the window. He scrambled out the window and walked to the edge of the roof.

I hated heights. Bracing my hands on the windowsill, I followed after him. In moments, I was soaked. The rain was smacking the ground, sounding like tiny pebbles hitting the ground.

"What are you doing?" Paul screamed over the booming thunder.

"Helping catch her. I'm not letting you go alone."

He opened his mouth to speak then closed it and nodded. "I'll jump first."

"Why not use the stairs?" I asked.

"They were bringing up equipment. This is quicker." Paul braced a hand on the roof.

I closed my eyes, refusing to watch him jump off. I was a person who preferred safer over quicker.

"Your turn. Instead of jumping, shimmy off the roof and I'll grab a hold of you and help you down. Or you can stay. We're losing her."

Staying wasn't an option. Taking a deep breath, I shimmied to the edge and let go once Paul's hands were firmly on my legs and I slid down his body, his hands quickly gripping my waist.

Once my feet were on the ground, I grabbed his hand and tugged him toward the parking area. "I have a golf cart. We can chase her down."

"First we have to find her."

Rain pounded us. The dark clouds hid all the sunlight. Even though it was early evening, it looked like it was midnight.

"Safety in numbers," Paul said, sliding onto the passenger seat of the cart. "We stick together."

"Might find her quicker if we split up." I jumped in the golf cart and held onto the frame as Paul pressed the pedal to the floor.

"Sometimes quicker isn't the best option."

Unlike jumping off a roof. The golf cart puttered over the asphalt, leaving it and driving onto the softening grass. The fastest speed was fourteen miles an hour, faster than Katrina could run down the road. The cart bounced over slight ruts in the backyard. Leaning forward, I stared out the small windshield, straining my eyes. There wasn't anyone ahead of us.

"I think she went into the woods. She's not sticking to the main path. Easier for her to get caught. I'm glad you got here in time." I just hoped no one found his timing convenient.

"Our suspicions were correct. Luna was one of Marie's PI clients."

I drew in a deep breath. Now was the time for telling Paul the truth. "I know. Edward told me today."

"What else did he tell you?" Paul slid a gaze in my direction that was unreadable with the low light. Lightning flashed across the sky. A moment too late for me to get a read of it. But I had a feeling Paul discovered what Marie was investigating and knew I tied into it.

"Someone threatened to reveal that Luna abandoned a newborn daughter, and Marie was helping her find the child."

"Why didn't you tell me when I called?" He slowed the golf

cart as we approached a thick section of woods.

I scanned the woods, straining my eyes as I searched for any type of movement. "I wasn't ready to face the prospect of Luna being a criminal...or the possibility I'm that child."

Paul's lack of reaction told me he found out talking with Marie's colleagues.

"Am I? Is there real proof of it in Marie's phone?"

"No. Just speculation. The time frame fits, and it was within fifty miles of the area Luna remembers traveling."

"I found a list in Marie's car. I thought it was a list of crafters and now I think it was the names of the women who were possibly Marie's daughter."

"Who else was on the list?"

"There were five names. Katrina was on the list and before Luna entered Marie's bedroom, Katrina ranted about Marie stealing her identity. I think she meant Marie no longer believed Katrina was Luna's daughter."

"And that made her angry."

"Yes." But was she angry enough to kill?

The *whoop, whoop* of sirens reached us. A police car turned in front of us and pulled to a stop.

The window rolled down and an officer yelled at us. "Head back to the house. Chief doesn't want civilians involved in this."

"The more people looking—" Paul said.

"The better chance someone innocent will be hurt." The officer's voice carried over the sound of the storm. "Head back."

"There's a good possibility she killed my cousin." Paul clutched the steering wheel. The rain shifted and pelted us from the side. We were both soaked.

"Another good reason for you to back off. We can't have anyone saying this woman was treated unfairly."

"Shouldn't you be more concerned that a possible murderer is running around the town?" I asked.

"I'd like to be," the officer snapped, "but that's hard when I have civilians chasing down said likely suspect. My priority now is deterring you from helping rather than looking for her."

He was right, we were being a distraction. "Let's head back. What if she sneaks back in? She was searching Marie's stuff."

The officer pushed out a frustrated breath and glared at me for a moment before switching his irritated gaze toward Paul. Okay, my comment wasn't the best as I basically was still inserting us into the police's investigation, but someone should guard Marie's room considering there was potential evidence in there.

Paul stared back. The men were in a silent duel. Neither wanting to back down.

"We're soaked," I said. "It's dark. Katrina won't stick to the road, and it's not safe walking through the woods right now."

"She's not that smart. She broke into Marie's room while people were in the house," Paul countered.

I held back my frustration. Paul wasn't usually this argumentative. Of course, it was usually me sticking myself into police business and not Paul. I was probably not the best person to convince him otherwise.

"Which makes her desperate. Dangerous," the officer said. "Go back and let us do our jobs without worrying about you or your friend getting hurt. It's dark and raining. I don't want either of you being mistaken for the runaway person of interest."

Neither did I. Plus, there was one item I was interested in. The binder. It must have Marie's case notes in it. That was why Katrina wanted it. But why had Katrina asked me to get the items from Luna's car? To get me out of my trailer so she could search it without worrying I'd catch her in the act? It would take me a few hours to get to Harmony, run Luna's and my errand, and return. Who stole the list of names? Katrina was back at the set.

We needed the binder. I firmly believed it contained information about Marie's death—and also about my parentage.

SIXTEEN

After stopping at my RV for a change of clothes, Paul and I took his truck back to Luna's house, planning on packing up Marie's items. We figured they'd be safer in the RV than remaining there. Katrina might return and take or destroy everything, or Luna might decide pitching it all was a way to stop everyone from poking around in her house.

Ebenezer was in a frenzy as there were two people in his vicinity and neither giving him any attention. I scooped him up and took him with me into the bedroom and placed him on his favorite spot on the bed.

"We'll play later. We have an important mission."

Ebenezer cuddled on my pillow and promptly fell asleep.

My phone vibrated. A message from Bright. And another. And another. Quickly, I changed into dry clothes and then brought up the messages.

Not true. Was the first message from Bright. *Luna NOT your mother.*

Are you sure? I responded.

Ran info I know about your past and also what I could find about Luna. Doesn't match.

We don't have all the details. What I have on Luna is from a second party. Might be rumors only.

I'm sure of it. Bright responded back immediately. *Besides, if you compare pictures of you and Luna, there is no resemblance.*

There was a tap on the door. "You ready?"

"Yep." *Going to take a look for more info. Will message any new findings.*

Paul was waiting for me by the door when I emerged from my room.

"Let's go see what we can find out." Paul stepped outside and headed for his truck.

My stomach was knotted with a slew of conflicting emotions, dread, excitement, sadness. Did I want to know more about what Marie found? What if Luna was my mom? What if she wasn't? I wasn't sure which was better or worse.

"You okay?" Paul asked.

"I'm just worried about what we'll find out."

"Me too."

It took us a few minutes, in complete silence as we were both lost in our own thoughts, to arrive at Luna's house. There were a few cars in the circular driveway. Paul dropped me off front then drove around back to park in the crew lot. I waited out front, watching the finishing touches being placed for tonight's scene and the crew cleaning up the debris of leaves from the thunderstorm. The sun was just starting to dip from the sky, the light fading. In two hours, it would be pitch dark. Enough time for us to clean out Marie's room and leave before filming started.

Fortunately, with the crew making the final touches for the party scene, we got inside without any difficulty. We just had to hurry before Luna realized we were back in Marie's room.

I scrounged up the boxes I had used for the craft items and placed them in the room. It was still a mess like Katrina had left it. Paul stood in the middle of the room, glancing around, face showing he was unsure of where to start.

"Did you want to pack everything and take it home with you or set some aside now for donation?" I carefully folded and placed clothing into a box.

"We'll take it all back and let her parents decide. I don't know what they'd consider important." Paul picked up a thin blanket and placed it on the end of the bed. "Whatever might be Ms. Carmichaels, we'll leave on the bed. What was that woman looking for?"

The binder. I picked it up from the floor and held it out to Paul. "Katrina was holding this when I confronted her."

Paul flipped it open and thumbed through the pages. With each turn, a frown deepened on his face. "Did you look at this?"

"No. She started rambling about Marie stealing her identity and then Luna showed up, livid at us for being in Marie's room." I walked over to Paul, almost pressing myself into his side to get a look at the papers. The page Paul stopped at had my name on it and details about my birth. From the notes, Marie was undecided on whether I was Luna's daughter. She had written more research needed to be done. I sure wished she wrote down where she planned on looking next so I could complete it. Now that my birth parents might be in front of me, I wanted to know who they were.

He flipped back a few pages. "Katrina Emerson is in here. At the top Marie wrote no."

"Katrina still believed she was Luna's daughter and Marie was taking that away from her. Hence the stealing her identity." I tilted the book toward me. "Who else is in there?"

"Sharon Zimmerman, a no at the top of her page. Olivia Highman, no with quite a few bullet-point notes about Olivia's adoption. Yours, undecided with a bit of details about your life. Most of it was what I had told Marie. And a Desiree Young. Nothing on top of hers either or any notes."

That explained why Marie interviewed Sharon for the crafting job. She was actually looking for Luna's daughter, and once they eliminated her, moved onto another likely-the-child-of-Luna candidate.

"Do you think it's possible?" Paul asked. "That you're Luna's daughter."

"I'm going with a no." Luna stepped into the room and held out her hand. "I do believe that's my property. I'd like it back."

Paul closed the binder and tucked it under his arm. "All the notes are in Marie's handwriting. It's hers. And being her family member, it's now mine."

Luna narrowed her eyes on him and took a step forward. "I don't think so. I hired her, so whatever was found is mine. I paid for it."

"My cousin paid for it with her life." Paul tightened his grip on the binder.

"Being a little dramatic aren't we." Her gaze was steely. Was the woman so determined to protect herself, she'd keep the truth silent?

"I collected your items from the sheriff's office," I said. "The tell-all manuscript Marie was mailing the morning she died wasn't in the box."

Her eyes widened and she grabbed the door frame, locking her knees for a moment until she became steady again. "She told you that?"

"She mentioned it was one of her errands that morning. Along with getting you coffee."

"I'm surprised she was sharing details about my private business. That wasn't like Marie." Her features hardened and she shot to her feet, pacing around the room like a predator.

"Then she told me for a reason. Like she was afraid someone was in danger."

"By someone you mean her."

"Or you," I said.

"If that's really true, it's a good reason Marie's cousin nor you should have the information in the binder. It's dangerous. I don't want anyone else dying because of me. It should be turned over to the police." Luna leaned back toward the door. "I need security in here. Now."

My phone vibrated in my pocket. I tugged it out. A messenger notification. Bright. Only a smidge of the message appeared, "you're not." I swiped the message away and responded with Desiree Young followed by a question mark. "Can we make a copy of it first? There are some things I'm interested in researching some more. And since it involves me..." I let my words trail off when two security guards appeared behind Luna.

"You're not one to leave well enough alone," Luna said, almost proudly.

"Not this. I'll either start over from scratch or continue where Marie left off. Have you looked at her phone records? Who did she call last?"

"I think that information is best given to the local authorities. The sooner the matter is settled, the better it is for me." Luna faced the guards. "Escort this man to my office and allow him use of the copier. Once he's done copying the material, collect the binder, along with the original notes, and call the chief. Tell her I have some documents that will enlighten her on a few matters."

Paul and the security team left.

"You should tell her about the manuscript and ask the sheriff about it. He was the first on the scene. Maybe he didn't put it in the box for a reason."

"I'm sure it was just an oversight. Randolph isn't the most thorough sheriff, following rather than leading is more his style. He'd have happily remained a deputy, but his father and grandfather wouldn't tolerate that. What some people won't do for the ones they love." She sighed. "I'll let Chief Quinn know about the missing manuscript, tell her I noticed it wasn't in the box you picked up for me. It's better if only a small pool of people knows about its existence."

"Katrina already knows that I know. She had asked me to get the box from the sheriff," I said.

"That doesn't mean she knows you had knowledge of the manuscript. Or even if she does, the manuscript might have no bearing on Marie's death."

"Why did Marie tell me about it? What's in there that she might have been concerned about and someone wanted kept quiet? The truth about your daughter."

Luna heaved out a sigh. "Yes, about her. The daughter I gave up for adoption forty-six years ago, around Christmas time. Her existence in my life would be uncomfortable for someone else in my life and I decided it was time for the truth anyway."

"Because you want your daughter in your life?" I asked. "Or because someone threatened to tell the world?"

"Because someone thought it's their place to share about my past misdeeds. And it's always better if you're the one who fesses up before someone announces it for you."

"Giving a child up for adoption isn't horrible," I said.

"Depending how you do it," Luna said. "Handing the month-old infant to your traveling companion to drop off somewhere is reprehensible. Especially when you never ask where he placed the child. The book will tell the world I do have a daughter and I'll add her in my will."

Month old. I was days old when my parents found me on the church steps on Christmas Eve. It wasn't me. Relief flooded through me. Was the other potential father the one who sent the letter to Edward? Edward had said it was possible he was the father of the baby. Or was it Luna's traveling companion? Could those two people—the companion and the father—be one and the same? Why was the truth being forced from Luna now?

"The baby's father just let you take her?"

"He didn't know. I knew I wanted to give the baby up and he'd never agree so I didn't put his name on the birth certificate."

"Have you told him now?" What game was Luna playing? Why had she led Edward to believe he was the father if he wasn't?

"I will when the time is right?"

"What about your daughter?"

"Again, when the time is right."

For a long moment, all I could do was stare at her. "Is this an attempt to atone for your mistake?"

"I'm doing what is best," Luna said.

"For your child or you?" I asked, bitterness creeping into my voice. Luna was too blasé about the whole situation. "Marie might have died because of this secret. You should tell the sheriff or the chief who the fathers might be."

"And besmirch a good man's name. Once I know the truth, the world will."

"But—"

"I'm a simple woman, Merry. The fact is I don't like anyone forcing a decision on me. Someone wanted this information out in the world and gave me no choice but to find this woman and make some type of amends. I'm doing that."

"You don't really want to find your daughter." Tears pricked my eyes. I drew in a breath, an attempt at settling myself down. She wasn't my mom. There was no reason to take it personal, but I was. Part of me feared it would happen to me when—or if—I ever decided to find my birth mom. What if she once again didn't want me?

"She's had forty-six years of memories with other parents. Better parents. I wanted her name, that was all. My plan was once I died, she'd get some jewelry, some money and learn I was her mother. Simple. No fuss. Marie was the one who decided it was best I meet all the candidates. Probably figured I'd change my mind." Luna fixed a soft smile on me. "I know my flaws, Merry. I'm not the mother type. As one man told me, I have accessories, not family members. No sense hurting another innocent person because I can't be who they envision I am."

SEVENTEEN

I stood in silence, watching Luna waltz out of the room as if the conversation we had was about the décor for the scene rather than the possibility she was my mother, or one of her potential daughters was a suspect in Marie's death. It was like none of it fazed her. The only reason she was searching for her daughter was to mitigate any damage the truth might do to her reputation and career, no matter the heartache she was creating for the woman she intended to cast aside once she "made amends." Of course, her original plan was just adding the daughter to her will and letting the woman find out that way. It was Marie who insisted Luna meet her daughter.

Was that what Luna and her soon-to-be ex-husband Vernon argued about and ended their marriage? Had he been upset she was changing the will, or was it about her treatment of her potential daughter? Had Luna told any other of her daughter candidates about adding her to the will? She had told me, but I was asking a lot of questions about it. There was one woman currently in the house I could speak with: Olivia Highman, Luna's personal chef.

I headed for the kitchen. I hoped I didn't get thrown out before I talked with the chef. The last time I tried entering the kitchen, her sous chef acted like he was protecting the White House.

The large dining room and living room were transformed into a Christmas wonderland. Lights twinkled. The ornaments I made for the tree were artfully arranged and the lights showed them off. Right in front were the merry and bright bulbs I made. The word "merry" was on a higher branch than the "bright" but both were easily seen. The remainder of the words were scattered around the tree, broken up by the white glazed plastic bulbs. Leaving off a word decal on those were the perfect choice. It was nice having a place for the eye to rest.

The crew was setting up the lights and mics. Carefully, I made my way through the cords and pushed open the swinging door leading into the kitchen and was almost ran over by a woman tottering around on high heels, trying to hustle in a tight evening gown while balancing a tray of unbaked cookies.

Olivia's gaze fell on me. She opened her mouth wide, like gearing up for screaming at me then thought better of it and heaved out a loud sigh instead. "We lost half the food for tonight's scene. Are you good in the kitchen?"

"Christmas baking is one of my specialties." I was taking a huge risk offering up my baking services, the items Bright was sending filled out some of the areas but there was still more that needed to be made. This was the only way to get into the kitchen and check for any other cups like Marie's and also chat with Olivia. "I have some crafts arriving tomorrow morning so I can volunteer some time."

"Good. Pick up a recipe that's quick and makes a lot," she said. "There's also some premade cookie dough."

"I know a great one for peanut butter and jelly cookies. They're always a big hit."

"No peanuts in this house," Olivia said. "Allergies."

"I can use the premade dough for Italian Christmas cookies."

"Sounds good. The ovens are in use so just set them on the trays, and once an oven is open, we'll toss them in."

From the attire of others in the kitchen, some of the extras for the scene were roped into baking and cooking. Ike was also in the kitchen, happily arranging cheese slices, olives, and deli meats onto a large, wooden cutting board.

The scent of fresh bread filled the room as the sous chef entered carrying a box overflowing with different types. He placed the box on the counter. "I bought out the local bakery."

I crumbled the cookie dough into a bowl and added some cream cheese and the other ingredients, kneading it together then shaping it into small balls and placing them on the trays. There was too much commotion, and people, to ask Olivia any questions. The countertops were filled with a mix of appetizers, cookies, bread, and dips. There was enough food to feed a small production company.

Garrison leaned into the kitchen. "Edward wants all the extras on deck. With the police scurrying around outside and the lights and sirens, he says it's the perfect time for filming the night scene that takes place after the murder."

I held back a grimace. "I'd check with the police first. I have a feeling they'd have something to say about that." Like no. I couldn't image they'd like their real person of interest search showing up as a scene in a Christmas movie.

A mass of people headed for the door. Garrison stepped inside, pressing himself against the counter while the extras and some crew members left the kitchen. "It's his fight. He says he'll do it discretely."

Ike wiped his hands on a dishtowel. "Everything is under control in here, so I'll leave you to it."

The only people left in the kitchen were the sous chef, the chef, a caterer, and me. Olivia took inventory of all the food. "Let's make a vegetable plate and put some crackers and the pita chips on a platter."

The sous chef nodded and began chopping the vegetables while another worker in a chef's jacket unpackaged crackers onto a Christmas themed plate.

The chef watched them work for a few minutes before spinning on her heels and walking toward the back of the kitchen. I followed her.

She stood in the large pantry area, twisting jars and cans so the labels faced the front. "This is why I hate people in my kitchen." She shook a box, grumbled under her breath and threw it over her shoulder. It clunked against my shoulder. She spun around and pressed a hand against her chest.

I picked up the empty box and tossed it into the garbage can that was behind me. "Sorry for startling you. Can I ask you some questions?"

"Why?" She pivoted back toward the pantry and rearranged some spices.

"It seems you and I were on a particular list that involved Luna." I hedged into the conversation, not sure how much she knew. For all I knew, Marie had eliminated Olivia from it without talking with her.

Olivia paused then slowly turned around, eyes wide. "You too. A daughter of Luna? That makes three. How many others?"

"Five in total. Who else do you know about?"

"Katrina Emerson. She pushed her way in here a day ago, demanding to know why I was pretending to be Luna's daughter. It's why I banned people from coming in. I told her I was hired as Luna's personal chef, and as far as being her daughter, I didn't care."

"How did Katrina know about you?"

"She mentioned overhearing Marie speaking with someone about it. A guy. She didn't see who it was."

"Do you remember when?"

"Around the time you showed up."

"How do you know when I showed up?"

"Because Luna was very interested in it. I heard Marie telling her you had arrived and wanted to know when she wanted a meeting arranged. Luna said not until the other matter was settled."

"What matter was that?"

"I'm assuming Katrina being informed she wasn't Luna's daughter." Olivia pulled a box from the shelf and tucked it under her arm.

"When did Marie talk with you?"

Olivia stepped out of the pantry and closed the door. She held the knobs for a long moment before turning and facing me. "I told her I didn't want to know. If it was me, tell Luna I wanted nothing from her. I'm leaving Luna's employment after this movie is over. I've lived forty-six years without a mother and I'm not interested in having one now. Luna is a complicated woman that thrives on drama. I don't want that in my life."

"Maybe she'd change for you."

Olivia laughed, a disbelieving sound. "I've been around her long enough. Finding her daughter won't turn her into the mothering type. Luna cares about one person. Luna. Regardless of who else is in her life."

EIGHTEEN

With Edward discretely using the police as background props for the movie, the rest of us were being sent home as the indoor part of the scene was rescheduled for tomorrow. The only one pleased was Olivia who now had time to ensure the food brought in was safe for the people with allergies. The crew was a little irritated as they now had to go into town and pay for a meal since originally dinner was being supplied by Luna. The cafeteria was closed tonight.

Now that Olivia had extra time, she no longer needed—or wanted—my help. I slipped out the kitchen doors and headed for the stairs. I'd go back upstairs and finish packing Marie's belongings before Katrina found a way back into the house and took something. The front door opened, and a weary looking Chief Quinn walked in followed by an irate Sheriff Rhodes.

"I'm shutting this production down now," Rhodes said.

I paused on the stairs, interested in the conversation. The sheriff was shutting everything down. Had he learned more about Marie's death? What would he think about the information Paul was copying? I glanced up the stairs and wondered if I could warn Paul before he came down with the items.

"Then all potential suspects leave. Sounds like a great plan, Sheriff."

The sheriff grabbed Quinn's arm and spun her around. "You already managed to do that. You ran off my best suspect, asking questions about an investigation that is not yours. It happened in my jurisdiction.'

Quinn glared at the hand latched onto her arm. "Maybe not."

I drew in a sharp breath then slapped my hand over my mouth.

Two heads turned in my direction. I quickly swiveled to appear like I was coming down the stairs rather than going up. "Is something wrong?" I fixed a confused expression on my face, hoping they bought it.

The sheriff was more interested in the chief's last statement than my presence. "What did you mean by that?" He reached for her arm again.

Quinn side-stepped away. "I let you get away with that once, Sheriff, don't test your luck."

"I'm not the one testing it. Someone should take a good hard look at your cousin." The sheriff crossed his arms and a sneer worked its way across his lips. "There's a lot of history between him and Luna. Also heard he had an argument with Marie the day she died."

"Don't slander my cousin." Quinn clenched her jaw.

The hairs on my neck bristled. I heard the warning in her tone. What was it about? Edward's words played in my head, one of the possibilities. Was Vernon the other candidate for the baby's father?

"I'm just sharing some tidbits from my investigation into Marie's death. A professional courtesy even though you inserted yourself into it." The sheriff pulled out a pen and paper and scribbled on it. He folded the note and handed it over. "I'm sure those crew members wouldn't mind repeating what they told me. Since you don't believe me."

"I have my reasons for my decision," Quinn said.

"I'm sure you do."

Paul came down the stairs with a large box in his arms.

"Thanks for grabbing those items I need for the last few craft projects. We have to get right on them to complete them for the craft bazaar scene," I said in an overly bright voice. "Ms. Carmichael will have a fit if they're not done."

Eyeing me oddly, Paul nodded and walked down the stairs, excusing himself around the sheriff who tried peering into the box.

"I hope it's an easy craft because I'm not a fast learner."

"That's why we're doing it now." I linked my arm through his and practically dragged him out of the house.

Paul followed along, not asking any of the questions I saw in his gaze. I made my way through the cast members and extras who were heading into town. Some were walking and others were taking golf carts. There was still some light in the sky but in an hour or two it would be gone. Hopefully the police found Katrina before nightfall. I hated thinking about her running around in the dark—especially if she was Marie's killer. Would she hurt someone else?

I tried blocking a shiver working its way up my spine.

"Are you okay?" Paul slowed down.

"We'll talk in the RV." I continued hauling him toward our destination.

My RV stood out from all the other trailers in the living quarters area. Not just because it had wheels, but the large Christmas decal that stretched from rear tire to front tire. I couldn't help pondering if making the RV so unique was such a good idea considering how often I found myself in trouble. Or rather inserting myself into trouble.

Again, a shiver worked its way through me and this time I couldn't stop it. Instead of the issue I was facing now, my mind conjured up the most recent Christmas past and everything that had gone wrong. Murders. My mom's failing health. Loneliness.

Paul halted. "Tell me what's going on."

"Debating whether customizing the outside of the RV was such a good idea."

I tilted my head to the side and studied it. It was Santa's sleigh and a team of nine reindeer flying over a row of houses, each with a different color string lights and wreath on it. Bright and I had come up with the design together.

Christmas had always been my thing. Ever since I was a little girl, I loved the feeling surrounding the holiday. The love. The wonder. The hope. The anticipation. Last Christmas, fear, grief, and melancholy had stolen the holiday from me. Loss had hit me hard, not just the people who had died but all the small things that made up the holiday were changing. Traditions were fading as my adult children began their separate lives away from me. My mother's health issues showed me that love couldn't conquer all.

Maybe the goal shouldn't be conquering everything but coming to term and accepting the new way of life. Find new traditions. A new way of doing Christmas. I started over before. I could do it again. I just wasn't looking forward to starting over again without my mother. But it was coming, and I could no longer pretend it wasn't a reality I'd ever face.

"Merry?" Paul placed a gentle hand on my shoulder.

"All this talk of adoption has me wondering if I should find my birth parents."

"It's not..." he trailed off.

"No. Luna said the baby was a month old. I was days old when I was left." A bitterness crept inside me. Almost hatred. I hadn't really thought of my past much, but who left a days old baby out in the cold? In a stocking. Had my parents hoped I wouldn't survive? Or had they placed me on the church steps on Christmas Eve, knowing the Christmas Eve service was letting out soon and I'd be saved.

"You're good at piecing together information. I'm sure you can find out."

"Do I want to?" I voiced aloud my biggest dilemma. "Do I want to know why? What if it just some selfish reason?"

Paul guided me into the RV. "You just have to figure out which is worse...knowing or not knowing."

"I'm not sure." I opened the door and was greeted by Ebenezer's disgruntled whistles. "Did you go back and search Marie's room?"

"The security guard wasn't having any of that. We were lucky enough Luna relented and let us copy her notes."

"Whatever is in Marie's room will now be fought over. The sheriff and chief were arguing over who had jurisdiction over the case. The sheriff wants the production shut down and the chief disagrees."

"Can't say I blame her. If the murderer is someone from the cast or crew, which is likely, they'll be able to leave and take evidence with them."

"Evidence could get ruined or contaminated with all these people walking around." I opened the bedroom door and Ebenezer tore out, running for the living room. "What did you find out today at the coroner's office?"

"The full autopsy isn't back yet, so they don't know what type of sleep aid or how long it was in her system."

"I'm surprised the coroner told you anything." I stared into my craft cabinet. What could we make that was easy and I had enough supplies to fill a booth?

"Professional courtesy. Law enforcement agencies will sometimes share with others in the field like first responders."

"Maybe you can get the sheriff or the chief to share with you."

Paul snorted. "I highly doubt it. So, what's your plan? I have a feeling the sheriff or chief will stop by and see what we made."

"I agree and for no other reason than to see what you were carrying out." I took out a clear fillable ornament. Easy project for the booth as the rest of the clear ornaments I had remained blank as this was a customizable project for the customer. "I'll make a floating photo ornament. This ornament opens in half and I'll stick a photo in it. It'll be the example for the photo and the other ones will be left blank for the customer to add a photo."

"Where will we get a picture? Who carries around a photo to a Christmas bazaar?"

I refrained from rolling my eyes. "I'll take one on my phone and print it out on my photo printer. People might not carry physical photographs with them, but they do on their phone. They can send it to the printer and then it'll be turned into an ornament. Not that we'll actually have to make them I just need the sample ornament done and then set up the space as a custom ornament booth."

"Great. Let's take a picture of us." Paul wrapped an arm

around me and pressed his cheek against mine.

For a moment I froze, the gesture seeming too intimate for our stage of friendship, or rather the fact Paul had been honest at wanting more. He respected my decision on keeping our friendship at just a friendship, yet the close proximity gave me thoughts of what more we could have. Something I wasn't ready for. At the moment, my life was complicated enough.

I forced the thoughts out of my head and smiled, raising my arm up and snapping a couple of photos on the iPhone. After scrolling through them, I picked the best image and sent it to the printer.

As I watched the photo print, my memory flashed onto Luna's study or rather the framed photographs. I had been amazed at the close resemblance between the young aunt and nephew picture to Luna and Garrison. What if the resemblance was close because those were real family photographs?

"I think Luna and Garrison are related." That would explain the private conversations between Garrison and Luna, though others on the set were interpreting it differently.

"Why would they hide that?"

Good question. "Luna is a complicated woman."

"Complicated?" Paul's eyebrows quirked up. "Don't you mean selfish?"

"That too." Olivia's comments raced through my head. Was that what she meant by knowing Luna wouldn't turn into the mothering type? Was Garrison Luna's son? "How could no one else know?"

"Know what?" Paul frowned.

I took in a deep breath and told him the theory my mind conjured up. "Why hasn't anyone connected Luna to the baby or Garrison before? What if he's her son?" I told Paul about my conversation with Olivia.

"Maybe he doesn't want anyone knowing."

"Or she doesn't. Why?" I paced around the room.

"Has to be hard keeping one child after you got rid of one."

The harshness of the statement had me cringing. “She’s been the queen of Christmas for decades. Portrayed herself as sweetness and light. As being the spirit of Christmas.” With each word, I heard my anger growing. “She’s a fake. I can’t believe someone hadn’t found out the truth about her.”

“Someone did,” Paul said. “That’s why Marie was here. Find the daughter so the ugliness wasn’t released.”

“Why would that stop—” The daughter. “The daughter is the one who sent the letter. She wanted Luna to acknowledge her. The people who would know about what happened to the baby were the daughter, the father...”

“How would the daughter know?”

“My parents told me the situation about how I was up for adoption. It’s likely her parents did as well. And she might have tracked Luna down through genealogy research. DNA tests are popular. She might have taken one and was linked to Luna.” I stopped pacing and fought back a smile. This was too serious for happiness. But I was excited answers were finally coming to me rather than more questions.

“Luna doesn’t seem the type to take one of those.”

“Garrison might have,” I said.

“How are you going find out?”

For once I’d go easy route. “Ask him. The possible daughters are Chef Olivia, Katrina, Sharon, Desiree Young, and me. We know I didn’t send the letter and I’m not her daughter.”

“You’re sure? Luna might be lying about how old the baby was. I don’t trust that woman.” Paul sat on the couch and pulled out the notes he copied from the box.

“There was no reason for her to lie.”

“Marie never crossed your name off the list or Desiree Young. There has to be a reason.”

“Maybe she hadn’t finished researching us.” I plopped down beside him and leaned into his shoulder, getting a good look at the document. Desiree’s name was first with an underline underneath it. When I created a list, I always underlined the title at the bottom, the topic. Marie had underlined Desiree, and only Desiree, because that was the name of the birth mother who now went by the stage name of Luna Carmichael. It made sense. That was why no one had ever found out this information about Luna before. I jumped up. "That's why no one knew Desiree. The name is underlined. Luna is Desiree. Luna Carmichael is her stage name."

"That makes sense. Information like that wasn't as easy to dig up decades ago as it is now."

"Probably also the reason no one has connected Garrison and Luna. But why keep it hidden?"

"There are two people who could answer that," Paul said.

Luna and Garrison. I had a strong feeling Garrison was the most likely of the two. "What do you say about heading into Carol Lake and eating dinner at the diner?"

NINETEEN

The closer Paul and I got to town, the more the summer night turned into a scene in a Christmas movie. Lights were strung on trees and the stacks of wood I'd seen on the ground a day—or was it two days? —ago were now booths. There were twenty booths placed strategically in the square. Pie booth. Cookie booth. Soaps. Wreaths. Ornaments. Personalized signs.

In the background, the lake shone with the Christmas lights casting what looked like stars over the surface of the water. Christmas music from the jukebox of the diner flowed out and into the street. The town was getting into the spirit of the movie, or the owner of the restaurant enjoyed Christmas all year-round.

We stepped into the diner, and I immediately regretted not bringing a sweater. The cold air prickled my flesh and I rubbed my hands over my arms and scanned the diner. There was a Christmas tree in the corner near the front door. Bells of different colors, shapes, and sizes hung on the branches. Other than that, the décor was fifties retro diner: black-and-white checkerboard floor, white walls, and the bar in the back of the restaurant extended nearly from one wall to the other, large white Formica top on a chrome and black base, paired with black barstools with red vinyl cushions. Booths and tables filled the dining room, the color combination a mix of red and white.

An older woman with gray hair piled on top of her head in a bun was at the counter and stopped ringing a sale and pointed at the back of the diner. "Rest of the movie folks are back there. In the banquet room." Her voice carried over all the other sounds. She was one of those people with a natural buoyant voice that floated into every nook and cranny of a room.

"Thanks," I said.

Paul leaned into me. "Do we stick together or split up? The main room is packed and there's a vacant chair at the bar."

"There's a reason Luna picked this town as her home base. Might be best for one of us to chat with the locals."

"Agree. Maybe they knew Luna as Desiree Young and aren't using her real name because Luna Carmichael is bringing business."

"I'll take the movie folks and you talk with the locals," I said.

"Sounds good. We'll share intel when we head back."

I headed for the back room. Boisterous laughter drifted from the back. I stepped aside and let a waitress carrying a tray with a pitcher of soda and appetizers by. The room was packed. There was a large group crowded around a table in the corner wearing Yale Productions baseball caps. One of the men was pushed back from the table and cradled a DSLR with a zoom lens in his arms, hat tipped low and shielding his face.

"Merry, I'm happy you're here." Anne rushed over and grabbed my hand, tugging me toward the back. "There's a quiet table in the corner."

I still hadn't found out what Anne almost told me. Now was a good time. I looked over my shoulder. Paul was at the bar already engaged in a conversation with two people, one had a baseball cap with the emblem of the local volunteer fire department.

As we walked by the table with the camera crew, a young guy picked up a stainless steel cup and held it out. "I found it on the set, Ms. Lindsey."

The words on the cup caught my attention: Drama It's What I Do. It was the second cup I had seen with the emblem.

Using only the pads of her fingers, she took hold of the cup. "Thank you."

Another small group was heading for the corner table, so I quickly maneuvered my way through and took a seat. The group frowned and I smiled apologetically and nodded toward Anne who was making her way toward me. I hoped they were more understanding knowing I snagged the table for her.

Gingerly, Anne placed the cup on the table and pushed it toward the wall. She sat down and stared at it like it was the bane of her existence.

"Something wrong?"

"Why was it on the set? It shouldn't have been there. Right?" Tears rushed into her eyes and she blinked them away. "Marie had the cup with her."

A coldness swept over me. No. No. It couldn't be. Anne couldn't have something to do with Marie's death. "What?"

"I'm sorry. I was eavesdropping and heard you asking Vernon about the cup. The crew knows me better, so I thought they'd look for it if I was asking about it. Most of them were a little distrustful of Marie."

"Why?"

"Because she was Luna's assistant and the two of them didn't get along. No one wants even the appearance of crossing Luna. Luna's assistants were usually quiet and stayed in the background. Marie was a force to reckon with. She wouldn't allow anyone around Luna. I'm surprised she let Chef Olivia and her sous chef stay in the house. Vernon and her butted heads constantly."

A waitress came over and placed two menus on the table. There was something bothering me about Anne's confession. Marie had been a police officer. If she was here protecting Luna, I'd assume she'd want more allies than enemies. She needed the crew and cast to trust her.

"I'll have the special," Anne said, "and whatever is your most popular beer."

"Me too," I said, handing back the menus.

The waitress nodded and took them, heading for the table of rowdy crew members. Anne had quickly switched the conversation away from the cup. A cup that I was told Marie had commissioned for all of the cast and crew, yet there was only one I had seen—

maybe two if this wasn't Marie's cup.

"Have you seen other cups with that design on them?" I carefully tugged the cup toward me, running my finger over the bottom portion of the cup and searching for a dent. It took me awhile until I found the dent among the smoothness of the cup. I drew in a breath.

Anne shook her head and frowned. "Are you okay?"

"This is the cup I was looking for." I tapped it closer and peered at it. There was something I was missing from the customized cup. "You didn't get one? I was told Marie had them created for the cast and crew."

Anne frowned. "No. Who told you that?"

"Maybe I misunderstood them. I'll double check." Had Luna been mistaken, or had she lied to me? Why? The more I learned, the less I understood. "What did Marie and Vernon fight about?"

"About some past issues. And those problems were causing difficulties with Marie doing her job. Not to mention being the real source of Luna and Vernon's marital woes."

"You didn't hear this did you?" There was something about the way she was explaining it that had my guard up. I wasn't sure if it the unemotional way she spoke or the faraway look in her eyes, as if she was trying to remember what was told to her. "Someone told you. Who?"

Anne bit her lip and looked away. "I probably shouldn't say..."

Everything in her posture said she would tell me after some convincing. It would make her feel better if she didn't easily supply me with the information, though she had done so about everything else.

I leaned forward and clasped her hands. "It's important."

Tears gleamed in her eyes. "I'd feel like I was betraying hi— them. And they've been betrayed enough by the people close to them."

Garrison. I'd seen the two together a few times and Anne had defended him to Ike.

The waitress brought our food and we ate in silence. Either

Anne didn't want to talk any more or she said all she wanted. But I had one more question for her.

"The other night when you helped me sort through the items from the fire, you had started saying about something not being innocent. What did you mean?"

"In Luna hiring Marie. She wasn't a personal assistant. I know it. Garrison knew it. I think even Vernon knew and that was why he was angry with Luna. I think he thought she was looking into him for cheating on her. Very ironic since Luna had been spending quite a bit of time with Sheriff Rhodes...until that night of the fire."

There was a loud commotion in the main dining room. Diners leaned over and others stood, walking out of the banquet room for a better look. Anne's phone buzzed. She glanced down and her eyes widened, face turning pale.

"What's wrong?" I asked.

Without a word, she jumped up and ran for the door, nearly colliding into a panicked Chef Olivia. I side-stepped around Olivia, blocking out the worried look on Paul's face. I wasn't sure if it was about my fleeing the diner or whatever Olivia was rambling about. The woman was gesturing wildly in the air

"Anne, wait." I sped up, my breath coming in spurts. I couldn't remember the last time I ran. Heck might have been when my kids were in elementary school, and now the youngest was twenty-two.

Instead of heading back toward the film lot, she headed for the opposite side of town. Her sandals clacked against the wooden planks of the bridge. Why was Anne so distraught?

"Stop."

"Garrison's in trouble." Anne's words floated to me.

"Let me help," I called out.

Someone ran into me from behind, knocking me against the railing of the foot bridge. A hand pressed down on my back, the air in my lungs escaping as my stomach flattened onto the wooden railing. Bracing my arms on the railing, I tried righting myself. I kicked my feet, trying to rid myself of the person who collapsed on top of me. Scream. Scream now.

I drew in a breath. Another arm went under my knees and before I knew it, I was falling into the dark. The scream finally left me. A splash sounded as water filled my mouth. I closed my mouth and struggled to remember which way was up as water closed around me.

My head broke the surface. The world was blurry, and I barely saw two feet in front of me. I had lost my glasses in the fall. Near me there was another splash and a dark shape went underwater. Anne had been on the bridge. I scanned the area searching for who or whatever else went into the water.

"Merry! Merry, are you all right?" Paul's frantic voice called out.

"Yes." Treading water, I shoved my wet hair off my face. "I think Anne was thrown over also."

Where was she? I paddled in a circle, straining my gaze as I peered into the water. The darkness paired with the ripples caused by either the water or my sight issues made it impossible for me to distinguish anything. Panic was setting in. I tried calming myself, knowing I wasn't helping me or Anne by letting fear win. Something slithered against my leg. I yelped. Was it a snake? Or Anne's hair. A few feet from me was another splash.

"Hang tight, Merry."

"Something touched my leg. It might be Anne. I'll check." I drew in deep breath, hoping I'd manage underwater just fine.

"I'll look for her. Swim to the left. You'll reach the shore quicker."

I wanted to argue with him, but Paul was better suited for rescuing Anne, especially since she hadn't surfaced yet and he could see. Maybe it wasn't Anne. Could've been anything and Paul was risking his life.

"Get out of the water!" A large blurry group of people were on the bridge. "There are snakes in there."

Like this was my choice.

Paul broke the surface, an arm wrapped around a still form. "I have Anne. She's hurt."

I turned in the direction Paul said and headed for the shore. Swimming wasn't a skill I had really mastered, but I was okay at the doggie paddle and headed for the shore. I always said I had enough skill not to drown for a nice length of time and hoped not to challenge that theory. A few meters into my swim, the water level lowered, and I placed my feet on the ground and trudged my way through the rest of the lake.

Everything was a blur. The ground felt different under my feet. I made it onto on the bank. I walked forward a few paces and stumbled, my foot smacking into something hard that yielded a bit. I fell forward, faceplanting onto a body.

Quickly, I pushed myself off and over. I turned my head. Sightless eyes stared into mine. It was Katrina. A dead Katrina. I screamed.

TWENTY

The lights blinking around the pavilion were a distraction as I tried focusing my mind on the barrage of questions Deputy Paugh, Chief Quinn, and a state trooper threw at me. I wasn't sure if they were trying to confuse me, hoping I'd confess, or if my tired and strained mind just had a hard time sorting out which law enforcement member was speaking to me and which was talking to one of the other people gathered in the food pavilion area.

A hot wind drifted into the open space area, bringing with it the scent of coffee. I drew in a deep breath, hoping the smell cleared my mind. An officer had escorted me back to my RV long enough for a quick change and to retrieve my spare glasses. I grabbed the first two items and was now wearing a t-shirt proclaiming every day was Christmas and an old pair of jeans with ripped holes and a multitude of paint splotches all over it. These were my board prepping pants, and as I was a messy painter, I had one outfit set aside for the task so I didn't ruin all my clothes.

One by one, members of the cast and crew who thought they had possible information were being dismissed. Ike and Edward, though no longer being formally questioned, remained near the coffee urns. Every now and then, Ike checked the list in his hands. I assumed it was the names of everyone on the cast and crew.

"Ms. Winters." The aggravated tone returned my attention to Deputy Paugh.

"It's been a long day." I shuffled backwards, feeling like I'd been on my feet for sixteen hours. "Hope you don't mind if I sit."

"By all means." Paugh took a seat on the bench across from the table where I sat. Turning sideways, he placed the notebook and pen on the table then faced forward, resting his elbows on his knees. "Are you sure you don't need to be checked out? I can run you to the hospital."

I wished I remained standing, now we were face-to-face, almost nose-to-nose. His intense blue gaze was unnerving. "No, I'm fine. Just an unexpected swim. Have you heard anything about Anne?"

"She's still unconscious."

"Did she hit her head when she was thrown into the water? Or before? I didn't hear her scream."

"I'm not a doctor. I couldn't say." He jotted something down. "Let's talk about Ms. Emerson fleeing the Carmichael house. When did you first notice her in Marie's room and what was she doing?"

At least he wasn't asking again about what I was doing in there, or why Katrina hadn't noticed me right away. Saying I was hiding under the bed would come across as suspicious.

"She started throwing Marie's items around the room and I confronted her. I was afraid she'd ruin something."

"That's when she told you she believed she was Ms. Carmichael's daughter?"

"What she said was that Marie was stealing her identity."

Paugh stared at me with one eyebrow raised.

"I kept prying and that's when she told me about being Luna's daughter. Which she isn't." My last comment was a little too forceful and once again the detective's brow arched up.

"Is that so?"

"The binder she was stealing was filled with Marie's research on Luna's possible daughters. Marie had eliminated Katrina from the list."

He made a noise at my choice of word.

My gaze left the deputy and roved around until it fell on Paul, who was at the coffee station. From my vantage point, I didn't know if he was getting a cup or eavesdropping on Ike and Edward's conversation.

"Why isn't the sheriff here? I'd think he'd be interested in the fact that a possible suspect was killed, and Anne was injured. Whoever threw us into the lake might be the killer."

"Why do you think Ms. Emerson was murdered?" Deputy Paugh drawled out, eyes narrowing into a slit. After a few moments of staring at each other, Paugh sat back.

"Because you wouldn't be here asking me and everyone else a ton of questions."

"You ladies were thrown into the lake. You don't think that warrants an investigation? Why do you think it was the killer who threw you in? From what you said earlier, you and Anne were heading toward the side of the lake where Ms. Emerson was found. The person had come up behind you. So, they'd have come from the side of the lake where the diner is. No one passed you. Correct?"

"That's right."

"We've had a lot of comments saying you and Anne ran out together. In a huge rush."

"Anne looked upset, so I followed her. Right before the person tossed me over the railing, she said Garrison was in trouble." The breath locked in my throat. Garrison! Where was he?

Jerking forward, Paugh braced his palms on his thighs, rose, and scanned the area. "She went in search of Garrison Tyler?"

"I'm assuming that was where she was going." My stomach was twisting into a knot. I wasn't liking where this was going.

"And the direction Ms. Lindsey went was where Ms. Emerson's body was found. Make sure you stay in the area. I might have more questions for you later." Paugh rose and strode across the pavilion to where the sheriff was in a heated conversation with Chief Quinn. The deputy whispered something to the sheriff, who had just arrived, and both men left.

The chief watched them walk away then focused her attention on me. She hitched up her gun belt and came over. Anger rolled off of her. "What did you tell Deputy Paugh?"

"I was just answering his questions." I stood and wrapped my arms around myself. The air was still humid, but a coldness was entering my body. There was something going on that I was missing—that I had just created—and I wasn't liking it one bit. I hated being the cause of strife. And there was something I was forgetting. Something important that might change the direction my comments had sent the sheriff and the deputy.

"What were those questions?"

I had brought my suspicion about Marie's death to the chief and now I was reluctant to repeat the information to her.

"Ms. Winters, I expect an answer. This is an active investigation. Deputy Paugh might have convinced you that Marie McCormick's death is their case but Katrina Emerson's murder, and there is no doubt that is what it is, happened in my jurisdiction."

I repeated what I had told him. Did Paugh think Garrison had hurt Anne? Killed Katrina? Why would he call her and then attack her? Was he the one responsible for Marie's death? Why? To protect Luna—who might be his mother or aunt? I just knew there was a family connection between them. And there were only two people who knew what it was—Luna and Garrison.

Visually, I took attendance of everyone present. There were three people missing: Luna, Garrison, and Vernon.

"You have no idea why he was in trouble?" Quinn's question drew me from my thoughts.

"No. I'm guessing it has something to do with Katrina because of Paugh's reaction. After I said that, the deputy left and said he might have more questions for me later."

"Why were you hesitant about telling me?" Anger flashed in her eyes. "What have Rhodes and Paugh been saying about me?"

"Nothing. There's a lot of animosity between you and the sheriff and I don't want to get mixed up in a turf war." Especially over Marie's murder investigation. It was unseemly and, in a way, made her death even worse. Paul didn't the need the two local law enforcement agencies at war with each other rather than working together to find the truth.

Though I hadn't mentioned the cup that was given to Anne and how uncomfortable she was about it. A cup we had left behind at the diner. I groaned and smacked my hand onto my forehead. Well, I guess the good thing about leaving it was it didn't end up at the bottom of the lake.

Was it Marie's cup and not the one I found in Marie's room? Before today, I had only seen one of those cups, and then I saw two. Was it the same or a different one? Had someone planted the cup in the room and Katrina grabbed it and dropped it somewhere else? Had she jumped for the window to get rid of evidence, or at least move it and point the blame at someone else?

"What else did you remember?"

Cringing, I told her. "I can't remember if Katrina took the cup from Marie's room or left it behind."

Quinn frowned and narrowed her eyes. "I do believe she took it with her."

"That means—"

"That crew member might know who saw Katrina last. Do you know the man's name?"

"No. Anne might."

Chief Quinn pressed her lips together and sighed. "She's still unconscious. There's nothing you can tell me about this guy?"

"He worked with the film crew." I regretted not being able to help more. Since he gave Anne the cup, I should've memorized something about him. I let a great opportunity of finding Marie's, and now likely Katrina's, killer go.

"I'll head into town and ask around. The waitress might remember him."

"The table he was at was rowdy."

"Then she'll likely remember him or someone from the table." Quinn placed a hand on my shoulder. "Do me a favor and keep this between us. I don't want anyone tipping the guy or anyone else off. The best thing for you to do is stay in your RV where it's safe. Stop asking questions. Two people have died because of—I'm not sure yet. And I don't want the body count going up."

"Shouldn't you tell the sheriff?"

"Some things are better not shared with him. And this is one of them."

TWENTY-ONE

A loud knock on the RV door startled me awake. There wasn't an ounce of light in the sky. I groaned and rolled over, tapping my cell charging on the wireless base. Five thirty. There was movement in the living room. Since he was up, I'd let Paul deal with it. He had returned from the hospital a little after midnight. Anne had regained consciousness and the doctors insisted the police wait until morning before speaking with her.

I snuggled back under the sheet. Ebenezer roamed around on the bed until he found a way under the covers and pressed himself into my back. At least another hour of sleep before I tried making sense of what was going on. I wasn't sure if finding Luna's daughter was worth it, whoever the woman was, it might be best for her not to know. It wasn't like Luna actually wanted a relationship with her. Who wanted all of those ugly details about the circumstances of their birth and adoption? I was leaning toward leaving my past behind me. There were some things better left buried. Could be this last woman was like Olivia and happier not knowing. Maybe that was why there were no notes on Desiree Young. She asked Marie to drop it.

Then why kill Marie?

I groaned and tugged the blanket over my head. Stop thinking. I'd never fall back asleep with my mind whirling away.

There was a light tap on my bedroom door. "Merry, Ike's here. Says it's of extreme importance he talks with you."

"Tell him to try again at a more reasonable hour."

"Either I speak with you or security will," Ike's callous voice filtered past the door. "Or I could call Sheriff Rhodes since you're such good friends with him."

"How about you tell me?" Paul asked.

"Director Yale insisted I give Ms. Winters this message directly."

Whatever this was about, it wasn't good. I had a bad feeling the talk had something to do with what I told Deputy Paugh last night. The director wouldn't be happy with one of his stars—his son—being dragged into the police station for questioning. With shaking hands, I exchanged my nightwear for a t-shirt and shorts.

Paul leaned against the kitchen counter, holding a mug of steaming coffee. His stance spoke of a casual protectiveness. One word from me, and he'd put down the mug and throw Ike out. Ike sensed it as he took up a spot as far from the door and Paul as possible.

"How can I help you?" I asked

"Edward sent me to pick up Ebenezer. There is just one scene left for him, the Christmas party scene, and then he's no longer needed. As Edward doesn't want to reshoot scenes, using your pet is the only choice. After the scene is done filming, Edward wants you and your friend off the property."

"I'm not giving you Ebenezer." I was being fired. Easy to do as I had already completed most of the craft items needed and handed over the ones I bought from Sharon.

"We don't have much time." Ike's voice was twinged with anger. "The sun will be out soon. The scene won't take long at all. I promise I'll have him brought right back over."

I didn't care how mad I made him or the director, Ebenezer wasn't going anywhere without me. "Right. Your crew will take as good care of him as you did the sheriff's cat."

"The cat wasn't our fault. It disappeared sometime in the middle of the night. No one was over at the house besides Luna's personal staff."

"Then how come Luna didn't know the cat was gone until I told her later that morning?" I picked up Ebenezer and cradled him against my chest.

"Luna doesn't notice what she doesn't want to." Ike sighed. "The cat was no concern of hers so its appearance or lack thereof wouldn't register until she needed him for the scene. It's how Luna treated every living thing. It was invisible until it served a need for her. As for you no longer being welcome, you can't really expect staying on the premise was an option once you accused one of the stars of murder."

Paul choked on a swallow of coffee.

"I didn't accuse anyone of murder," I said.

"After speaking with you, the sheriff and his deputy dragged Garrison off."

Ike scanned the room and made checkmarks on his clipboard. "All are present."

He was doing everything possible to ignore my presence and not create a scene. The director made it quite clear he was not happy with us being there. I held onto the strap of Ebenezer's carrier, a slight reminder that without me, Ebenezer wasn't available, and they'd have to reshoot a lot of scenes.

Edward stared hard at me, finally diverting his attention to the assembled cast members. "The chief of police is threatening to shut the production down later today. So, we have one chance to get this right. Since Anne is still on her way back from the hospital, we'll shoot the reaction scenes after the victim collapses and the part when the police arrive and ask questions of the party guests. After that Anne and Garrison should be here. Anyone not an extra or film crew member, leave the set."

"I'm here with Ebenezer and I'll be staying and monitoring him. He has a knack for finding his way into trouble."

Edward pointed upstairs. "His scene is in the study. It'll be shot last. You can wait up there with the pet."

The director yelled roll as I walked up the stairs. The carrier bounced against my hip with every step. For once, Ebenezer was nice and quiet. The movement must've lulled him to sleep. There was yellow police tape strung across Marie's door. Grief welled up in me. Marie. Katrina. So many deaths surrounding the movie. Even with Ebenezer in it, this was one Christmas movie I'd never watch.

"Let's check out your set." I hoisted the strap onto my shoulder and opened the door to the study.

The room looked the same as the other day, except for a disorganized pile of papers on the desk. I placed Ebenezer in his carrier on the overstuffed chair in the corner then lifted up the corner of the area rug and shoved a lamp cord underneath it. "I'm going to make sure there's nothing on the floor you can nibble on."

Ebenezer whistled and pressed the side of the carrier.

"I know, buddy, you want out. You need to stay in there until it's show time. I've already irritated the director enough."

On my hands and knees, I crawled around peering underneath the desk and the chairs. Scooting backwards, my feet hit the bookcase that was right behind me. There was a thud and a clink. I groaned and lowered my head for a second. Hopefully, whatever it was didn't break it.

I rose and dusted off my knees, turning and facing the massive bookcase. One of the photographs had fallen over. Carefully, I picked it up, relieved that the glass hadn't broke. It was the photo of a young woman who resembled Luna and a young child who I could envision was Garrison. The resemblance was uncanny.

I brought the photo closer to my eyes, studying it. The script called for Luna's character reconnecting with the estranged son she had sent to live at a boarding school while she traveled the world for her modeling career—a son she told everyone was her nephew.

Garrison had called her Luna. Not Ms. Carmichael as the other male members of the cast. Marie had said only men related to or married to her called her by her first name. Had Luna written the script based off her life? What if the movie itself was Luna's tell-all? Was that what Sheriff Rhodes had meant the other night? The sheriff knew Garrison and Luna were related and it was a secret that needed to be revealed. Who wanted to keep the relationship quiet, Luna or Garrison? How did Garrison feel about Luna searching for her long-lost daughter? His sister. The most confusing question was why hide it?

The door opened. I shoved the picture back into its spot. Or at least tried. It was too close to the edge and fell onto the ground by a pair of feet in black oxfords. Garrison. He gazed down on it and then at me, tilting his head to the side.

"Checking out the décor," I said.

"I see that." He squatted down and picked up the photograph, gazed at it for a long moment before sighing and placing it back on the shelf.

"It's amazing how the director found a picture of an aunt and nephew that resemble you and Luna so much."

Garrison closed the door and stood in front of it. "Yes, it is."

I should've moved toward the door before I mentioned anything. I studied Garrison's expression, hoping to gauge his attitude. It was hard to tell; the man was so calm. No frown. No smile. Completely and utterly neutral. Was he acting?

He moved away from the door and sat in the office chair. He placed his hands on the desk, palms up. "Just ask me. I'm trying to be as unthreatening as possible."

"Ask you?"

"I'm not stupid, Merry. You know there are secrets being kept on this set and one...or some of them...is why Marie and likely Katrina were killed. For the record that person wasn't me."

I grabbed the straps of Ebenezer's carrier and lifted him from the chair, wanting him in my arms for a quick escape. "Is Luna your mother? I never believed the rumor saying you were having an affair with her."

Garrison grimaced and turned a little green. "Yes, she is."

"Anne knows the truth, doesn't she? I heard her demanding Ike defend you to the crew or tell Luna so she could stop the rumors."

Garrison let out a bark of a laugh. "That explains why Anne

has been hovering around me so much. Kind of sweet she wants to protect me."

"Was that why you texted Anne last night and said you were in trouble? You knew she'd help you."

His eyes narrowed. "I never contacted her. If I was in trouble, Anne would be the last person I'd call. I'd never want her hurt, especially because of me."

"Anne said you were in trouble. That was why she ran out of the diner. She went looking for you."

He paled and plopped onto the office chair. "Someone texted her about me."

"You didn't?" I knew what I heard. Anne had said Garrison was in trouble. Had someone called her threatening him? "Who did?"

"I don't know. That's why the police let me leave after checking my phone."

"Anne's phone! They should—"

"It's gone. Either the person who knocked her out and tossed her into the lake took it or it's lost in it. Anne can't remember who contacted her. The doctor says it's not that unusual after a head injury to be confused about what happened. The sheriff said it'll be days before they can get the records."

There was one reason Anne might've been concerned about Garrison being in trouble, someone else knew the truth about him and Luna. Something the pair wanted hidden. "Why did you and Luna hide the fact that she's your mother? How were you able to?"

"Luna has always been good at hiding parts of her life. Luna Carmichael is her stage name. It's rare to see a picture that isn't of her being part of a cast. Plus, it was easier forty-some-odd years ago to keep secrets. Information wasn't at everyone's fingertips."

"Desiree Young. That was her real name."

"No." An emotion flashed in his eyes and he quickly blinked, chasing it away. "Where did you see that name?"

I wasn't sure I wanted to answer, so I went with asking another question. "Do you know if there are any other secrets your mother is keeping?"

"You two done gossiping about me," Luna snapped at us.

We spun toward the door. We were so engrossed in our conversation we hadn't heard the door open.

"It's not gossip, Mother, if it's the truth." There was no mistaking the snideness in Garrison's tone when he said mother.

"I'm just trying to understand what's going on," I said.

"You're not my daughter so there's no reason for you to care."

"Marie was killed. Katrina was killed. That's more than enough reason for me."

"Wouldn't even matter if she was." Bitterness flowed from Garrison. "Not all moms care about their children. Luna played the mom role once and it didn't take. It was the year that picture was taken. Apparently, it wasn't the first time she tried and decided it wasn't for her. I should appreciate the fact she left me on my father's doorstep and didn't dump me in a trash can."

Luna grabbed his arm, her whole body shaking in anger. "Who told you that? Edward? I didn't throw anyone away."

"Really? Because I've watched you do it my whole life, including to my dad. You know he'd never say a bad thing about you." He peeled her fingers, one by one, from his arm. "Even it was true. As you said there's no reason for us to care. The person who has the most to lose about the truth coming out is you—and you're one person I no longer care about."

TWENTY-TWO

I adjusted the glitter bowtie the stylist insisted Ebenezer wear for his part in the scene. My little buddy was to grab a ribbon and scurry off with it. The original plan for the cat was tying the ribbon onto his collar and scaring the cat, filming it from the side so it looked like the cat had the ribbon in its mouth. With Ebenezer's love of ribbon and all things string and rope, getting him to grab the ribbon and race away with it was easy, having him not eat it was the hard part.

Once I voiced that concern, Edward gave me permission to stay on the set so I could take the ribbon away from him. No one else was interested in taking something out of his mouth even though his teeth were tiny.

"Places everyone." Edward sat on a chair near the camera.

Filming was starting. I had to get in my spot, near the kitchen where I was out of the way, but close enough to snag my runaway pet. I wiggled my way through the sea of extras, eyes fixed on the door. "Excuse me."

Luna stood near the archway leading into the living room, squaring her shoulders and slipping the clutch under her left arm, her right hand a few inches from it. The expression on her face was definitely not Christmassy. I wasn't sure if that was because the scene being filmed required that attitude or a result of the scene between her and Garrison an hour ago.

The cameras were facing toward her and the party goers in the room. Garrison was near the tree talking to a young woman who was gazing at him in adoration. I wasn't sure if that was part of the script or just a natural expression from being so close to the man.

A hand wrapped around my wrist. "This way," a gruff voice said. Vernon.

"My spot is near the kitchen. They're not filming in this direction. I can make it in time." I leaned away from the Vernon. The tight grip he had on my arm was scaring me.

"No, you can't. A camera is focused on the kitchen door. You can stand with me out of the way from all the cameras. We'll have a great view of the scene," he whispered and tugged me past the foyer where other non-actors were loitering still and quiet in the shadows. He kept his head down low almost like he didn't want anyone to notice him.

"I'm needed by the kitchen. That's where Ebenezer is running."

"I have to tell you something," he pleaded, still controlling the direction I walked. "There are some people who shouldn't overhear me. They'll be furious."

I was kind of furious right now from being manhandled. I broke from his grip. "Talk now before I create a scene."

He hunched over, bringing his mouth closer to my ear. "Please, it's about Katrina. And it might relate to Marie's death."

Okay, I'd listen. It wasn't like I was in danger. There were people all around.

Vernon placed a hand on my back and maneuvered me to a small alcove where I guessed a small built-in bookcase had once been. Now, it was turned into a small bench.

"It's sturdy enough to stand on." Vernon smiled and held out his hand. "It'll give you a better view of the scene and your pet."

"I'm here because of the information you have on Katrina."

"We need a reason we're over here. Plus, you'll hear me better if you match my height."

Slipping off my Christmas-themed canvas sneakers, the only Christmas attire I allowed myself in July, I stepped up. I was in the shadows, out of the way, but able to see everything. Vernon eased into the space between the bench and the wall. I had the perfect view of the living room where the majority of the party scene was taking place. I knew Luna was perishing in this scene, near the buffet table, and from my hiding spot, I'd see it without anyone blocking my view.

Vernon's shoulder leaned into mine. "I told Katrina Luna was her mother."

I spun toward him, nearly toppling off the bench. Vernon snagged hold of my waist, keeping me from falling down.

"I found a letter from her to Luna amongst the discarded fan mail when I was packing up my stuff after Luna threw me out of our home. I thought if I found Luna's daughter, I'd win her back. Never considered I was hurting Marie by agreeing with Katrina." There was a deep regret in his eyes.

"Did you tell the sheriff or your cousin this?"

"Roll," the director shouted.

Actors and actresses moved about, some putting presents under the tree, others kissing cheeks. Garrison was standing in front of the Christmas tree, a glass of eggnog in his hand. Anne was sitting in a chair near the director with a security guard standing behind her and glaring at everyone who dared approach. I wondered if they'd worked a guard into the scene or if one was dressed as a party goer.

Luna slapped her purse into Garrison's stomach. "I will not be lied about."

Garrison tossed the purse onto a table behind him. "It's not the time, Auntie. Besides, one person's truth is another person's lie and who knows which one it is."

She smoothed the sides of her hair and adjust the drape of her necklace. "When you allow other people access to your story, they muck it all up. Sometimes to live the life you want, you must create it yourself. That doesn't make it a lie."

"Doesn't make it the truth either."

She drew in a deep breath.

"Cut. What is going on here?" Edward flipped through the script, a perplexed expression deepening on his face.

"I'm improvising. Deal with it." Luna's heels clicked on the marble floor as she headed for the dining room. She passed by the area I was standing. "Roll the film."

Edward frowned and rolled his wrist in the air.

From the corner of my eye, I spotted a movement low on the ground, sneaking past the Christmas tree. It was Ebenezer. Without a ribbon. It wasn't time for him yet. Either he escaped from the crew member or the person responsible for releasing Ebenezer was confused with Luna's improvisations.

As the extras moved with Luna toward the buffet, I hopped off the benched and merged into the crowd, keeping my head low, hoping my t-shirt wasn't spotted among the formal wear. Just a few more feet and I'd snag Ebenezer before he ruined the scene.

Anne leaned forward, placing a hand on the director's shoulder and whispered in his ear. He nodded and motioned her forward. She slipped off a coat draped over her shoulders and headed for the front door. I guessed she was entering into the scene to fix everything or find out, using her own dialogue changes, what Luna was doing. The guard followed her outside.

Luna snatched a goblet of water from a tray an extra was carrying and chugged half the glass before depositing it on the table. She dabbed at her mouth with a napkin, crumbling it into a ball before tossing it on the floor.

The extra sent a panicked look at the director. Everyone was thrown off by Luna's ad-libbing.

She ate a few pita chips and chugged down the glass of water in the flute. She tossed it over her shoulder.

Anne jumped back, the plastic cup nearly clunking her in the head. "Are you all right, Mrs. March?" Anne asked, using the name of Luna's character.

Ignoring the question, Luna snatched another plastic champagne flute filled with water and stumbled to the other side of the buffet table, knocking extras out of her way. Her gaze desperately scanned the room. She waved, trying to gain Garrison's attention.

Slapping a hand over his eyes, Ike moaned. "Is she drunk? Shouldn't you end this?"

Luna was sober when I spoke with her an hour ago.

Edward covered up the mouthpiece of his headset. "Let's see where she's going with this. Luna said she was improvising. Maybe the death scene wasn't splashy enough."

Luna coughed and reached for another water glass and tried drinking it. Water dribbled down her chin, dotting her silk gown with drops. She patted her throat, lifting her chin toward the ceiling. The glass slipped from her finger. Her head jerked around until her panicked gaze found me.

The extras and other cast members chatted with each other, trying their best to adapt to Luna's impromptu changes to the script. Luna grasped the edge of the table, now hitting at her throat and making a gagging sound. The director leaned forward, grinning. I guess he liked the changes.

Luna looked over at us. Eyes wide and panicking, hands clawing at her throat. I frowned and slipped forward, no longer caring what Ebenezer planned on doing. Her gaze locked onto mine.

"She's choking!" I screamed. I took a step forward, Vernon grabbed my arm and dragged me backwards.

"You can't interrupt a scene like that," he whispered harshly. "Let her finish it."

Luna twitched and her body went slack. She crumbled to the floor and laid on her side, one hand splayed out and the other on her neck. The fear in her eyes grabbed onto me. Something wasn't right.

Cast members gasped. Someone screamed. "Call an ambulance."

"Cut. It wasn't perfect but with some editing it'll be great." Edward sounded so pleased.

I broke away from Vernon and watched Luna's chest. It wasn't rising. Oh my god! Luna wasn't acting. I ran over. Splotches of red dotted her face, throat, and hands. Her lips were swelled.

"Doctor," I shouted, turning her onto her back. "She needs a doctor!"

No one moved. I placed my shaking fingers on the pulse in her neck nothing. I grabbed her wrist with my other hand. Her pulse was weak. I stared at her chest. It wasn't moving. Luna Carmichael was dying.

I removed my gaze from Luna's inert form and looked at Edward who was standing behind the camera. "She's not breathing."

The director clapped his hands. "Print. It's a wrap everyone."

"This isn't ad-libbing." I shouted over the din of voices and movement. "Luna needs help. She's dying."

TWENTY-THREE

Garrison pushed stunned crew members out of his path and ran over to Luna. He dropped beside her and rested his head on her chest. He fumbled around for her wrist and held onto it for dear life. He tapped her cheek. "Come on, Luna, talk to me." He cast a frantic gaze around the room. "Get the medic!"

A security guard began performing CPR.

Nearby, I heard an authoritative voice asking for an ambulance and the police. Paul. He was at the RV. I texted him. I wasn't sure how long it would take for an ambulance to arrive. My mind was numb as I tried comprehending what was happening. Anne sobbed, hands covering her face.

I inched back on my knees, giving Edward and Garrison space. Tears glittered in his eyes and his hands shook as he tried bringing her around. Luna's lips and face were turning blue. We were running out of time.

Someone grabbed my arm, yanking me away from Luna. Olivia's eyes blazed and she shook me. "Did you put peanuts in the cookies yesterday? She's allergic."

I shook my head. "No, you said someone was—"

The front door opened and slammed shut.

"What?" Edward stared at the food on the buffet and paled. "No one told me that."

"Does she have an EpiPen?" Paul placed his fingers on Luna's pulse, face grim.

"Find her EpiPen," Olivia shouted. "She always carries one with her."

Paul patted Luna's sides then her legs. "I'm not feeling one."

The red purse. "She was carrying a red glittery purse when the scene started," I said.

The cast and crew started looking around the room; someone dropped to their hands and knees and peered under the couches. Vernon started tossing the purses from the party guests onto the floor, desperately searching for Luna's purse prop.

"Hang in there, darling," Vernon said. "We'll find it."

Most of the extras backed up, while a few inched closer and snuck cell phones out of pockets to snap a photo. Slipping off his suit coat, Garrison held it out, blocking the view of Paul performing CPR on Luna. Olivia and the catering staff positioned themselves around Luna, blocking the photo takers.

"Show some respect," a tall and muscular crew hand said, holding out his beefy arms. "Anymore photos and we'll physically remove you."

"I don't see it," a man said.

"Try under the tree. Maybe it got mixed in with the presents."

Oh no! Had Ebenezer taken it? I scanned the room. Where was he?

"Why would it?" Vernon hunched over the presents, pushing them out of the way.

"It has to be somewhere," someone said.

"Maybe she has one in her vanity." I scrambled to my feet and bounded up the stairs.

In my haste, I almost tripped and face-planted on the stairs. I grabbed the rail and kept myself righted and on my feet. My mind was whirling, trying to remember which drawer the EpiPen was in. The top drawer. I ran down the hall and yanked open the door, reminding myself to slow down before I collided into the clothing rack that was likely in front of the door.

The rack was there. Why the stylist and Luna thought that was the perfect placement I had no idea. It was cumbersome and squealed as I pushed it out of the way, took less time than fighting through the vast array of dresses, sweaters, and slacks.

A window slammed shut. The hair stylist waved her hands around in the air and kicked something under the vanity. "What are you doing in here?"

"Luna is having an allergic reaction. Need her EpiPen. Can't find the one she was carrying."

The woman's eyes widened, and she ripped the drawer open on the vanity. "How did that happen? Olivia doesn't allow anything in the house with peanuts."

"There was a mishap with the food delivery yesterday. The chef had some of the cast and crew helping prepare the food." The perfect opportunity for slipping in the allergen.

"Where is it?" The woman's voice grew frantic and she threw items out of the top drawer of the vanity. "She always keeps one in here. Said that every year, she discovers something new she's allergic to. A week ago, she found out she's allergic to red dye."

"Did she tell anyone?" I ran through all the foods being made in the kitchen. Was anything red? The drinks? Luna knew about her allergy; she'd avoid consuming anything red.

"Her new assistant knew. The woman tried giving her a bottle with a strawberry drink. I'd assume Olivia knows also." The stylist let out a happy cry and pulled the EpiPen from the drawer. "Here it is."

I snagged it and ran, taking the stairs two at a time, heart pounding as I feared too much time had passed. "I have it."

Paul took it from me and pressed it into Luna's outer thigh. She remained unconscious, lips still blue and face pale and splotchy.

"Why isn't it working?" Vernon sounded panicked. "Shouldn't she be better."

Paul met my gaze. I covered my mouth, holding in my gasp. The look in his eyes said he didn't think Luna would make it. We were too late. I scanned the room and everyone in it. No one was holding the purse though an extra was cuddling a rather pleased Ebenezer. Where was the purse? Who took it?

Sirens screamed from outside and a few moments later,

paramedics raced in. Edward and Ike moved everyone away, giving the medical team plenty of space to work. Quickly, Luna was placed on the gurney.

Paul handed over the EpiPen and told the paramedics everything that he'd done. Vernon hovered by the door, shifting his weight. The paramedics raised the gurney and wheeled Luna toward the door.

Vernon stepped toward them. "She shouldn't be alone. I'll go—"

"No. I'll go with her," Garrison said.

"I'm her husband." Vernon pushed Garrison back into the house.

"And I'm her son."

Vernon gaped at him and stumbled backwards. Silence blanketed the room followed by murmurs.

Anne squeezed Garrison's shoulder then wrapped her arms around herself, tears flowed down her face. "Call me, okay."

Garrison nodded and hurried after his mother.

"I'll inform Sheriff Rhodes," Edward said. "Keep me updated on Luna's condition, son."

Vernon stepped outside only to be dragged back in by his cousin.

"No one else is leaving until I find out what happened," Chief Quinn said.

"I need to be with my wife."

"I don't think she'd want you there. She is divorcing you." Quinn kept a tight hold of her cousin's arm. "Someone start explaining."

"She had been patting her throat. She seemed frantic." The words fell out of me fast and furious. A coldness washed over me and I wrapped my arms around myself. "I thought she was choking. Real choking not fake choking."

"We believe she ate or drank something she was allergic to," Ike said.

"I thought that was why Luna employed a private chef and never ate in town." Quinn frowned. She released her cousin and nodded toward him. An officer walked over and stood beside Vernon, keeping an eye on him.

What had the chief found out that had required her putting a guard on Vernon?

"There was an incident with the food for the scene," Ike said. "We were a little haphazard—"

"We weren't haphazard," Olivia screeched. "I still monitored everything that was prepared. There were no peanuts used. Matter-of-fact, no nuts at all."

"Or red dye," I said.

The sound of glass shattering had everyone staring at the sous chef standing in the dining room. He held a silver platter in his hand, one side tipping down. Shards of glass were around his feet.

"Red dye." The young man shook. "Ms. Carmichael couldn't have red dye?"

Olivia shook her head. "It was on her newest list of allergens. Didn't you read it?" There was a sharpness to her words.

"I thought I read the most updated one." His voice shook. "The candy cane cookies used red dye."

"The candy canes bought were mint," Olivia's voice rose with every word. "There was no red in it. They were green and white."

He shook his head back and forth, horror growing on his face. "Mint isn't used in the dough. Candy cane is the shape of the cookie. I split the dough and colored one red and left the other white, then I made strips and twined them together."

Gazes went to the dessert buffet table. There were a few candy cane cookies on the cookie plate. The white-and-red dough wrapped around each other, making the strips for the cane, and the tip of the cookie was curved down

"Luna didn't eat them," I said. "I saw her drink water and eat some pita chips and some dip. None of those were red."

"Or made with peanuts," Olivia said.

Fear churned through me as my mind listed all the pranks that had befallen on the movie. But putting an allergen in the food was something different. It was vicious. Dangerous. Murder. But—

"We'll collect the food and save it." Quinn motioned for two officers to step forward and begin collecting what might become evidence. "Tests will be run to determine what caused her reaction."

"What if someone did it on purpose?" My gaze locked onto the buffet table.

The extras holding plates dropped them to the floor and edged away, looking as if the items on the plate could jump up and do them in.

Ike paled. "No one would do that."

"Really. Marie is dead. Katrina is dead. Anne was attacked. And now—" I turned and focused my gaze on Vernon who hovered near the door. "What if they didn't think it would kill her? Just make her sick. The cat escaping. The fire that took out some of the props. The coffee urns spigots being jammed. The food cart being knocked from the caterer's grasp yesterday."

"That was an accident," Ike said.

"Not from where I saw it," I said. "I was in Marie's room and watched what happened. Vernon bumped into the guy. On purpose. Who knew about her allergies?"

"Me. Garrison. Ike." Anne shivered and wrapped her arms around herself. "Luna didn't like everyone knowing."

"Her assistants," I said. "Probably ex-husband."

Vernon flushed. "Rhodes knew about it also. I swear it was an accident. The siren startled me."

"Rhodes isn't here," Quinn said.

Vernon's eyes widened and he shook his head, inching back toward the door with his hand reaching for the doorknob.

Chief Quinn walked purposefully toward Vernon. "What did you do?"

He swallowed hard and held up his hands. "I didn't do that on purpose. It was an accident. I'd never hurt her."

"A convenient accident," Edward said.

"Chief, I found these in the trash." An officer held up an empty jug of peanut oil and a funnel.

Olivia gasped. "The pita chips were fried in olive oil. I don't keep peanut oil here. There would be a difference in the smell." She turned to her sous chef. "It was olive oil. Correct?"

The man grew paler and shook his head. "I'm so sorry. I don't remember. The bottle said olive oil and I used it. I didn't pay attention to how it smelled. I never thought..."

Chief Quinn's gaze zeroed in on her cousin who was inching toward the door. "Take the pans and the bottle of olive oil."

Vernon slammed into Sheriff Rhodes who was coming through the door.

The sheriff took hold of Vernon's arm. "Why are you rushing out?"

"I know what you're thinking. I didn't hurt Luna. I love her." There was a mix of anger and despair in Vernon's face as he stared at his cousin. "You have to believe me."

"Isn't that the problem?" Sheriff Rhodes commented. "She has been listening to you and ignoring evidence. Unlike your cousin, I checked your phone records. You and Katrina had called each other quite a few times. Her last two messages were to Ms. Anne Lindsey and you."

"Katrina Emerson's case is mine," Quinn said. "You have no right poking around in it."

"I found proof it tied into mine. That gave me the right."

Quinn removed her handcuffs from her utility belt. "But the sheriff is right, I have believed you and look where that's gotten me, Vernon. I have no choice. I'm bringing you in for questioning on the attempted murder of Luna Carmichael."

"Based on what?" Vernon's face turned red.

"Really want me announcing that here?" Quinn asked.

Vernon opened his mouth then closed it, swallowing hard before trying again. He turned, placed his hands behind his back, and leaned forward. "Take me in. But I'm not saying anything else until I consult my attorney."

TWENTY-FOUR

Ebenezer raced around the RV, chasing after a plastic, round Christmas bulb I gave up for his entertainment. It was the only thing that enticed him to leave me alone while I worked on piecing this mystery together. After speaking with the police for hours, I was escorted back to my RV with the order of remaining inside until the police and sheriff were satisfied all evidence had been collected. So far, it was a long, boring, and headache-inducing afternoon.

I drew diagram after diagram, list after list and I kept coming back to the one thing connecting Marie, Luna, and Katrina: Luna's search for her daughter. Marie was looking into it and Katrina believed she was the one. Who wouldn't want the truth coming out? The father of the child? From what Luna had said, she hadn't been entirely sure where the baby had been left. Was the father the person who actually abandoned the child, and if so, where had he left the baby? Edward admitted he was one of the possibilities of the baby's father—who was the other?

From what I knew about Luna, she wasn't a woman who made random, spur of the moment decisions. She chose Carol Lake for a reason.

Sharon Zimmerman. Luna moved close but not too close to her. Sharon must've been the strongest choice and why Luna made Carol Lake her home base. The rest of us, Katrina, Olivia, and me, were gathered here. The only person Marie had no notes about was Desiree Young. Garrison had said Desiree Young wasn't Luna's stage name. Then who was she? Had Marie found out and this woman didn't want to be known? But enough to kill? And two people at that. It didn't make sense.

I tapped my nails on the keyboard. Or had Marie immediately discounted the woman? Maybe the woman didn't want a relationship with Luna and hadn't wanted her birth mother to know anything about her and Marie agreed to let it go.

Instead of pondering it all until dinnertime, which was fast approaching, I moved the cursor over and opened up Messenger. Bright would have some ideas. So far, she had tracked down pretty much everyone in her family tree. Hopefully, she had some spare time for tracking down Desiree Young. A quick search on Google resulted in a lot of options. It would take months to sort through them all.

Hate to bother you with non-crafting work but can use some more research help.

Two minutes passed by and I received a response from Bright. *Does this have to do with Luna Carmichael's death?*

I froze for a moment. Death? Luna had died and the word was already out. I snagged my phone and called Paul. He had followed the ambulance in case Garrison needed someone. Paul hadn't been in the house when Luna was poisoned and thought it was safe for him to leave.

"Did Luna die?" I blurted out the question the moment he answered.

"How did you find out?"

"From Bright."

Paul sighed. "We shouldn't be surprised. A movie star dying during the shooting of a film was news. Someone at the hospital must've leaked it."

Messenger pinged. I glanced at it. A row of question marks from Bright. I pressed the phone between my cheek and shoulder and quickly typed, *Yes. In a way. Trying to find information about the remaining possible daughter. She might like knowing who her mother was.*

Are you sure? It's not like she'd be able to have a relationship with her. Might be more painful.

I sighed.

"You okay?" Paul asked.

"Bright isn't sure I should still look for the daughter now that Luna is gone. Might hurt her."

"How would you feel? Would you want to know? At least the woman would know her mother had spent the last few weeks looking for her. That might matter."

"You're right. Regardless of Luna's reasonings, she had wanted her daughter to know the truth." Or at least the truth about who her mother was. The father would likely remain a mystery. Unless Edward Yale decided he was okay with being named the father regardless of the truth.

I'd want to know. I typed and hit send.

I'll help. Name?

Desiree Young. Found notes on the candidates. Nothing about her except the name.

Anything that can help me narrow it down?

Birth date would be around Christmas. 1974. I tapped on the photo icon and enlarged the picture of the notes on Sharon, jotting down the key points then doing the same thing for Olivia and Katrina. *The states we were found aren't the same. I'm West Virginia. Olivia, Maryland. Katrina, Pennsylvania. Sharon, Pennsylvania.*

Last names and cities.

I sent Bright the information and stared at the screen, waiting for her response. What would she find out? Would it answer our problems?

This might take a few hours, Bright responded. *I'll let you know as soon as I dig anything up.*

I flipped back and forth through the photos of Marie's notes. There was something I was missing. Why was Sharon the strongest choice of being her daughter? Luna brought us all here. The key was the location. Carol Lake. There was a reason Luna wanted everyone here. Which meant Desiree was here in Carol Lake. Either she was working on the film or lived in Carol Lake. Ike and his list. If Desiree worked on the film, I'd find her on it.

After securing Ebenezer in the bedroom with enough food and entertainment, I went in search of Ike. A few golf carts with cast and crew members drove by heading for town. I waved, seeking out their attention. Why was everyone leaving?

Finally, a young woman stopped. "Can I help you?"

"Where's everyone going?"

"Into town to finish wrapping up the movie. The Christmas bazaar scene is tonight."

"Even after..." I stopped talking. Maybe everyone else hadn't heard that Luna died.

"Yes, even after this morning's incident as Director Yale refers to it. He said even if Luna died, she'd want the film finished. It was important to her."

Was it the movie that was important or what she was revealing through it? Had Luna feared for her life and the film was a backup plan, so the truth got out if something happened to her? Or did Luna just love toying with people?

From what I knew about Luna, she was a love them, marry them, and divorce them type. Chief Quinn had mentioned the break-up between her cousin and Luna seemed to happen overnight. One moment, they were happily married and the next split up. Luna had said she hadn't known the baby was thrown away. She handed the baby to her traveling companion. Not the baby's father. Why use the word "companion" if she meant the father?

Was Vernon the companion and because of the letter, Luna had found out the baby had been thrown away and that caused the sudden end of the marriage? She kept him around in case she discovered the baby had died, so the person responsible was nearby to take the fall. But why would Vernon stay? Had he planned on making sure the truth remained quiet? Were the pranks ways for him to divert the truth or get rid of something?

The boxes. I froze. The answer might be in one of the trash boxes. Had the garbage been taken yet? Should I head for Luna's house or look for Ike? The chances were the police were at Luna's and searching through everything and had taken anything that was possible evidence. The best thing for me was finding out if Desiree Young lived in Carol Lake or was part of the crew or cast.

Unfortunately, Ike took the golf cart back this morning, so it was a long walk into town for me. On a very hot summer day. I wiped the sweat trickling from my brow. Only one more mile left until I reached the town limits of Carol Lake and then about a half-mile until the town square where the scene was taking place. The hum of an engine grew closer. I stepped off to the side. The golf cart stopped in the middle of the road.

"I'm needed in town for a scene." Garrison patted the seat beside him, a forced smile on his face. "Why don't you come along? You can see all your hard work being staged in the little shops."

"You sure you want to give me a ride? I was given the impression the power-that-be firmly believed I tried ruining your life."

"My dad gets overprotective at times. Hop in."

Overprotective enough to kill? I pushed the thought away. "You couldn't get today off?"

"Why should..." He trailed off and the smile fell. Grief flashed in his eyes and his shoulder slumped forward. "This is the last movie my mother will ever be in. I want it finished. There's just one more scene."

"I'm sorry for your loss." I slipped into the seat. "I'd think they'd give everyone some mourning time. Or haven't they told the cast and crew yet?"

"It won't affect them. Fans will miss Luna Carmichael, the queen of Christmas. Cara Michael, the real person, people won't miss. She was a very self-centered woman. She only had people in her life for her benefit."

"But she was still your mom. It's okay for you to miss and

grieve her."

The engine hummed and we putted down the road. The slight breeze from the movement of the cart cooled me down. I twisted my hair off my neck and fanned the back of my neck with my hand.

I eyed his attire. The poor guy was wearing a sweater and blue jeans. "Aren't you roasting?"

"Just wait until I have to put on the scarf, gloves, hat, and coat." He briefly glanced back at the pile of winter wear in the area usually reserved for golf clubs.

"Has to be miserable."

"It's one of the drawbacks of starring in a Christmas movie. But I'd rather roast for a while than not be in it."

"What is it about this movie that made you want to star in it? I know my Christmas movies and you've never been in one before."

"Luna asked. She never wanted us working on a movie together. Afraid someone would notice our resemblance." His voice broke and he drew in a deep breath. "Christmas crafter. That's an unusual career choice."

"It wasn't my only job. While my children were growing up, I also worked as a golf shop pro and a tax preparer. It's hard raising a family on crafting income."

"The father didn't help you out." He sent a sympathetic gaze in my direction.

My face heated. "No. I was fortunate that my ex-husband always supported his children. If there was something his children needed, he'd provide it even if it wasn't written in the decree. He's a good guy."

"What made you divorce him? If I'm being too nosy just tell me."

"I don't mind. We both just felt like we couldn't truly be who we were with each other. We saw the world in different ways, and it caused some turmoil. I grew up in a happy home and wanted that for my children, and unfortunately that meant my children having one home with their mom and one with their dad. We did the best thing for us and our children though some people would argue we didn't because we divorced. Relationships are complicated."

"That they are." There was a deep sadness in his tone.

"What got you interested in acting?" I asked, hoping a change of topic brought some cheer back into our conversation. It was hard prying when a person was guarded.

"As you know both my parents are in the business, so I grew up around it. I spent a lot of time on sets, it was the only time I really spent with Luna. My father thought it was best we were at least acquaintances."

My heart ached for him.

"Though," Garrison continued, "I always leaned more toward directing. Being in front of the camera isn't comfortable for me, but I couldn't turn down the opportunity to act with my mother. It was important to her."

"Luna wanted you to have a role in the movie?"

"She wanted me in the leading male role. Said it was her way of giving my career the boost it needed. I knew there was something else going on."

Luna was trying to make up for not being a mother to him. She knew her relationship with her son, or lack of one, would also come out and would let everyone know the way she treated her daughter wasn't a one-time mistake by a scared teenager, but part of who she was. "She wanted you here if her daughter was found."

"Yep. She wanted the whole family together." His grip tightened on the steering wheel.

Edward had told me he was one of the possibilities. "The baby she gave up was Edward's daughter. She had two children with your dad." And, in a way, abandoned both.

"He thinks so. Luna told me it wasn't him. There was never a second possibility. She wants a father for the daughter and knows my father is the kind of man who'll step up and be there for this woman."

"Does the man know Luna is looking for the child?"

"Yes. She contacted him."

"Who is he?"

"She wouldn't say. Said she and the man came to an understanding then, and now, that benefits them both."

"Do you think this man, the baby's father, killed Luna?"

Garrison nodded. "But the sheriff and the chief have closed the case."

"Why?"

"Because they have found the murderer."

"Who? Why don't you believe them?"

"Because they say the murderer is Katrina. Apparently, a note was found in her old room that ties her into this and an EpiPen was hidden in a shoe."

"Who found the note?"

"A security guard along with the Chief Quinn and Sheriff Rhodes. Rhodes didn't trust Quinn, and Quinn didn't trust him, so the security guard went with them."

"That does seem rather convenient," I said. "Did they say what was in the note?"

"They wouldn't give me many details just that it appears she'd been researching Luna a lot. Luna wasn't the first celebrity Katrina had tried claiming was her mother."

"Why hadn't anyone discovered this beforehand?" At least Marie. Why hadn't she made sure that Luna was protected from Katrina...unless that was what the argument between Marie and Katrina was about the first night I was here.

"Because Luna wanted her here anyway. Luna convinced Anne to let Katrina be her assistant, even though the woman didn't have any experience."

"Your mother wanted Katrina here in case she was her daughter and once Marie knew it wasn't true, she wanted Katrina gone." And Luna sent Marie to do the dirty work.

Something was troubling me about this conversation. Edward hadn't said he shared the letter with Garrison, so how did he know about it? I squirmed in the seat. Why hadn't I picked up anything from Katrina. You'd think I'd be better at reading people—especially killers by now.

"How did you find out?" I scooted over to the end of the seat and gripped the bar on the passenger side, preparing to bail if necessary.

"Luna. She told me she was being blackmailed about her past and I'd soon hear she had a daughter. She was getting all the key players together. I asked her who was the dad and she said it wasn't an important detail."

The barn-like building loomed in front of us. The diner was packed. The parking lot was filled with motorcycles, trucks, cars and a section of the lot was portioned off with ropes on the ground with a sign stating it was for golf carts only.

The cart rolled over the rope and Garrison pulled to a stop at the end of a row of carts. Each one had winter gear stored in the back. Everyone was waiting until the last moment to don their gear for the scene. Couldn't say I blamed them.

"Do you know everyone who's on the cast and crew?" I asked.

"Pretty much. Why?" Garrison turned off the engine and pocketed the key.

"Did your mom tell you all the names of the women she thought were her daughter?"

"You. Katrina. Olivia."

"There were two more. One of the women Marie had no information on. Everyone has been tied to the movie in some way, either hired or considered to work on the film. I think she either lives in town or is working on the movie."

"What's her name?"

"Desiree Young."

There was a flash in his eyes, like a moment of recognition before he blinked, and the expression faded from his gaze. His shoulders slumped forward. "Marie was at the end of her list and died before confirming for Luna that this woman was her daughter. That's a shame."

Was that what Marie was doing? Eliminating the candidates first before moving on to the next. In a way it made sense, why give a woman false hope about their birth mother looking for them, but it also seemed to draw out the process longer. Paul would know his cousin's work process best.

Maybe the only tie to Carol Lake was it was a small town, not too far and not too close to Harmony, and perfect for the movie's home base. The large town might have more people asking questions, diving into Luna's past while the small-town people were less trusting of the movie folk and kept their distance.

"I'm going inside for a drink and a sandwich. You can join me."

"I wanted to check out the bazaar booths in the town square and make sure they have everything." And chat with Ike.

I headed toward the center of town. Birds chirped and flew around. How was the crew dealing with that? Maybe that was why a lot of the scenes, especially the outdoor ones, were filmed at night. No birds or other wildlife running around.

Twenty booths created a circle in the town square. There were food booths and craft booths. The stuffed creatures and critters I bought from Sharon were split into two booths. The Christmas themed ones filled up one while the magical and other animals were in another. The ornaments I created were hung on small artificial trees that filled up a booth near a movie camera. I couldn't help the excitement racing through me knowing it was a featured spot in the film.

I spotted Ike in the middle of the circle, checking off his list. The man was as enamored with his list as Santa Claus. Hopefully, he had Desiree on it. I wasn't looking forward to going shop-to-shop and asking if anyone knew a Desiree Young.

"Is a Desiree Young a part of the cast or crew?" I asked.

"Why should I tell you?" Ike held the list protectively to his chest.

"Because she might be important to what's been happening around here." It was the best answer I could give him without revealing too much.

"She's responsible for the pranks?"

I stared at him, debating with myself on running with that

theory or remaining vague. I waited too long and Ike's eyes widened.

"You think she's involved in Luna's death. Why isn't the chief or the sheriff asking me about her instead of you?"

It was a good question. "Because they think they have the murderer. If they're wrong someone else could be in danger."

"Like who?" His eyes narrowed.

"Anne. She was thrown into the lake. Katrina was likely already dead when that happened." Something the police and sheriff were overlooking. "Please can I look at your list, or can you tell me if Desiree Young is on it?"

"Fine, I'll look, but I'm telling the chief about this conversation." Ike flipped through his list, running a finger over everyone's name. "You'd think I'd have them memorized by now."

I shifted my weight, doing my best not to lean against Ike and read the list myself. After ten minutes, I caved to temptation and crowded into Ike's personal space. "Do you have the cast members listed by their real name or stage name?"

Ike tugged the clipboard away from me. "I only need the names used on set. There's enough here to keep track of without remembering birth names."

"Does anyone know?"

"Yes, Edward and Vernon."

"Vernon?"

"Yes, he's a financial attorney and since he already knew some of Luna's financial business from having been her husband, and he was a hometown boy, he was hired for the film. We had to make sure we were following all the tax laws and rules for Indiana."

Vernon knew everyone's name.

TWENTY-FIVE

I hurried across the bridge, staying in the middle, as I crossed to the other side of the lake where Katina was murdered. The spot was far enough away from the town square that none of the crew putting together the booths would've seen or heard anything. The construction noises would've covered everything up, and Katrina might've been dead when she was left near the lake. An easy place for her to be discovered.

Was Vernon still in custody? They couldn't have let him off that easily especially if he had ties to Katrina. The woman couldn't have murdered herself—unless the police discovered evidence that Katina had killed herself knowing she killed Luna. What if only Chief Quinn was there? Would she believe me? Arrest him? She had to know the other work he did for the film besides being a security guard. Or was she working with her cousin?

I pulled out my phone and called Paul. It was better someone knew where I was going. He answered on the second ring and I rushed out what I had figured out.

Paul drew in a deep breath. "That theory makes sense with Marie asking about you a few weeks ago. She said Luna was having trouble finding the perfect crafting expert for the Christmas movie and wondered if you'd be interested in applying. Mentioned your Christmassy name fit right in. She knew that wasn't your birth name. Marie probably figured your birth parents might have originally had a birth certificate with your real name on it, but once they left you, your parents named you Merry."

"My parents said nothing was left with me. No note even

saying the day I was really born. But we know it's not me," I said, in a way desperate for it not to be true. I hadn't ever given much thought in finding them and now with it implanted into my head, I didn't want to know that my birth mother was now dead, especially knowing the end of my adoptive mother's life was approaching. Tears pricked my eyes. I couldn't deal with it.

But did it matter? I had a great mother. Gloria Winters loved me with everything she had, gave her all for me just like my adopted dad had. I had a wonderful childhood with people who treated me with nothing but love and acceptance. They couldn't have loved me anymore even if they had been my birth parents. I knew that for sure.

"Then who does it leave?" Paul asked.

"Anne." The name rushed out of me.

"Anne?"

"Luna had a reason for everyone she hired. Why hire Anne, an actress with little lead role experience, for the role? It fits with the other hiring decisions Luna made and since Edward knew about the letter, I bet he went along with it. Anne was thrown into the lake. What if the daughter was the one who wrote the note and wanted the truth out? The only person that leaves who didn't want it known was the father."

"Would this guy really kill his daughter?'

Sadness welled up in me. "He tried before."

"Let me check the copies I made of Marie's binders and the papers that were in the box you retrieved from the sheriff."

"You took them with you?"

"I didn't want them left in the RV...with you." There was rustling in the background.

He was protecting me.

"All I see is a copy of a script with notes," Paul said.

"Why would Marie make notes about the script? She wasn't Luna's real assistant and wouldn't have been annotating the script for Luna, especially since Luna wrote it. Wait, Marie said she was taking Luna's autobiography to the attorney for a read through.

What if the script and the notes on it were the draft of the manuscript? I never found one."

Luna's dialogue changed the day of her murder. Why? Luna did nothing without a reason. Who had seemed the most affected by Luna's off-script comments? Garrison. Edward. Vernon.

"Merry, I get worried when you're quiet."

"The one consistent thing everyone said about Luna is she didn't make random decisions. There was a reason for everything she did, and her decisions were driven by self-preservation. Luna went off script. She wrote the script and was ad-libbing the scene the day she was killed."

"Then no one knew about the change. How could that have set the murderer off?"

I started to speak then stopped. Paul was right. "Maybe Luna was worried she was next on the list and was leaving us a clue."

"Why not just tell someone?"

All of the players possibly involved ran through my head: Sheriff Rhodes, Vernon, Chief Quinn, Katrina, Olivia, me, and even her own son Garrison. Was the father there as well? The secret was likely to harm two people: Luna and the birth father.

"Maybe she didn't know who to trust," I said. "Why bring the possible daughters and not the father, the one person Luna could point at as the real culprit for abandoning a baby in an unsafe place."

"Something that could ruin him."

"Someone like an attorney," I said. "Luna filed for divorce after Edward showed her the letter about exposing the truth about the baby. What if Luna hadn't known the baby was thrown away?"

"But she abandoned her child anyway."

"Yes, but she had meant for the baby to be in a safe place. Like my birth parents had done for me. Luna didn't want ties to Vernon."

"But why keep him around?"

"Because she was waiting for the perfect time to tell everyone the truth."

"She was going to do it during that scene."

"Yes. Vernon insisted I stand near him. Said he had news about Katrina. I bet he wanted an alibi."

"Don't do anything until I get there. I'm grabbing all the evidence and I'll meet you near the police department."

"Anne could be in danger," I said.

"She's on the set."

"That didn't help Luna."

A strong instinct was rising up in me, telling me something was wrong. I wasn't sure the feeling was about my choice in listening to Paul and heading for the police station instead of checking on Anne or my conclusion was wrong. Vernon made sense. Everything fit. Opportunity. Motive. And the fact his cousin was the police chief. He likely thought she wouldn't see him as the murderer. She'd protect him.

Yet something was throwing me off. It felt like bugs were crawling up and down my arms and my scalp. There was this heavy anxiousness in my stomach weighing me down. Almost begging me to slow down and reconsider. But reconsider what was the main issue. I didn't know what I was doing wrong.

I slipped my phone from my pocket and clutched it tightly. It was becoming my security blanket. I didn't leave without it on my person or in my hand. The humid air wrapped around me, nearly stealing my breath. Even with night approaching the heat was unbearable. Laughter and loud music came from the diner across the pond. The place was ablaze with lights from the ones shining through the window and the Christmas lights strung across the top roof, giving it the effect of a runway for Santa's sleigh. Some of the lights dripped down the sides of the building. It was a huge beacon.

Was that why someone—Vernon—picked the grassy area right off the bridge to leave Katrina's body? He knew someone on their way would spot it. Or was it a rash act? He needed a suspect for Luna's and Marie's death, and she was the perfect person. The only wrench in his plans was Anne and he tried getting rid of her.

There was a small side street, barely big enough for a car, splitting the area between the convenience store and the police station. Even though the streets were empty, I still paused and looked both ways before jogging across the street. There was a movement at the end of the street. I strained my gaze, peering down the street. A shadow slunk its way behind the police station. I leaned forward and narrowed my gaze, straining to make out the shadow again. Was I wrong?

Nope. There it was again, a slow movement, low to the ground. Not a large shadow but enough to show movement and confirm something or someone was back there.

I ran for the station, scanning the area and looking over my shoulder. Everything in me said Luna's accident wasn't a simple mistake of an allergen getting into her food. It was deliberate. The sheriff's cruiser wasn't parked out front. He either returned to Harmony to work on the case or was tying up loose ends. Had he taken Vernon with him or left him in Chief Quinn's custody? Either way, Anne was safe as along as Vernon was still in custody.

I tugged open the door and hurried inside. There were two officers hovering over the calendar marking something on it. Both looked over at me and frowned. Quinn was stalking around her office, arms waving wildly as she glared at her cousin who was sitting with his back ramrod straight. With his back toward me, I couldn't read his expression, but Chief Quinn was livid.

It was hard to make out every word, but a few leaked out. I caught the words "what" and "thinking," along with "Katrina," and "withholding information."

The younger of the two male officers placed a steaming cup of coffee on the desk then dropped into a chair. It groaned under his weight and the back shifted, nearly toppling him onto the floor. He scooted closer to the desk and turned on the computer monitor.

The older officer hitched up his utility belt and walked over to me. "How can I help you, ma'am?"

"I saw some movement behind the station, like someone

crawling."

"Stay here with Officer Albertson." He tapped on the desk. "Let the chief know I'm checking out something behind the building."

Quinn braced the back of her legs against the desk and leaned forward, placing a hand on Vernon's shoulder. Her gaze flickered toward us, head tilting to the side for a moment before focusing on Vernon. She spoke something quietly, squeezing his shoulder tightly.

"I have some information about the murders."

"Do you now?" The officer finished typing and with a flourish, turned off the monitor.

"Yes, and I don't think the chief will like it. Is the sheriff returning? I know their cases are overlapping."

A clattering and a crash came from the back of the building. There was a shout. More banging and clattering. A curse. The officer shot to his feet. I rose from the chair.

"Stay put." He rapped on the chief's window and pointed toward the back of the building, hand resting on the butt of his holstered gun.

The chief rushed out of her office, a fierce look on her face. I wasn't sure if it was about what had been going on in her office or what was now happening out here.

"There was a noise outside. Like fighting. Your officers went out there."

"Keep an eye on him." Chief Quinn jerked her heard toward Vernon who was hunched over, rocking himself back and forth.

Watch him? A criminal. A possible murderer. Though the man didn't look like a criminal who was caught but a man who just lost the love of his life, and I doubted the chief would leave me alone with a known murderer. In case I was wrong, I hung out by the door. A few shuddering sobs escaped him and then he drew in a deep breath. Sitting up, he squared his shoulders and stood.

My gaze scattered around the main room of the police station, searching for anything to stop him in case he attempted an escape. Besides standing, he hadn't moved. His arms hung limply at his sides; head lowered. Despair rolled off of him. My heart went out to him.

"I love...loved...her." His voice broke.

"I know." That didn't stop people from killing, sometimes it was the reason why. "Who's Desiree Young?"

"Who?" His features twisted in confusion.

"Desiree Young. Another potential daughter of Luna's." If he hadn't known about her then who else did? Who else could've found out the information?

"Do you think this woman killed Luna?" Slowly, he turned, his gaze burned with grief and hatred.

"No."

He fisted his hands. "I'll find who killed Luna, and then I'm going to kill them."

"That's interesting, because every piece of evidence I've found, says it's you." The male voice behind me was filled with as much hatred as Vernon's.

Slowly, I turned. Sheriff Rhodes had his gun drawn, aimed at Vernon's heart. With his other hand, he reached back and locked the front door.

"Merry, why don't you go outside?" Vernon's gaze was fixed on Rhodes.

"She has caused just as many of my problems as you. Both of you stay right there."

"She was just trying to make sure Marie's murder wasn't covered up." Vernon stepped away from me. "Not her fault you weren't doing a good job."

"I was doing my job. Following the clues. I didn't miss anything."

No, but I had. The clues. The cup. I described it to the sheriff. The one I found outside and later showed up in Marie's room was smooth. It wasn't a Yeti. I hadn't told the sheriff the brand. The Yeti brand name was raised on the base of the cup toward the bottom and the other tumbler was smooth. He had wanted a tumbler found near Luna's house because he took the one that had residue of the sleep aid and disposed of it.

The sheriff narrowed his eyes on me.

Sirens whirled from outside, heading into town.

"Sounds like something's going on, Sheriff," I said. "You should head over and help."

"Likely a fire. I can't do any good there. Such a shame the chief and her officers ran off leaving a criminal alone with a defenseless woman. Such a bad mistake." Rhodes raised his arm, the barrel now aimed at Vernon's head.

A chill ran though me. He knew I figured it out. The sheriff was the companion who dumped an infant in the trash.

Vernon lightly touched my shoulder, tapping me to move out of the way. "If you think I killed Luna and want to kill me, go right ahead. You have no reason for hurting this woman."

"You're correct. I don't. But you do."

"I'm not hurting her."

"Sure, you are. Because she figured out you were setting Katrina up for the murder. A dead woman." He pointed the barrel at us and gestured toward the main office area. "She was escaping, and you killed her. Move over there. Now."

I complied. There was nothing close enough I could snag as a weapon where I was near the chief's office. I hoped the new location gave me something.

"Be smart like the lady. Move it, O'Neal."

"I'm staying put." He crossed his arms. "Shoot me here."

"I can shoot her first and then you. Doesn't make a difference how I do it." Rhodes grinned. "Then again, she'll scream and that'll add a nice detail. One of the officers outside will hear it. Might be a better choice just in case the coroner could figure out the difference between the couple of seconds it'll take to shoot one of you first."

Through the window behind the sheriff, I saw the chief looking at us, a large orange cat held in her arms. I didn't know how to tip her off. She reached for the door. I watched the doorknob twist slightly. I cast my gaze in the direction of the sheriff, hoping she'd notice him and see the gun.

"I'll move," Vernon said. "How about you kill me, and she'll tell everyone you saved her? Right, Merry. You heard me confess."

The back door rattled. The sheriff's finger twitched. I stepped back, bumping into the desk. Liquid sloshed from a coffee mug. Hot coffee.

"I'll even write a note confessing to the murders. Tell me how you did it. I'll just get—" Vernon reached for a pen.

The sheriff aimed the gun at Vernon. "Don't move."

Carefully, I tugged the mug closer. I needed the sheriff looking at me.

"Let her go. She has nothing to do with this. How about I turn around and you can cuff me? Haul me to the sheriff's department. Lock me up. You'll have my written confession."

Rhodes let out a bitter laugh. "Right. So you can talk your way out of it? I'm sure your cousin is already covering things up for you. It's what she has done her whole life. Clean up your messes."

Messes. Katrina wasn't the only one who gathered Luna's stuff from the floor. So did the sheriff. There was one way to get his attention and save us both. I just hoped I didn't get killed before I put my plan in action. Grab the mug and throw the hot coffee in the sheriff's face.

"You helped me and Katrina pick up the items on the floor." I spoke loudly, with a slight hysterical twinge, I hoped the sheriff bought the act and the chief heard me. "You could've replaced Luna's EpiPen with an expired one. Just like you said Katrina did. And the cup. You planted it on the premise once I mentioned it to you. There won't be traces of the sleep aid in it because it's a different cup."

"That would be difficult to prove...if it was true." Rhodes roved his gaze from me to Vernon who he still pointed the gun at.

"Luna said a companion took the baby and placed the infant in a safe place. You were the companion. Luna hadn't known you threw the baby away until she started searching. She was going to tell the world."

The sheriff trained the gun on me. Before I gripped the handle of the mug, I was thrown onto the ground. A body pressing me down. There was a loud crack. The window exploded. Another crack. Sheriff Rhodes fell onto the floor a few feet away from me.

The police department was crowded with people. Deputy Paugh, who was likely now the new sheriff, separated those he needed to interview from those who were just plain nosy. The chief was sequestered in her private office while the officers and the deputy figured out how to handle the matter. After speaking with the State Police, I was stationed in a corner with Paul hovering near acting as my bodyguard. Paugh didn't want anyone talking with me until he spoke with me again. The sheriff's cat, Hercules, was wandering around the front room, rubbing his body against legs and meowing.

The chief killing the sheriff—a murderer—wasn't something anyone ever dealt with before and no one knew the proper, legal way of handling the matter. The only thing they agreed on was the chief shouldn't question anyone and it was better Vernon was transferred to the sheriff's department until it was certain what his role, if any, was in any of the deaths. From what I overheard, it was likely the State Police were taking over the case.

Paugh walked back over and handed me a bottle of water. "You're free to go. I have no more questions. The security tapes back up what you, Vernon, and the chief stated."

"The police department has security cameras." I reached down and rubbed Hercules behind his ears.

Paugh nodded. "Something Rhodes wasn't aware of."

"He's the one who switched out the EpiPens," I said.

Paugh nodded. "We searched Luna's car and found it plus a cup in the glove compartment. The plan was crushing the car, with the evidence in it, then carting it off for scrap metal. The sheriff had access into and out of the house and had free reign since he was investigating Marie's death. He replaced the olive oil with peanut oil. His prints were on the bottle."

"Which could've been explained away by him taking it as

evidence."

"Correct."

"Why did he murder Marie and Katrina?" I asked.

Paugh heaved out a sigh. "From what I'm piecing together, it looks like Katrina was after the proof that she wasn't Luna's daughter so she could destroy it. Rhodes thought that like Marie, Katrina was close to figuring out he was the one who threw the baby away. Since Katrina fled that night and she had access to Luna's vanity, he could pin the murders on her. Case solved. He was scared because if the lost daughter wasn't found—"

"That meant the baby had died and he was a murderer," I broke in.

"But I'm not dead." Anne stepped into view. Garrison and Edward were behind her. "The officer said we could come in. Was he..." she trailed off, gaze fixed on the red stain where Rhodes had fallen.

Garrison wrapped an arm around her, and she leaned her head on his shoulder.

"No," I said. "Though he and Luna had been friends..."

"Lovers," Garrison corrected.

Hercules trotted over and weaved himself first around Anne's leg then moving onto Garrison and then Edward. It was almost like the critter was testing everyone out.

"We don't know that," I said. "Your mom said companion, not father of the baby."

"Then who?" Tears filled Anne's eyes. "I never should've sent that stupid letter."

"You sent it?" Paugh asked.

Tears dripped down her face and she stepped away from Garrison. "My family is all gone. When my mother passed away, I inherited her diaries. I hadn't known she kept one. It told the real story about how I came into her life. My parents had always told me my mother placed me up for adoption through an agency. She was too young to be a mom and gave me the greatest gift by placing me for adoption. Then I read my Mom's diary about being thrown in a trash, my parents being my foster parents and then later adopting me. I was too young to remember any of it. I was furious. They lied to me. I wanted the truth and dug for it. Now I have it and I don't want it." She scrubbed her arm across her face.

"You have me," Garrison said. "No matter who your father is, you're my sister."

"I know." She tried smiling but it trembled, seeming more like a grimace. "But who's my father. Does he want me? Why did he—"

"It's Edward," Vernon blurted. "Luna told me. It's why she was divorcing me."

I frowned. "Because you weren't the father. That doesn't make sense." Garrison had said Luna told him that Edward wasn't the baby's father. Had Luna lied—or was Vernon?

Anne's eyes widened. Edward beamed. Hercules meowed loudly and stretched up, placing his paws on Edward's leg.

"No, because I told her I didn't want that guy in my house. She lied about him. Said they had only been friends."

I studied Vernon. He looked away. The man was lying.

Anne and Garrison swapped phones and were talking with each, and Edward stood between his children looking from one to the other as the spoke, Hercules cradled in his arms. They were in their own world. Thrilled with this truth—that I had a feeling wasn't the real one.

I pulled Vernon aside. "You lied. You're her—"

"I'm old. Too old to change who I am. Let it be what it is now. It's best for the girl. Luna and I are peas from the same pod. Neither of us cared about children. It's why I don't have any. Don't want any. I'm not healthy. My lungs and heart are bad. The girl wants a family. Let her have it."

"What about you? You really don't want to know her."

"I don't deserve it."

"It's not about deserving. Everyone can always use more family. Being connected. What about your cousin? She might like knowing her niece."

"It would be the best thing I ever did for her." Vernon's gaze settled on Edward and his children. "But no one needs someone like me in their family tree."

"Shouldn't they decide for themselves? Family is the people you choose to love and claim as being part of your life. I include my former stepdaughter and her grandmother as part of my family. Heck, I even include my late ex-husbands wife who I hadn't liked originally as my family. Edward and Garrison are nice guys, I bet they'll include you if you want to get to know Anne. Your family is as big or small as you choose. Choose big. Choose more."

"Maybe." He headed for the office where his cousin was sitting and staring at a wall.

"It's time to head home." Paul held open the door. I slipped out.

The sun was rising. I held back a yawn. Even though I was exhausted I was ready to leave. Go home. See my family. My children. My mom. My former stepdaughter. The friends I now considered my family.

"I'm ready for home," I said. "And I need away from here. I plan on driving for an hour and stopping at a rest stop for a few hours. I'll call you when I'm at home." How I longed for Season's Greetings and all that was familiar.

"I was thinking about following you back. We can stop and eat lunch or dinner together. Kind of keep each other company."

"That'll be nice." I smiled at him.

He smiled back. "I liked what you said about family. I'm wondering if there will ever be a spot for me."

I reached out and took hold of Paul's hand. "There's always room for one more."

Christina FREEBURN

Christina Freeburn has always loved books. There was nothing better than picking up a story and being transported to another place. The love of reading evolved into the love of writing and she's been writing since her teenage years. Her first novel was a 2003 Library of Virginia Literary Award nominee. Her two mystery series, Faith Hunter Scrap This and Merry & Bright Handcrafted Mysteries, are a mix of crafty and crime and feature heroines whose crafting time is interrupted by crime solving. Christina served in the US Army and has also worked as a paralegal, librarian, and church secretary. She lives in West Virginia with her husband, dog, and a rarely seen cat except by those who are afraid of or allergic to felines.

Mysteries by Christina Freeburn

The Merry & Bright Handcrafted Mystery Series

NOT A CREATURE WAS STIRRING (#1)
BETTER WATCH OUT (#2)
DASH AWAY ALL (#3)

The Faith Hunter Scrap This Series

CROPPED TO DEATH (#1)
DESIGNED TO DEATH (#2)
EMBELLISHED TO DEATH (#3)
FRAMED TO DEATH (#4)
MASKED TO DEATH (#5)
ALTERED TO DEATH (#6)

Henery Press Mystery Books

And finally, before you go...
Here are a few other mysteries
you might enjoy:

FATAL BRUSHSTROKE

Sybil Johnson

An Aurora Anderson Mystery (#1)

A dead body in her garden and a homicide detective on her doorstep...Computer programmer and tole-painting enthusiast Aurora (Rory) Anderson doesn't envision finding either when she steps outside to investigate the frenzied yipping coming from her own back yard. After all, she lives in a quiet California beach community where violent crime is rare and murder even rarer.

Suspicion falls on Rory when the body buried in her flowerbed turns out to be someone she knows—her tole-painting teacher, Hester Bouquet. Just two weeks before, Rory attended one of Hester's weekend seminars, an unpleasant experience she vowed never to repeat. As evidence piles up against Rory, she embarks on a quest to identify the killer and clear her name. Can Rory unearth the truth before she encounters her own brush with death?

PUMPKINS IN PARADISE

Kathi Daley

A Tj Jensen Mystery (#1)

Between volunteering for the annual pumpkin festival and coaching her girls to the state soccer finals, high school teacher Tj Jensen finds her good friend Zachary Collins dead in his favorite chair.

When the handsome new deputy closes the case without so much as a "why" or "how," Tj turns her attention from chili cook-offs and pumpkin carving to complex puzzles, prophetic riddles, and a decades-old secret she seems destined to unravel.

CPSIA information can be obtained
at www.ICGtesting.com
Printed in the USA
LVHW011813190720
661087LV00012B/831